PROSPECTS

D1707191

A NOVEL BY

PETER C. BRADBURY

Dedicated to my late mother Dorothy and to my late grandmother Edith, both of whom I still miss terribly.

PROSPECTS

SPECIAL THANKS TO:

Samantha Davis Darrin, Nob Hill Gazette, Intercontinental Mark Hopkins, Zuni, Absinthe Brasserie, Coi, 5A5 Steak Lounge, Raj Campton Hotel, Slanted Door, Allegro Romano's, Miller's East Coast Deli, Ottavio, Redux Lounge, Zatar, Sinbad's, Naked Lunch, Luna Ristorante, Annabelle's Bar and Bistro, Grand Hyatt Hotel, Huntington Hotel, Spruce, Gallery Café, Bix, Ruby Skye, City Lights Bookstore, Moe's Bookstore, Bookmark Bookstore, Scala's Bistro, Neiman Marcus, Vice, Sutter Station Tavern, Debbie Bradbury.

PROSPECTS

CHAPTER ONE

NOW REBECCA KNEW THE FULL

meaning of the word petrified. She was almost hyperventilating, as her breath came in short gasps and her chest rose with each breath. She couldn't see anything, nor could she yell for help, although it hadn't stopped her from trying. Apart from the blindfold and the gag, she knew she was also strapped or tied down at the wrists and ankles with both her arms and legs outstretched. It felt like she was being held down on flat metal. She thought a sheet was covering her but felt naked below it as the surface was cool on her back, buttocks, and legs. Her senses could smell animals but couldn't hear any. She had no idea what time it was, or indeed what day it was as she struggled against the restraints.

Rebecca had been sobbing almost uncontrollably since realizing her predicament. The blindfold was soaked, and she felt tears coursing down the side of her eyes. Never had she felt this vulnerable in her whole 24 years of life. She couldn't understand how she had gotten in this place, as she was always so careful and controlled. She couldn't help but think that she wasn't going to see her 25th birthday.

Where is Brad? She thought. *Is he in the same situation, is he already dead, is he close by?*

Her last memory before waking up to this nightmare was having breakfast in bed with Brad, which he had cooked, and then they had made glorious love again afterward.

What the hell happened? WHERE AM I?

CHAPTER TWO

AROUND 2700 PEOPLE

GO MISSING in the USA every day, and in California alone, almost 15,000 women are lost each year. Of course, many of these are explained away by the authorities as being voluntary or because of mental problems and so on, but it's enough of a problem that you no longer have to wait before filing a missing person report. It's fair to say that hundreds of young adult women throughout America go missing every year, and no one knows their fate. Except the folk who have been an integral part of their "missing" status.

One of these was "Brad." He didn't keep score of the women he'd taken, he didn't need to, as he'd barely gotten started. This was only his second, and the first time had been a mess. A bloody mess. One that he'd learned from and vowed never to recreate, as he really didn't like getting blood all over himself.

He didn't even like the killing. It gave him no thrill. And this second time was so much more satisfying, just knowing that she would be taken care of. That she would no longer be around and he'd have to make dumb small talk just to seduce her. The thrill for him was the chase, the research on the women, the deception, and best of all, planning their last days on earth.

He'd pulled out at almost the last moment on a few occasions, as he hadn't felt comfortable. He'd thought the woman would be reported missing, and he believed he'd be suspected. He hadn't been careful enough.

Then he was given a chance when he went into a packed and dimly lit bar in Walnut Creek to watch some football, and a newly divorced, very attractive brunette hit on him. She'd apparently been dumped by her friend as soon as they entered the bar and, seeing him alone, decided to risk talking to him.

This wasn't unusual, he was an extremely handsome man, with thick, black curly hair atop closely shaved chiseled features. He was six foot four with no sign of fat, and he still had a 30 inch waist. Brad always dressed in expensive clothes from his favorite store, Neimen Marcus. From his custom shoes to his polo shirt, he was every inch the dapper gentleman, even in casual attire, and the combination of his looks and obvious wealth was like an aphrodisiac to women. It was easy for him.

This one, though, was even easier. She was very horny, she actually told him so, and best yet, she didn't even want to exchange names, just to be taken somewhere with no questions asked and then a ride back to somewhere near her home. So he'd taken her for a ride, but didn't take her back to anywhere.

It had been totally against his modus operandi but the chance was too good to resist for him.

Brad's real name was Alec Savvas, and the only living relative that he knew of was his brother, George. Their parents had been killed in an auto accident near to their farm in Clayton, which was just outside of Walnut Creek and within an hour's drive of San Francisco.

Their mother had met their father while on vacation in Greece, and after they'd married in very quick time, they'd settled in the USA, although they did move around a good deal. In one way it paid off, as they made a lot of money in lobbying and in the bond market. On the other hand, they never really made any friends. Once they decided they had earned enough, they bought a farm and raised sheep, just as his ancestors had done back in Greece. The boys' mother also did some part-time work from home, helping people make their fortunes in the cities. For a hefty fee, of course.

It was a very enclosed family, they didn't really mingle or make friends locally. They didn't go out much, and the boys were more academic than athletic, although they did enjoy going to sporting events and they both rode horses. There was only a year difference in the boys' ages. They both went to college at Stanford. Almost immediately after George, the youngest, graduated, their parents were tragically killed.

The two sons were very intelligently gifted, but they only had each other both before and after their parents died. The money their parents made was more than enough to take care of the two boys for the rest of their lives. They had both taken the business degree route through college. It had been ingrained in them that they would never lose their money if they had strong business minds, and they also learned other languages, which could also never hurt them. They'd been brought up speaking English and Greek, but they also learned Spanish, French, German, Russian, Mandarin, and Japanese.

When their parents were ripped away from them, they thought at first to sell the farm and go their separate ways. Yet George had always enjoyed helping his father, and he expressed his wish to stay and take care of the sheep. Alec had never liked farming, horses were enough for him. He agreed that they would keep the farm, but he stipulated that he wanted to return whenever he liked but live in the city most of the time. So that's what they did.

It had been eight years now since the car wreck that killed their parents.

Alec didn't know why he wanted to take women. Maybe it was because his mother had been taken too soon. He just thought one day it would be a good and very exciting idea, although he didn't know if he'd have the nerve to do it.

When he took the divorced woman back to the farm, it seemed like the perfect time. George had let him know that he wouldn't be there that night, so Alec felt the world was all in alignment with his plans.

It went so perfectly, just the way he'd rehearsed it over and over in his head for so long. They had a fabulous night. She was beautiful and lithe, and he promised her that he'd take her back to her neighborhood before it got light. At 3 am he crept out of bed and after relieving himself, he made fresh coffee and orange juice for them both. He'd already prepared the crushed Donormyl, a non prescription sleeping pill that he'd bought online, and he put some into one of the orange juice glasses and one of the coffee cups. Once he had the tray ready, along with some sugar and cream in respective containers, he returned to the bedroom.

Putting the tray down on the nightstand closest to her, he turned on the bedside light and gently woke her.

"Honey, you need to wake up," he said in a voice just above a whisper.

"Mmm," she finally murmured, slowly awakening and taking in her not-too-bright surroundings. "What time is it?"

"It's 3:15. I promised you I'd take you home."

She looked magnificent to him as she slowly awakened, her wavy shoulder length hair all tousled, her make-up slightly smudged, and her great body still naked and arousing.

"Do you have any coffee or anything?" she asked in her still sleepy voice as she raised herself to lean back against the headboard.

'I have some right here. Would like you like sugar and cream? There's some orange juice as well."

"Just cream, thanks. No orange juice."

He prepared and stirred her coffee, handing it to her before taking a sip of his own orange juice and sweetened white coffee as he looked at her. She was holding her coffee in both hands below her breasts, not trying to cover herself in this strange bedroom or in front of this man that she'd only met the night before. He knew he'd have to have her one last time.

The coffee by now wasn't too hot, and she finally raised the cup to her lips and drank it steadily until she finished the contents. "I'd better use the bathroom."

He'd been sitting on the edge of the bed beside her, so he stood up so that she could get up. He was still naked and hadn't even considered covering himself as she put her cup down on the tray and stood in front of him. Even though she was tall, she still barely came up to his shoulders.

"We'll still have time before its light," he whispered.

"I think I'd like that," she replied, standing on her toes to give him a quick kiss on the lips before heading to the open bathroom door, not caring that she, too, was naked.

He watched her as she walked, her hips swaying above her slim long legs, and he wondered why she was now divorced.

Although she shut the bathroom door, he heard the toilet flush and the faucets run in the sink. He lay down on the pillow she'd been sleeping on and smelled her perfume, putting his hands behind his head as he looked forward to her return from the bathroom.

She opened the door and turned off the bathroom light. She hadn't tried to brush her hair, and she was still naked, her round breasts bouncing slightly as she walked, her nipples erect, her vagina shaved so that her pubic hair was just a vertical line. He was coming to attention again.

They made love again. It seemed they used the whole king-size bed and more, his knees also using the bedroom carpet, both coming loudly and most enjoyably after almost an hour of unabashed lovemaking.

"I'll never forget this night," she finally said after they were both sated, and she took a drink of her orange juice before molding her body back into his. "Just let me have a few more minutes before you take me home."

"Okay," he replied, kissing her on the lips, "this has been my greatest night ever." He wasn't lying.

She went quickly into a very deep sleep. He gave her a few minutes and didn't disturb her as he pulled out of her embrace and got out of bed. He rushed downstairs and retrieved from the bag he'd brought into the house last night the plastic sheeting, the knife, and the rope. Once back upstairs, he laid out the sheeting carefully on the floor, then carried her, still sleeping, and placed her in the middle of it. She never stirred. Taking the knife, a big carving knife that was very sharp, he straddled her and raised the knife high in both hands above her chest, then paused.

This is it, he thought. *It's now or never.*

He plunged down with the knife as hard as he could. He felt it slide by her breastbone, but that was about all. He was nauseous now, couldn't believe he'd done this, and he was covered in her blood. Sticky, gooey, thick blood was all over him, and it was horrible, he could even taste it on his lips. He was happy she was gone, no one else would experience this woman like he had. But he couldn't pull the knife back out.

She hadn't woken up with the stab, he'd heard her sigh very deeply with an "Ohhhhhh," like a very big relief, and he was very grateful that she hadn't woken up and struggled. He doubted if he could have stabbed her again. All he could do was sink back until his still-naked bottom was sitting between her knees in her still warm blood, and watch her now lifeless body that had a knife handle protruding between her breasts.

CHAPTER THREE

HE WASN'T SURE HOW LONG he

stayed like that, watching over her, but he felt the blood getting cold, and he kept fluctuating between elation and despair. Elation that he'd finally done this after so long of thinking about it, and despair because of all the blood. Why hadn't he realized that there'd be so much of it? He couldn't even move off the plastic, as it would drip everywhere.

Then he heard a car pull up and a door shut as someone got out of it. Truck really, as it could only be his brother. But why was he home so early? Would he call the police and send him to jail?

He listened as his brother messed around downstairs, and then as he came upstairs and headed toward his own bedroom.

"George!" he shouted. "Is that you?"

The footsteps stopped, then started approaching the bedroom.

"Alec? I thought you'd still be asleep."

It sounded like he was very close to the bedroom door, probably reaching out to open it.

"Don't come in, George, you might want to call the police. I've done a terrible thing, and I don't want you involved."

"What's going on, Alec? Are you in trouble, or do you need some help?"

The tone of George's voice had changed considerably. He was obviously very worried, and Alec saw the door handle slowly turn.

'Don't come in, George!" he yelled. "Just call the police."

"You'd better tell me what's going on, Alec, or I'm coming in."

"George, I've just killed someone, and there's blood all over the place. Just call the police."

"What the hell do you mean, you've killed someone? Did we get burgled or something?"

"No, George. There's no easy way to explain this. I brought a woman home, and while she was sleeping I stabbed her. She's dead."

It went very quiet on the other side of the door.

"George? Are you still there? Have you called the police yet?"

"I'm coming in, Alec." George opened the door and stood in the door way. "Oh Jesus, Alec, what the hell happened?"

Alec looked around at his younger brother. George wasn't as tall as Alec, nor was he as handsome, despite the same black curly hair. He was much stockier from working on the farm, and his facial features not as finely defined, more like their mother with her small brown eyes and pert nose, almost a permanent stubble. As usual, George was dressed in Levi's, a plain white tee shirt, working boots, and tattered baseball cap with a faded Stanford logo.

"I killed her, George."

George looked down on the scene. His naked elder brother was covered in blood. He saw the dead woman, the knife handle, and the plastic sheeting.

"Did you plan this, Alec?" asked George, suspiciously.

"I've been planning on doing this for some time, George, there's no point me lying to you. But not with this particular woman. It just kind of presented itself, and I took the plunge, so to speak."

Alec looked at his brother, who was obviously in a state of shock, his mouth agape at the scene in front of him.

"Call the police, George, I'll explain it to them. This has nothing to do with you, and I don't want you in the middle of all this."

There was no reply to this for a while from George, he was obviously deep in thought and torment.

"Wait right there Alec. I'll be right back."

With that, he bounded downstairs and out the front door, returning about 5 minutes later with a bucket of cleaning materials and a small stack of newspapers, which he deposited at the door. He disappeared again, re-emerging after another five minutes but now dressed solely in an old pair of overalls and barefoot. He picked up the newspapers and entered the room, taking care where he walked, placing sheets of newspaper down on blood spots, then making a route to the shower.

"Walk on the newspapers to the shower, Alec, and keep your hands to yourself. Don't touch anything. The shower is already on. Keep washing yourself until all the blood is washed away from you. I'll get some old towels that you can use when you're done. Now go."

"I told you, George, just call the police. Don't get involved in this."

"Alec, listen to me. I've been envious of you all my life. Your looks, the women you attract, your effortless intelligence, and the way you coped after Mom and Dad died. I've always had to follow behind you, and it's been very difficult, but this is the one thing that I can do better than you. So go and take the shower, and let me take care of this."

"But George, there's something you must know. If you let me get away with this, there'll be more. I won't be able to stop. Even though I'll have to rethink how to kill, I know I'll have to do it again. The rush I got, knowing that this woman would never leave this place, was wonderful. It was just the killing I didn't particularly like."

"You always were the squeamish one, Alec. Listen, if you want someone to go away, then just leave it to me. If there are going to be others, then I'll deal with them and get rid of them. We have the tools for that here on the farm. But only do it here. I won't go to San Francisco and help you there, only here. I can kill a sheep easy enough, I'll just do the same thing with your women. Okay?"

Alec couldn't believe this. It was perfect, just a pity he hadn't known this before getting covered in this god-awful blood. But at least now he knew what the feeling was like to take another's life.

Despite this conversation, neither of the brothers were that likable. Although popular with all women, Alec was very vain, especially rude to vendors, thought all American women were dumb, believed himself to be far more intelligent than anyone else, and was cheap with almost everything bar his clothing and hair.

George, for his part, was unfriendly with practically everyone, always seemed to have a chip on his shoulder, and was cheap with no exceptions.

As Alec took his shower and George started the clean-up, he already wished his older brother hadn't killed this gorgeous woman. George would have loved to have been able to spend some time with her himself, even though he wouldn't have been attractive to her in the way that Alec was. That though, was fine by him. He'd never told Alec, but he'd raped before, when he was in college and afterwards, and he'd loved it. Being with a regular looking woman was okay, but the beautiful ones, the type that Alec could get so easily, were always beyond him. He'd tried on more than one occasion, but he always got this look as if they wanted to say, "Are you serious?"

As he wrapped up the naked brunette in the plastic and tied her up, he again was envious of his brother.

He'd never had a beautiful woman like this in his arms, not willingly, and probably never would. He'd gotten away with his rapes by using his intelligence, sedatives, and threats, which was very satisfying to him, but with the drugs he had at his disposal, it was only going to get better. He would have no need to look over his shoulder, so he could take his time.

Don't kill them, Alec, he thought to himself as he threw the woman onto his shoulder and took her away. *Leave them with me for a while.*

CHAPTER FOUR

ALEC'S PENTHOUSE

APARTMENT IN SAN Francisco was located on California Street in a building next to the Huntington Hotel. He'd paid several million dollars for it, which he gladly did, as he was a big believer in property ownership, even when the economy sucked and values were decreasing everywhere. It had, however, largely escaped downtown San Francisco, as the local real estate market showed.

He loved his apartment. Being on the top floor, he could see for miles in all directions, but he especially loved the view of the bay. He could sit for hours watching the boats in between reading his many books. His books of choice were generally business related or autobiographies, and he'd buy them in different languages so that he could keep up his skills.

It was very much a man's apartment, in the sense that he liked to watch sports, so had a lot of flat screen TVs around. He hadn't employed an interior designer, although he had spoken to one, so he'd furnished the place himself. The figures the designer had come up with had been ridiculous, and he would probably have been uncomfortable at the end. So he bought oversized sofas and chairs, king-size beds, a large desk to work from, lots of mirrors, and basically whatever took his fancy. As long as the colors matched or contrasted well, then he was happy.

He also bought virtually everything at discount furniture stores, haggling and demanding free delivery. He'd kept the fitted carpets that were in place when he viewed the apartment. They were nothing special, just a basic cream color, and although he liked wood floors he also liked warmth beneath his feet. So he kept the carpets.

It was a large apartment, with three bedrooms and four bathrooms, although he'd converted one of the bedrooms into his office. It had a modern kitchen with newish appliances, a deck, and fireplaces with real gas fires. His only indulgence furnishing wise were the paintings scattered randomly about the place. He thought of paintings as a good investment and, like his parents, he liked European landscapes.

He had an extensive walk-in closet that contained all of his clothing, which he separated into winter and summer racks. It was very organized, very neat, and all color coordinated.

A housekeeper came in once a week and was made to work for her money by dusting and vacuuming the whole apartment, changing the sheets, doing his laundry, cleaning the kitchen and bathrooms, and replacing all the flowers. For this, he gave her the princely sum of $80 plus whatever she paid for the fresh flowers that she purchased on her way to work. Providing, of course, she had a receipt.

Although Alec was straight, a lot of guys thought of him as gay, with his mannerisms and clothing. He'd have been called a dandy in the old days. It never affected the women, but the gay community thought they were being mocked by him, so he was more or less shunned by both sides of the male community. He also had regular two week appointments for his hair, manicures, and pedicures, going to a women's salon because he believed that they took better care of him. He was quite the dapper gentleman.

Maria, his overweight Mexican housekeeper, dreaded the one day every week she had to go clean his apartment, and if she could have gotten another client for his day she'd have dropped him like a stone. There was never enough time to do everything. He always complained that she wasn't fast enough, or that the vacuum made too much noise, or that the washing machine was vibrating. She'd see the price tags sometimes of the clothing he'd bought and would be appalled to see he'd gladly pay over $300 for just a tee shirt, yet would begrudge her a measly $80. She also didn't like that he always stayed in the apartment while she rushed from room to room. He obviously didn't trust her, and he'd never given her a door key like her other clients. But then, that was true of everybody he knew.

Alec wondered if George had disposed of his second victim and how long it would be until the next. A few years ago, when he first got this urge, he began by singling out three prospective women by first finding them, researching them, and then finally sleeping with them. That had been the end result until the unexpected woman from the bar. Now he had more of a purpose, more determination, as he looked for another prospective woman so that he'd have three on the go again.

He was looking for a particular prospect, and as usual she had to be fairly young, very attractive and slim, hopefully single, with few friends or family, and most preferably a loner. Even loners need some kind of interaction, so he looked on the internet in chat rooms or various single websites. In local publications under the classified ads, and especially in bookstores and art galleries.

It seemed to him to be quite incomprehensible, that in this day and age, women were so willing to meet total strangers, with virtually no thought as to their own security. Not that he was complaining. Random meetings were what he preferred, and this willingness on the women's part was perfect. Ethnicity wasn't a problem to him, either. In fact, he very much liked different races, but only if they were westernized.

Most of Alec's time was spent alone. He liked doing his research and especially liked following his prospects, finding out their habits, patterns, social lives, hobbies, and such. He ate out a lot while doing this, not in the finer restaurants that he preferred and used to impress, but in convenient places close to his prospects. The rest of his meals he fixed himself, as he had a grocery chain deliver weekly supplies. He had few visitors. A couple of married women he'd met in the apartment building would occasionally stop by, not together and by no means regularly.

He would also sometimes take care of some of his mother's former clients and give them business advice. He had even got referrals from some of them, but it wasn't something he encouraged, as he didn't want work to take over his life.

CHAPTER FIVE

ALEC'S SECOND VICTIM

WAS REBECCA Young. They met shortly after Rebecca put an ad in the Nob Hill Gazette, saying she was a young business woman who was looking to meet someone in the Nob Hill area for friendship and to socialize.

A lot of ads from other women were in the publication, professional women like her who were finding it difficult to meet suitable men. It was an upscale publication so they listed their hobbies as polo, skiing, yachting, and dinner parties. Rebecca's ad was very demure, and she didn't leave a number, just a post office box that she always used for safety. She didn't know whether she'd get any replies, but being careful she didn't want to say she was pretty or that she modeled, so she was quite happy with her ad.

Rebecca hadn't lived in San Francisco for too long. She'd moved from Los Angeles, as she was always being propositioned there by agents who always told her they could get her into the movies or to the Playboy Mansion or other such places. Rebecca was a model and was also very attractive, so she wasn't just a "body." She had no shortage of suitors who first wanted her on their arm but then wanted to take her home or to a hotel, finally to be cast off. At first, when she was naïve and still fairly innocent, that had been exciting, and she believed it would help her career. But she'd hated it. She'd felt like a prostitute and was treated like one. Seeing herself in the tabloid press at some party only made her remember the date with utter disgust.

She'd always wanted to be a model, and when the opportunity arose, she took it with both hands. She and her much younger brother had been raised in a double-wide trailer in the northern part of Florida. Her parents were drug and drink addicts, and they were in a haze much of the time. She took care of her little brother as long as she could, but after doing some local modeling for various companies she was made an offer, and so she bade farewell to her parents and brother. She didn't think her parents were too aware of her departure, but her brother was, and she was desperately sorry she couldn't take him away. She even wrote him some letters once she got settled on the west coast, but she had never gotten a reply and had gradually stopped writing. It had been six years since she'd left.

The fashion modeling, which she wanted to do, was very difficult to stay in. She was always dieting, but even when she felt she was skin and bone, she was always told she needed to lose more weight. She got lots of work with different retail stores, but when she was offered a job with a major lingerie outlet, who didn't want her so thin, she was happy to take it. It meant moving to San Francisco, and although the work wasn't full time, it paid a lot, and she was free to take other assignments as well. Models don't make a lot of friends. She found it a very bitchy business on both sides of the camera, but she still liked doing it, and the loneliness didn't perturb her that much, just on odd occasions.

The mail she received from her posting ranged from junk mail advertising single domains to sex shops, and then letters from male and females who were obviously looking for a random sex partner. Among the dross, though, was a nicely printed note from a guy called Brad, who suggested they meet in a crowded coffee shop one morning. The note stated that if this was agreeable, then she could pick the place and reply to his post office box number. She replied and said she'd be in the coffee shop at the City Lights Bookstore in San Francisco the following Tuesday at 10 am, and she'd be wearing a Florida Gators baseball cap, black coat, and blue jeans. Brad replied, saying he'd be happy to meet her there, and he'd wear jeans, a Stanford cap, black blazer, and plaid shirt.

They seemed to arrive at almost the exact same time. She was in line at the coffee counter when he approached behind her. She wasn't aware that he'd been waiting for her outside, making sure she was alone before following her in. As she asked for a medium sized cappuccino, he butted in and said, "Hello Rebecca. I'm Brad." Directing his attention to the server, he continued. "I'd like a latte grande please, extra hot, and I'll get both. Would you like a muffin or anything?" he asked her.

"No thanks, just the coffee. Nice to meet you," she replied, offering her hand for a shake.

They shook hands and smiled at each other, moving away from the counter to the pick up area after Brad gave the server a $20 bill and received the change.

"You're a Gator fan?" he asked.

"Coming from where I do, there was no choice," she explained.

"So you're from northern Florida?"

"Yes, and you're from here?" She glanced at his cap.

"I am." He wasn't lying to her too much yet, as he didn't know how this was going to develop.

"Did you go to college there?" she asked, eying his clothing which she knew full well were expensive.

He had also done the same with her. She looked scruffy but was really very well dressed in designer attire. He suspected she was hiding a spectacular figure beneath the huge coat.

"Yes. Are you feeling the cold?"

"Now it's fall I am, but I haven't gotten used to the weather here yet," Rebecca replied.

They were informed that their coffees were ready, which they took. Rebecca thanked Brad for her cappuccino, and Brad didn't leave a tip. Rebecca found a table in the middle of the floor, and they sat opposite each other.

"So you haven't been here long?" He asked, referring to her last comment.

"No, just a few months. The weather here is crazy."

They were both weighing each other up. Both were attractive, even with their caps on. Other patrons were giving them glances, as they looked like a very good-looking couple. Already they thought they would meet again.

"It is, you never quite get used to it."

"So why did you reply to my ad, Brad? You don't exactly look like you need company."

"Maybe not, but you sounded genuine, and I have a hard time meeting genuine people. I don't like this modern attitude of casual encounters where no one seems to want to get to know each other," he lied.

"Me too!" She said happily. "What do you do for a living, Brad?"

She unbuttoned her coat to reveal another baggy garment beneath it, a navy sweater with a round collar. He noted her slender neck. Her long slim fingers were well manicured, and she had delicate wrists. Her blonde hair was like a mop beneath her cap, but it wasn't long, and she had high cheekbones, blue eyes, a cute little nose, and full lips. Not a lot of make-up, but what she had was adequate. He thought that if she had worn more, everyone in the store would have been looking at her.

"I help people with their businesses," he answered. "I'm like a consultant they use to help them streamline, or go public, or hire and fire their staff."

"That sounds interesting." She smiled, an almost perfect smile with dimples on each cheek.

"It is," he lied again. "Dealing with all these different people and their various problems is very challenging."

"Do you have to go to their workplace?"

"Not often. It's mainly by phone and online, but sometimes I do go and visit them."

She looked at him closer. God, he was good looking, even with the cap on. Tall, slender, beautiful hands, very clean shaven, he smelled and looked expensive.

"You're not married?" She asked, almost incredulous.

By now, her coffee was almost gone. She wasn't sure if she should ask him if he wanted a refill.

"No, not yet," he slightly laughed. "So, what do you do for a living, Rebecca?"

"I work for a modeling agency."

"You model?"

"Yes."

"I'm not surprised, you are very beautiful. Do you work here in the city?"

"Well, thank you, I work on Geary Street."

"I like being in your company, Rebecca, but I have an appointment coming up that I can't get out of. May I take you to lunch one day soon?"

"Yes, I would like that, Brad. Let me give you my number."

She wrote down her number on a napkin and handed it over to him, sincerely hoping he would call her soon.

After a little more small talk about the city and especially its weather, they left the bookstore together, shaking hands at the entrance as they went their separate ways. She to work and he back to his apartment.

He called her that evening from his new prepaid phone and arranged lunch with her for the following week. He didn't want to rush her, he had to stalk her first, find out things about her.

Over the next several weeks, Brad took her to very fine restaurants like Coi, and 5A5 Steak Lounge, and he followed her to and from work after he found out which agency she worked for by hanging out on Geary Street. He asked her if she confided in anyone or told her friends about him. Her response being no, he was her secret.

She would invite him inside when he walked her home from dates. But he made excuses, knowing she wanted him but if he let it happen then they would go no further. He'd kiss her on her doorstep and feel her wonderful body mold into his. It was a wrench to tear himself away, but it would be worth it, he just knew.

The right time was near after they enjoyed another especially fine dinner. She'd looked stunning in a little black dress that displayed her long lithe legs and a good amount of cleavage that he wanted to bury his head in. He asked her to go away for the weekend with him, to somewhere very special to his heart, and to wear the exact same dress. She agreed instantly.

When Brad got Rebecca to the farmhouse that weekend, he practically ravaged her, and she him, as they took out all their lingering sexual frustration on each other. It had lasted most of the night and into the morning. He'd even made her breakfast in bed, which she thought was most romantic.

Then she woke up to her nightmare.

CHAPTER SIX

SHE WAS STILL SOBBING AND

wondering where Brad was when she felt the sheet being taken away from her body. Then she felt warm water being sprayed over her, rough hands applying some kind of soap all over her, intimately, and she sobbed some more because she couldn't stop this from happening.

Finally, the water stopped and a man said, "This will hurt for no more than a second." She heard a "poof" sound, and felt a sharp jolt to her neck. Almost instantly, she felt her whole body relax. Her heart and breathing slowed down, she was so drowsy yet wide awake. *What the hell did he do to me*? she thought, panicking.

George had injected her with Rompun by using a blow gun. Rompun produces an almost sleep like state, with lower breathing and heart rate. George had seen large animals tranquilized this way, and thought it a great idea.

She felt herself being unstrapped and then lifted, being placed on a warm flat surface, like a bed of some sort. He hadn't taken off her blindfold or the gag, but she was covered by something. Then she felt the hands again, rubbing the covering against her before it was removed.

"You were still wet," he said, explaining his actions.

His voice was a little like Brad's but different, and she recalled the night when she'd gone to Brad's farm, his special place, not far out of San Francisco. He hadn't told her until they were almost driving through the gates where they were going, but by that time she didn't care if it was the cheapest motel in the state. She just wanted to jump him. Then she saw the farmhouse and it was delightful, two stories and about 10,000 square feet. It was a white, wood-paneled building, almost square, with steps leading up to a big porch on either side of the big front door and screen.

Once inside, she didn't see much of it until later, as he took her into the kitchen with its huge range. Pots and pans hung down over a big island, and there was a natural wood table with four wooden chairs. He made love to her there. She'd worn the same black dress, and she'd seen him watching the hem rise more and more as they made their way to the farm. She'd wanted to stop on the way, but he insisted on getting there, and after they arrived, they hurried to disrobe. It had been magical, more than she'd hoped for. She almost told him she loved him.

Afterward, she'd put on his shirt, and he stayed in his boxers as he showed her around. It was actually very feminine, with lots of flowery drapes, frilly lace window dressing, many empty vases, paintings of whitewashed buildings by the sea. Warm colors, knick knacks everywhere, and colorful bedspreads and pillows. He'd pointed out the room that had belonged to his departed parents, a room that his brother now occupied. His brother's old room was now an office/den. The family room had huge overstuffed furniture and a massive fireplace with a thick fluffy rug in front of it. Later, she rolled around with Alec in front of the fire. Alec's room was big, with a king-size bed, huge walk-in closet, and a bathroom with a Jacuzzi tub and separate shower. She could have fit her old double wide into just his bedroom area.

Her blindfold was taken off, and it took a few moments for her to refocus her eyes. She was in a room, not a barn like she'd thought, but she could still smell animals. The room was white washed and bare, apart from the huge table in the middle with faucets and a sink to one side. She couldn't move her head much but she could see she was lying on some kind of inflatable mattress, and she was totally naked.

A man was beside her, also naked, and he looked a little like Brad but was nowhere near as handsome or as tall and slender. This man looked more like a football player. He was smiling. She felt sick as he went down on her, and she couldn't protect herself. She wanted to kick and scratch his eyes out, but all she could do was lie there and take what he did to her. He took pictures, moved her this way and that, and didn't use any protection when he came into her, twice. Finally, he seemed to be finished, and she wanted to bathe for the next month to try to erase this.

"Rebecca," he said, and she wondered how he knew her name. "That was so enjoyable, and thank you for giving yourself to me. I will never forget this."

Again, she felt a sharp pain as he picked up a short rod from under the table and heard the same "poof" sound as before.

"You will go back to sleep soon and then wake up in your apartment, thinking this has been a dream. Good night."

Rebecca fell asleep as she watched him wash himself from head to toe at the sink, the soap suds and water rinsing away in the floor drain. Then she felt a sudden heat as she fell into her lifeless eternal dream.

CHAPTER SEVEN

GEORGE WAS ELATED.

REBECCA HAD been so beautiful, so shapely, his only regret was that he'd had to get rid of her. But he had taken photos, and his Smartphone enabled him to videotape the sex. He was going to download it onto his computer. That would keep him going until Alec's next conquest. For now though, he needed to do the disposal. He wrapped her up in the sheet he'd laid her on, and also the under sheet, leaving her there as he put on disposable overalls and shoe protectors over his bare feet. He then went outside.

One of doors in the room led to the barn, the other door was for a walk in freezer. He used this room to butcher his sheep, or when a neighbor gave him a pig or a cow in exchange for some lamb. He was a good butcher, so neighbors would often ask him to do their butchering, which was a nice little sideline for him, even though he didn't need the money. His freezer always had lots of meat. The barn was empty, he used to keep the horses in the stables there, but they got upset with the smell of animals being butchered. So he had another larger barn built about a hundred yards away, where he also kept the farm equipment, the farm office, and where his two workers would report when arriving and leaving.

This barn was now almost empty apart from a couple of pens that he used to keep the animals before butchering them. And the table, of course, with the shrouded body. He used a large autopsy table that drained blood into a container below, and he was able to wash the whole thing with the attached faucets and hose. Kept things hygienic, and if that's what they wanted, kosher, too.

Outside, it was still light, and shortly his weekend worker would return. He opened the door on the big incinerator. It was like a chest freezer, and he rushed back inside to pick up Rebecca. He carried her back out, and placed her, still covered, in the box like contraption. He didn't need to fold her, the opening was big enough for her to be completely outstretched. Leaving her there, he went back and gathered the towels he'd used, along with all her clothing, her purse, and her overnight bag, which he also deposited into the box.

He washed and rinsed off the table, then picked up the drainage container. He'd only used the table to wash her, so he poured the soapy water down the drain. This was the beauty of it. Not only could he put solid objects into the incinerator, like a pig carcass, but he could also throw in all the blood and entrails or whatever drained off the table. It just didn't matter.

He rechecked the whole house. The soiled bed sheets and towels she'd used were still in the washer, so he put them in the dryer. On his return he closed the door on the incinerator and set the timer. He nearly forgot his overalls and shoe protectors. He changed and threw them in, a minute before it started.

He'd been able to purchase this incinerator because he was a farmer and did some butchering, so no questions were asked.

The incinerator burst into life. All that would be left at the end of the cycle would be ashes that would be so environmentally safe that he could dump them anywhere. Sometimes a few tiny bone fragments might be in the tank, but they'd have no DNA.

"Goodbye, Rebecca," he murmured as he walked to the other barn. "It was really nice meeting you!"

CHAPTER EIGHT

THE FARM WAS IN THE foothills by

Mount Diablo, and because of its hilly terrain, it was perfect for the sheep. It was just over a thousand acres to take care of, but it wasn't a money making machine. George could have made a lot more money out of it if he'd wanted to, with trail riding or camps and such. He'd been asked many times to open the land to the public, but he was happy with what he made. The butchering and carcass disposal kept his fridge full and also brought in a little more money. But then, like Alec, he was already well-off thanks to his parents and didn't need or want the public intruding everywhere.

Like Alec, he had taken language lessons, but he hadn't kept up with it like his brother, although he continued speaking Spanish with the hired help, Mexicans who spoke very little English. His farmhands worked full-time, and one of them also worked weekends, while his housekeeper came in once a week. She also did some cooking for him. He had his groceries delivered, and he also loved to watch sports.

Since tomorrow was Sunday, he'd take the Bart from Concord and meet up with his brother at the bar before the 49er game. He and Alec had season tickets to the Giants, the 49ers, and the Stanford Cardinals. Sometimes they'd go watch the A's and Raiders.

Although the farm was in the East Bay, which usually meant they'd be fans of the A's and the Raiders, their allegiance was across the bay. It was now football season, but Alec and George also enjoyed the other major sports. They also liked soccer, the Olympics, and golf, one of the few sports they played, but not often.

Unlike his brother, George had a girlfriend. She was the local vet, and he'd been seeing her for quite some time. Jane Lowell was 28 years old, and they both thought they'd eventually marry. They had one of those relationships that appeared to an onlooker as if they'd been married for years. It seemed devoid of the passion you'd expect from a couple not even engaged yet. Yet that's how it was. Jane was by no means a looker, but she kept herself trim and presentable. Jane was mousy. She kept her brown hair short and close-cropped. Her nose was pointy, and her eyes were brown and slightly beady. Being primarily a large animal vet, it made no sense to her to keep herself well groomed when she'd literally be up to her armpits inside a cow every day, and she was devoted to her work.

Jane had actually asked George out the first time. She had to attend a veterinary dinner and didn't have a date, so she'd approached George on one of her visits to his farm. He agreed to go with her, he behaved impeccably, and she'd invited him inside her home and slept with him. Since then, they'd gone out regularly and were now a couple.

Like George, she wasn't very outgoing. She'd always preferred animals to humans. Jane liked to take the horses out, preferably with George, around the farm and its hills.

But she also liked sports, so she didn't mind the almost non-stop sports coverage around George. She didn't go to many events with him, and she didn't really like his brother, as he seemed to always look down on her whenever they met up. George could be the same with other people, but not as much as his brother did, and she was determined to stop him from acting all superior.

CHAPTER NINE

ALEC FELT REVITALIZED.

WHEN HE got back to his apartment, he checked Rebecca's phone, the only thing he'd taken from her, and went through the recent calls, contacts, and favorites. He'd taken some revealing photos as a memento on his own phone, but there were none of him on her phone. He smiled as he saw his number and name. Alec quickly figured out her work number. The phone didn't have any missed calls or messages, although he found some old text messages. He knew from talking to her that work was light at the moment and that she sometimes did work for other agencies. Sending a text wouldn't create any alarm bells. When he sent a text to her agency, he just added one more text to the list.

"Need to go to Vegas for a few days, got a last minute gig. Will call when I get back. R." He pressed send.

Alec checked the phone again thoroughly for any mention or photos she may have sneaked of him. Satisfied, he removed the batteries and the sim card. Although he was going to the 49er game later, he was going out this morning for a walk along the Embarcadero. Alec wasn't really into gym work or a keep fit regime. His metabolism was extremely good, but he did like to cycle or walk sometimes.

A couple of weeks ago he'd seen what he hoped was another prospect walking along the Embarcadero. He'd been down there a couple of times since, trying to spot her, with no luck, but this was the first chance he'd had to try to spot her at the same time and day as the first time. He wanted to do it on foot this time, there would be more chance of some eye contact.

He may well have been going out for some exercise, but he was freshly showered and shaved, dressed in a Gucci pacific blue tracksuit, matching striped tee shirt, and white Prada sneakers. He smelled, as always, of the Jack Black range he liked. Looking at himself in the bathroom mirror, he liked what he saw, and he tousled his hair a little before heading for the front door. Alec picked up his keys, a bottle of water, his phone, the phone he'd discard, and a $20 bill.

It was all downhill to the Embarcadero. The weather was still mild, and the streets were fairly quiet. He disposed of the phone in different places, he didn't want one of the many homeless to find the whole phone in one trash can and put the thing together. He was sure that he wasn't eyed with any suspicion as he threw the parts away.

Arriving at the Embarcadero, he wasn't surprised to see walkers, runners, and cyclists already doing their thing, and he headed west toward Pier 39, the tourist destination of San Francisco. He rarely went down there by choice, but today was a little different. Many fine looking women passed by, most accompanied by their boyfriends, husbands, or girlfriends, but he saw no sign of the one he was looking for.

Turning around at Pier 39, where the vendors were already selling boat tickets for the Alcatraz tour, he saw her approach about a hundred yards away. She was walking, not jogging. She was wearing a black, tight, jogging suit, and the pants ended at mid calf. She also wore white running or walking trainers, a thick watch that could have been a heart monitor, and white ear buds that connected to a white iPod. The highlights in her straightened, shoulder length hair were emphasized by the light breeze as she walked briskly toward him.

As he got closer to her, he realized that she was as beautiful as he remembered. She was a young black girl, maybe in her early 20s. Probably 5'9", very slim, and not big-breasted. She had long slim fingers that were obviously manicured, and she was getting a lot of backward glances from most of the guys and even some of the girls. She seemed to be into whatever she was listening to, taking no heed of the other exercisers, her face set in concentration as she got even closer. She didn't seem to be wearing any make up, she didn't need to.

Alec was happy to note that her left third finger didn't have a ring. She did wear gold rings on both of her index fingers, but nothing gaudy. And if anything, they only accentuated her long, slender fingers.

"Good morning," he said loudly, making sure she heard him as they got very close to one another. "A fine day to be out for a walk."

Her concentration broken, she returned his gaze. Her brown eyes hinted at a smile.

"Good morning," she replied pulling off an ear plug. "Yes, it's perfect." Her voice was soft, almost seductive, and he was disappointed that she continued past him.

He looked back, admiring her shape and her well-defined rear, exchanging knowing looks with another guy who was doing the same. *Maybe she's not into white guys*, he mused, almost miss- ing her quick glance back at him.

Or maybe she is, he thought happily, as he proceeded back to the east.

He slowed down a fraction, just in case she turned around where he did and caught up, but he was already happy with his greetings and her response. Her glance was another positive sign. His process varied with his prospects, depending on circumstances, so he was in no panic.

As he gradually approached the Ferry building and prepared to take Washington onto Battery, he was very pleasantly surprised when she passed him and said, "Have a nice day!"

"You too," he quickly replied. "It was very nice to meet you."

She looked back, not stopping, but she smiled broadly and waved.

He'd be back next week.

CHAPTER TEN

ALEC AND GEORGE ALWAYS

MET in the city before games and took the muni public transportation to the 49er game. They had tried driving to the stadium, but it was a pain to get out after the game, so they had resorted to using the muni. George would get the Bart train to downtown. They'd meet up, have a beer, and head to the game. It was always the same routine if it was on this side of the bay, and today the Cowboys were visiting.

Alec wasn't sure how the 49ers would do this season, but the previous years had been barren, and they had once again changed the head coach. At least this time the coach inspired some confidence, as he'd been very successful with Stanford. But the pre-season had been all but cancelled, so it was anyone's guess as to how well they would do. At least they had started the season with a win, so that was a plus.

Candlestick Park where the 49ers played was notorious for its weather. You never knew what it would do. A wind blew nearly all the time, and it could also get very cold as well. So Alec and George always dressed accordingly. They wore warm jackets and baseball caps, discarding the jackets if by chance the weather was warm and calm. They both remembered very well the nights they went to the baseball games there, before the Giants moved to the city, and they would literally freeze their butts off watching the game. Neither of them would be sorry when the 49ers moved, even though it would entail a longer journey, as they really disliked the present stadium. Although it had been a few years since the Giants vacated the stadium, they still looked across from the 40 yard line at the temporary stands that used to get wheeled away for the baseball games.

It didn't matter to either brother that they didn't know any of the other season ticket holders around them. Alex and George said hello if greeted, but that was about all. The brothers didn't even share high fives with their neighbors if the 49ers scored.

Today, they'd been together for almost a couple of hours. They hadn't spoken much, which wasn't unusual, but considering what had happened just yesterday, Alec thought that perhaps something needed to be said. It was well into the second quarter before his curiosity got the better of him.

"Any problems yesterday?"

"No, not at all," replied George bluntly. "It went very well."

Alec looked at George and at all the folk in close proximity.

"I don't need to know all the details, just that it's out of the way."

"Completely. Will there be another one next weekend?"

"I don't know. I doubt it. Maybe in a couple of weeks."

"Just let me know, and I'll make sure the coast is clear."

What George meant, and what Alec was aware of, was that he'd make sure that Jane wouldn't be around. If she was, then the prospect would be safe. Alec looked at his younger brother again, wondering, but not wanting to know, if he'd done something to Rebecca before he disposed of her. If she screamed or fought, or if he touched her. He shivered, then brushed it off, changing the subject back to the present.

"You think we'll get to the play-offs?"

"I don't know, Alec. We have a good defense, I'm just not sure if we'll be able to score enough points. What do you think?"

"I hope we do, I've backed them to, but we won't win the Super Bowl. We can't do as badly as we have done, we just need more offense."

Alec liked to wager. Not big sums but just enough to keep his interest, and he was fairly good at it. He had an online account with an offshore bookie. George didn't bet much, not even between them unless they played golf. George was the better golfer and liked to take money off his brother, which Alec didn't mind doing, as he knew he was way better off because of all the various investments he'd made.

"Have you a bet on today?" Asked George.

"I got the 49ers and the points. I couldn't bring myself to back the Cowboys."

The 49er fans and the Cowboy fans didn't get along and generally disliked each other. Alec and George were no different.

"I may have disowned you as a brother if you'd bet on the Cowboys."

"Even if common sense told me so, I couldn't do it. It wouldn't feel right to win with the Cowboys."

As it was, the 49ers should have won the game but couldn't put the points on the board, a familiar story with them. And although the game went to overtime, the Cowboys won it with a field goal.

Both brothers felt encouraged with the 49er performance. They thought they could have a good season, and Alec didn't lose any money, as he had the points. Once back in the city after the game, they went their separate ways, one to the farm and the other to the apartment. Both spent the rest of the day watching more football and checking on all the other sports as well.

CHAPTER ELEVEN

ALEC HAD TWO PROSPECTS ON

the go, and he hoped the Sunday walker would be number three. He kept his eyes open for number four, but he wouldn't actively pursue it until he was down to two again.

The day after the game, he met Ruth Stevens at the Raj Campton Hotel for lunch. He'd met Ruth while shopping at Neiman's when he was purchasing some body lotion, and she'd commented on his good taste. Apparently, she was buying toiletries for her father, who now lived in Florida with her mother after his retirement several years ago. His birthday was coming up, and she wanted to get him something different, something he wouldn't normally buy for himself.

Ruth was tall, around 5'7", but in her heels she was 6'. Although Alec was usually seen with younger women, he actually preferred older women, and Ruth was older than he by at least ten years. She wasn't slim like a model, but she wasn't fat, just what people described as a real woman with curves and a nice shape. Her shoulder length blonde hair was wavy and bounced around her neck, and when she'd complimented him, her smile had showed off her white even teeth. Alec noticed that she had some wrinkles around her green eyes and her mouth, but her lips were full, so he barely noticed the lines. She didn't wear a ton of make-up, didn't need to, but Alec thought she used a little mascara and shadow to highlight her eyes, some blush, and a subdued red lipstick. That day at Neiman's he could have kissed her there and then. She'd looked like a businesswoman in her skirt suit and blouse, and although she wasn't revealing her legs or breasts, he could tell from the fit of her suit that she was very well formed.

Alec had thanked her for the compliment, and once he'd bought his lotion, he'd suggested some of the products she should perhaps buy for her father. She took him up on this very happily and didn't flinch when the saleslady had asked her for almost $300. While she paid, he noticed her wedding finger had a tan line where she had once worn a ring. As soon as she'd collected her shopping bag, he'd impulsively asked her to join him for a coffee.

The coffee had gone really well, as had subsequent lunches and one dinner. He'd resisted taking her to his apartment or entering her home, but it had gotten more difficult.

By now he knew that she was an accountant who worked from home. If she needed to meet her clients, she would do so either at their place of work, their home, or in a restaurant. She'd been married but her husband had left once it was determined that they could not have children. It had come as a surprise to her, because they had decided not to have children years before, so she hadn't even been trying. She wasn't maternal, had gotten tired of her friends pushing their little ones into her arms, and she'd gradually stopped seeing them, as she always felt uncomfortable. She had no family here, she'd moved here with her husband when he was relocated by his firm, but she still had cousins and such back in Chicago, where she hailed from.

Alec had been in a quandary from their first meeting. He immediately had been attracted to Ruth but not just physically. He had also felt at one mentally with her as well. She was softly spoken, obviously intelligent, worldly, and mature. He hadn't gone so far as to use his real cell phone number with her, but he was using his real middle name, Christos. He wasn't sure if he wanted to get rid of her just yet, because he liked spending time in her company.

He'd watched her enough to know that she didn't lie to him. Most of the time she was ensconced in her house on Filbert, in the Russian Hill part of town, and when she did venture out she either went shopping or met her clients for lunch or at their offices. He had even followed her lunch "dates" to make sure they weren't romantically involved. Some of the men had ogled her, but that was as far as it had gone, although he was sure that she'd been propositioned a few times, which she had readily talked about. But then "Christos," as he now was, also had to concede that he was propositioned on a regular basis, as she had noticed women looking at him very lasciviously.

For his part, Christos had told her that he was a business consultant in a thriving firm, that he sometimes had to go away to see to his clients or to entertain them here in town. Christos told her that he'd been engaged to be married, but they'd recently broken up, as she didn't trust him. He explained that she thought he was too good looking to resist temptation. He had strenuously denied this, he knew that he wasn't that handsome, but her jealousy had been too much. He hadn't been married before, but he didn't sleep around either.

Ruth had more or less believed him with this comment. Christos had several opportunities to bed her, yet he'd resisted. Much to her disappointment.

Monday was rainy and chilly in San Francisco, and for once Christos was inside the hotel when Ruth arrived in a taxi. He met her in the lobby after the doorman opened the door for her. Christos was dressed in a blazer and pants. He had an open shirt collar, and his coat hung over his arm. Ruth wore a black trench coat and held her closed umbrella.

Christos welcomed her with a kiss on her lips that tasted of strawberries. "Great to see you, Ruth, it seems like an eon. Let me help you with your coat."

"You too, Christos. I've missed you," she replied warmly.

As he helped her remove her coat, he was delighted to see her outfit was shorter than normal for her, a black skirt and green v-neckedtop. They perfectly highlighted her figure, a little cleavage, the long legs, her tan from the salon, and her eyes.

They looked like younger versions of Kim Basinger and a curly haired Pierce Brosnan to the rest of the crowd at the Taj Campton Hotel, and as Alec held one of her long delicate hands and took her to their table, they both felt the eyes of the restaurant following their every move.

As Christos helped her with her chair, he got a glimpse of her black bra beneath her top and a little more of her well-defined legs as her skirt rode up a little. He ordered some Chardonnay as he took his seat opposite.

"You look more beautiful every day I'm fortunate to see you." He smiled.

"Thank you, Christos, that's very kind of you."

The wine came quickly, and they sat and watched as the waiter did his little show of presenting the bottle, pouring a drop, waiting for the approval, then pouring into each glass. The waiter knew they hadn't looked at the menu yet so he said, "Unless you're ready to order, I'll come back in a few minutes."

"That's fine," replied Christos. He turned his attention back to Ruth and covered her left hand with his right. "Do you have any clients this afternoon?"

"No, I'm free for the rest of the day. Why do you ask?" As she said this, her eyes were smiling, and the tip of her tongue touched her top lip.

He leaned in closer. Her perfume intoxicated him with its subtlety, "I want to book a room upstairs and take you there for the rest of the day and night, have breakfast in bed, and maybe stay there for the rest of the week," he whispered.

She leaned in to him, her face millimeters from his and whispered her reply. "Christos, I have a better idea. Take me home. I have some Champagne in the fridge, plenty of eggs, and, more importantly, a change of clothing. I also have something this hotel may not have."

She had the sexiest smile he had ever seen. "What would that be?"

She looked around, as if to make sure no one listened to their conversation, before giving him her full attention again. "Thick walls. I'm very lucky in that I'm able to have multiple orgasms, but they make me yell out loud. Will that bother you?"

"Ruth." He beamed and lifted his glass to clink with hers as she did the same. "Let's order a very quick lunch. I need to take you home."

They drank their wine, ordered their food quickly, and practically gulped it down, such was their haste to get away.

CHAPTER TWELVE

GEORGE HAD BEEN

BUSY THAT same day. A farmhand had radioed in to say one of the sheep had a broken leg, so he'd taken the all-terrain vehicle out to the location. The animal was in agony, so George put it out of its misery, loaded it up, and brought it back to the barn to butcher. Although by now he was quite an accomplished butcher, it still took him a lot of time.

The walk-in freezer was a good size, not too large, but the 12' × 12' space was about right for his farming operation. Most of the meat he was able to sell. He kept some for his own consumption, and when the neighboring farmers sent a cow or two over, he was glad of the space. First thing that morning he'd taken out a couple of steaks for himself and Jane, who was coming over that evening.

Once he'd finished with the sheep, he deposited all the skin, entrails, bones, blood, and waste into the incinerator and set the timer. The dust from Rebecca still remained in the chamber, but he didn't remove it.

He left it to mix with the sheep remains. He'd throw it all away tomorrow.

When he was a boy, he'd never imagined he'd be this callous or nonchalant when it came to taking life or butchering the remains. He wasn't into torture, he couldn't sever limbs from a conscious animal or anything. But he had no qualms with what he'd done to Rebecca. The only memories he'd taken from it were pleasurable to him. Much better than the rapes he'd done. He smiled to himself as he cleaned up the room. He didn't even think he'd raped Rebecca, it wasn't like he'd brought her here.

Jane came over at around 6:30 pm. She helped George with the cooking. He was okay grilling but not doing any sides, so she brought some onions and mushrooms that she sautéed and prepared the salad, which she had also brought over. They shared a bottle of cabernet as they cooked their meal and opened another one while they ate at the kitchen table.

The TV was on without sound with a Monday night football game, and George kept glancing at the screen to keep up with the score. Jane was well used to this behavior by now. Most of the time she didn't mind, as she had an interest in football as well, but she was more into her beloved Aggies from Texas A&M, where she'd learned her veterinary skills. She had thought about going to college nearer to home. UC

Davis had a great vet program. But she'd wanted to have a college education to make her independent, and going to Texas had done just that. She'd loved her time there.

"Do you think we'll ever get married, George?" She asked when she was about halfway through her steak.

Surprised but not shocked, George put down his knife and fork. He'd thought about it a lot. It made sense, and he did want to be a father some time.

"I hope so," he replied, "but I need to ask you to marry me first, don't I?"

Jane also put her knife and fork down. "Only if you love me, George. Do you love me?"

The only time that either of them ever mentioned the word "love" was when they were having sex. It was never spoken about at other times, but George could tell this was important to her, just from her mannerisms. She was serious about this. He didn't know whether he loved her. He loved his parents and his brother, but this was different. He was content with Jane, he could live with her and raise a family. But love her? He didn't think so.

"Yes. I love you Jane, very much."

"And I love you, George. I want to have your children, George, and I want them before I get too much older so that I can enjoy them more. My practice is doing well, I could hire another vet, and I'm ready. Are you ready?"

"I'm ready, but where would we live? Here? Your place?"

"I was thinking we could maybe build our own place on the other side of the farm. We have the money, and I know this is also Alec's home, which he wants to keep. I'd prefer us to have our own place."

George resumed eating, thinking about this as he chewed. It was actually a very good idea, even though he didn't want to fork out for a new house. If he was married and Alec brought someone home that he wanted rid of, then having Jane around would make that very difficult, if not impossible. Alec would have to take them elsewhere. If he did that, then he, George, wouldn't have his time with them or be able to dispose of them. He'd already told Alec that he wouldn't help him if he was away from the farm, so the only option, if he married Jane, was to agree with her and build a new house.

He put down his knife and fork again. "You're right Jane, we need a new house. You know a good architect?"

Jane got up quickly and ran to him, straddled him as he sat, and kissed him over almost his whole face.

"Oh thank you, George. We are going to be so happy!"

George had never even proposed, yet it was all a done deal. Jane knew an architect who she would call first thing in the morning to get things moving. She declared there and then that she was ditching the pill and was going to conceive. If not tonight, then soon.

For the first time, their lovemaking was exciting, and George barely thought of the memory of Rebecca.

CHAPTER **THIRTEEN**

CHRISTOS LINGERED

AT RUTH'S HOME, as he'd thoroughly enjoyed himself. She hadn't been kidding when she'd said she was loud when making love. But what was more gratifying was that she came easily and often, and although she was a lady in public, she was almost a slut in private. He didn't return home until late Tuesday morning. He didn't have to, but he wanted to check on someone.

Jenny Charles lived on Sansome Street on Russian Hill. She was another blonde, but her hair was cut very short in a spiky style. She was very slim, with vivid blue eyes and a small nose and mouth. She was almost boyish but very attractive, and she usually wore a little make-up on her dimpled cheeks and around her eyes. Jenny wore minimal jewelry, diamond ear studs, a small gold cross and chain, and two discreet sapphire rings on each hand.

Alec had met her in the City Lights Bookstore, a favorite place of his to find books and to meet prospects.

When he met Jenny, she was browsing through the financial section. He recommended a Warren Buffet book to her, and they started talking. It turned out she was another accountant who worked from home. She had her own private clients, and she loved the city but had discovered it was difficult to meet people for someone like herself who was mainly alone.

Alec wondered if he was starting to have a thing for accountants after dating so many models and actresses. She wasn't very worldly. She had a penchant for saying "like" a lot, but she had a nice giggle, and her voice was typical Californian. Apart from her mathematic intelligence, Alec found her boring. She liked to talk about movies and TV shows, but she had no interest in sports, and it was difficult for him. He kept up to date with all kinds of news, including movies, but when it came to TV he was at a loss, especially with the reality shows and soaps.

He'd been following, or stalking her for a couple of weeks now, and her life was truly uneventful, from what he'd seen. Most of her time was spent inside her apartment, and when she did venture out, she walked to nearby stores to grocery shop, to the pharmacy, or to pick up fast food.

Once he had seen her go to a salon for a hair cut and manicure, but that had been on a day they had a date. She'd also gone to a matinee at the movie theater alone. Shopped at Victoria's Secret, and window shopped around Union Square. All in all, it was very uneventful and perhaps quite sad.

Today was no different. Alec was as scruffy and as inconspicuous as he could be. He hadn't shaved, and his hair was uncombed. He wore sunglasses, denim jeans and jacket, and a baseball hat. Even his brother would have paid him no heed if he passed by.

San Francisco is plagued with hundreds of homeless people roaming, sitting, and sleeping on its streets. No one paid any attention to Alec as he sat in the empty doorway of a business, watching the movement at Jenny's apartment block just across and down the street from him. Jenny hadn't stirred from her apartment. He knew she was home, as he'd called her from the prepaid cell phone that was dedicated to her.

Watching was Alec's favorite way to pass the time. It was exhilarating for him to watch his prospects go about their daily lives without knowing he was there, especially when they seemed to sense that maybe someone was following them and they'd glance back. He'd smile when he saw that, especially if he was across the street and saw them increase their pace or look around with uncertainty.

Alec knew that Jenny had a car, a Mini. She told him once that she loved her little car and that it was perfect for city living, as she didn't need much room to park it. Not that she appeared to be taking it out today. The only time she emerged was almost at lunchtime to walk down to the local deli and buy what looked like a sandwich, which she took back to her apartment. After Alec had followed her there and back again, he went back to the deli and bought a sandwich himself, taking it to the doorway to eat. He stayed in her neighborhood for a couple more hours, walking around occasionally to keep loose and taking an interest in some of her attractive neighbors. Alec kept his eyes open to the comings and goings of the community while staying incognito.

When he returned home, he was careful to avoid his own neighbors because of the way he was dressed. Alec jumped into the shower as soon as he got inside.

Maria would be over in the morning, and his laundry basket was already full. She'd have a busy day. He mainly bought clothing that was washable and rarely sent anything to the dry cleaners, much to her annoyance. Maria had to wash and iron everything.

Tonight he was meeting Jenny at the Slanted Door restaurant at the Ferry Plaza. It was well within his walking range and would be for her as well, as it was almost around the corner from her apartment.

He checked his phones for messages. He kept his prepaid phones in a very secure locked cabinet in his office. The cabinet was lined and also wired for his phone chargers and watch winders. Anything of value to him, including large sums of cash, he kept in this cabinet. He could go anywhere with the contents of this space, and he was very careful with it.

Now that he'd set out on this current road, he'd been in contact with the accountants that he and George used in L.A. He didn't think they were going to get caught, the police were way too stupid to do that. But just in case that he or George made a mistake, the accountants were moving the ownership of all their holdings to an offshore location. That way, either one of them could keep their money, no matter what happened. He sure as hell didn't want to lose any money to the family of one of his victims.

Ruth had left a message saying she was missing him already and that she wanted to see him again soon, so he called her. Ruth invited him over for dinner tomorrow. She was cooking, but he agreed to bring some wine and a toothbrush.

He checked the weather before dressing. It was still mild, and no rain was forecast, so he picked out a checked shirt with a hint of blue, a blazer that matched the blue, and black pants and shoes. As usual, he'd pay cash for dinner, so he took a few $50 bills out of his cabinet, along with one of his watches and Jenny's phone. He still took his wallet, but he wouldn't use his credit cards. If things developed with Jenny that he wasn't envisaging, then he'd be extremely careful where he left it. The last thing he wanted was for her to see his driver's license and learn his real name.

Satisfied with how he looked and smelled, he picked up his house keys and left his apartment to walk down to the restaurant. He was early by design and was happy to see Jenny arrive by foot and alone. She was wearing a black wool coat that fell to her knees and blue shoes with sensible heels for San Francisco and its hills. Not that she would have to walk up any tonight, but she wasn't to know that.

He met her as she stepped inside, greeting her with a big smile, a hug, and a kiss on both cheeks. She wore make-up, nothing extravagant, but she did wear mascara, blush, eye shadow, and natural lipstick.

"You look wonderful, Jen. Let me take your coat."

"Thank you, Robert. That's very kind of you."

He stepped behind her to take her coat from her shoulders, taking in her perfume as she slipped off her coat.

"Wow Jen, you look great!"

She did. She wore a bandage dress that was mid-thigh, v-necked, and sleeveless. It was the same blue as her eyes and shoes, clinging to her every curve. Alec could see the guys at the bar giving her the once over, so he was quite proud to give her another kiss on the cheek as he took her hand.

"Thanks, Robert. It's nice to dress up a little now and then. I sometimes feel like I was born in jeans."

"Well, maybe you should do it more often. The guys at the bar are drooling at you."

She looked over at the bar and realized that she was getting looks. She felt slightly embarrassed yet elated, and a huge smile swept across her face.

"Let's see if our table is ready," Alec continued. He led her toward the hostess, although he already knew where they'd be seated, as he'd checked in earlier.

They were seated immediately, and Alec ordered some Sauvignon Blanc, sitting opposite Jenny as they waited for their wine, ignoring the menus before them.

Alec had been able to get a table with a view of the bay, and when their wine arrived they toasted to, "a fine meal, and more evenings like this one," and they both admired the view and each other.

It was a Vietnamese restaurant, and Alec ordered an appetizer of mesquite grilled local sardines, which they shared. He had estancia shaking beef, she had the chicken claypot. Alec ordered Syrah for their main course, and they had cocktails with a dessert of crème brûlée.

Alec mostly feigned interest in their conversation, but he was alert when he got her to talk about her family and upbringing in L.A. She was the oldest of three daughters. Her parents were divorced, but both had remarried. Although her stepfather was okay, he was fonder of her younger sisters, as he'd been more of a father to them. She still kept in touch with everyone, but not regularly or too many visits. They had never come here to San Francisco, but she still went home for Thanksgiving. Her friends from school and college had, "like, all disappeared," but she was thinking of going to her high school reunion in a few weeks. She hadn't liked L.A. that much, it was too big, too false, and too dishonest for her, she much preferred it here. Her business was doing well, and she was thinking of joining some social clubs to make more friends.

She was obviously very attracted to Alec. Her eyes never wavered from his, and she touched him whenever possible.

Jenny had asked "Robert" about his family and upbringing, and he'd more or less mirrored her replies to create a similar bond. He was an older brother to younger siblings. His father, like Jenny's, had remarried a younger woman. His mother had struggled to raise them in Chico, but he'd managed to get a good education and worked for himself as an advisor. Like Jenny, he had very little contact with his family, and they never came to visit him.

The restaurant was very good, and they both enjoyed their meals, lingering at the table with decaf coffee and brandy nightcaps. He let her talk about her shows and the current movies that she wanted to see.

When Alec escorted Jenny home, she held his hand very tightly, and she asked him to come up to her apartment. He replied that he liked her very much but that he wanted to develop their relationship long term. "Robert" said that he wanted to keep seeing her to find common interests that they could enjoy together. Not that he didn't want to go up to her apartment, he really wanted to, but he wanted to show a little restraint, to show he was serious about her.

Jenny accepted this, albeit reluctantly. When Alec kissed her good night outside her apartment entrance, she pressed herself into him and felt his arousal, which made her feel a whole lot better. After kissing her, Alec was extremely tempted to go upstairs with her and peel off her dress. He'd wanted to do that all night, but there was a reason behind all this, and he was deter- mined to see it through.

"I'll call you tomorrow, Jenny. Keep your weekend free. If you're agreeable, I have plans for you," he said with a sly smile.

"I can't wait to hear what they are," she softly replied. She put her lips to his again and played with his tongue, pressing her midriff into his groin again and hoping he'd change his mind and take her upstairs.

Alec eventually pulled himself away and said good night, that he'd call her in the morning. After she went inside, he wondered if he should have gone upstairs with her.

Oh well, he said to himself as he walked away. *Think how hot she'll be the next time!*

CHAPTER FOURTEEN

THE FOLLOWING MORNING,

AFTER A breakfast of avocado on toast and white sweetened coffee, Alec called Jenny, then his brother, and finally Ruth. He told Jenny how much he'd enjoyed dinner with her, how he regretted declining her invitation to her apartment, and that he'd like to take her away for the weekend, if she liked. He told her that he had a friend who had a ranch with horses, so they could go and ride, and he'd teach her if necessary. She agreed instantly. He'd heard her say once that she liked to dance, so he also informed her that on the way to the ranch, they'd have dinner and go to a club. She said that she thought that was a wonderful idea and she couldn't wait. He said he'd pick her up Friday night at 7.

He then called his brother to say he'd be staying at the house that Friday night. George sounded excited, at least for him, and he said he'd make himself scarce.

Finally, using his third phone, Alec called Ruth and confirmed that he would be over that evening. He said that he could barely wait.

He spent the rest of the day checking on Maria, exploring the internet, following the sports scores, and doing a little reading but not eating a great deal, as he wanted to keep his appetite for dinner.

The baseball season was almost at an end. The play-offs started the following week, but the Giants wouldn't be involved this season. The teams were scrambling to extend their seasons, so the games were getting exciting and edgy, and they held his attention. He was rooting for no one in particular, but he had backed the Rangers to reach the World Series.

Christos spent the evening with Ruth, and it was just as amazing as the first time with her. This time he didn't linger for too long in the morning. He told Ruth that he had some business to deal with for the next few days but that he'd call to keep her updated. Christos said that he'd be free of his client by Sunday, so perhaps they could go out for dinner.

Ruth wasn't too happy with this, but she agreed to Sunday and said that she would look forward to his call.

Today he was heading over to Berkeley on the Bart. Alec liked Berkeley. It felt compact and cozy with its narrow streets and the stores spread out like in San Francisco. Berkeley didn't have a huge mall like in other cities.

He'd thought of driving over there, but the Bart was much easier, especially if the Bay Bridge was gridlocked, which it could be at any time of the day. He didn't see anyone in the elevator or in the lobby of his building, and he strode with his usual confidence down to the Bart station.

He liked to walk, it was good exercise. With the hills, it was a good workout, and the streets were always interesting.

The Bart train wasn't very busy at this hour but it still had its usual mixture of interesting, dowdy, attractive, youthful, aged, and dangerous characters. He didn't socialize on the short ride, he only exchanged smiles with a couple of housewife looking ladies who seemed stressed and harried.

These were hard times for many people. Alec could never imagine how difficult it was for them, but even for him, someone who had never had a monetary worry in his life, he didn't like the behavior of the politicians and bankers. Alec was as selfish as they come, but even he was appalled at the greed they showed. He had shares in many companies, but he'd never condone the executives awarding themselves huge bonuses when the company was losing money. When he advised people, he'd have them streamline or fire staff if he thought it necessary, but he'd never suggest a huge payday for someone unless they truly deserved it. As he looked around at the diverse passengers, hardly anyone seemed totally calm and at ease. Perhaps it was a reflection of their current financial plights.

Departing the train at downtown Berkeley, he made his way slowly to Moe's Books. It was another mild day in the bay area, so all the students in town were in their usual attire of tee shirts and jeans. Some had sweaters, but even this close to San Francisco it felt warmer here, and it didn't take long for Alec to take off his coat and carry it over his shoulder.

Once inside the bookstore, Alec found a book to look through, a baseball book that detailed a pro's life in the major leagues. He purchased a large vanilla latte, then found a huge armchair to sink into and watch the activity in the store. A matching armchair was next to the one where he sat, but it was unoccupied.

He wanted a particular type of woman to approach him, someone who was confident in herself and knew what she wanted. Although shyness was attractive to him, he didn't want to go through the work and time it entailed to lure a coy woman. The best part about Berkeley and its students, though, was that a lot of foreigners were enrolled. They were alone and far from home, and at times they craved some attention.

It took quite a while. Two or three folks sat down beside him, two women and a man. Although one of the women was attractive and obviously into him, he wasn't interested in another married woman, and he eventually brushed her off.

He finally got what he'd been waiting for.

"Excuse me," she said in perfect English. "Is this seat taken?" She indicated the adjacent armchair.

"No, it's all yours," he replied warmly.

He'd seen her browsing the aisles and had admired her. She had jet black, straight, shoulder-length hair. Her tight blue jeans emphasized her slim legs, and she wore boots with heels, a navy college tee shirt that wasn't tight but fit perfectly, a long neck, high cheekbones, oval face, and perfect teeth. She was a quite beautiful Chinese woman.

Sitting down, she crossed her legs and smiled at Alec as he quite openly admired her.

"Are you reading anything interesting?" She asked, her voice clear but not loud, just a hint of her Chinese upbringing.

"It's about a pro's life in the baseball major leagues. And your book, is that as interesting?"

"I hope so," she replied, holding the book's title up to him, "I've just picked it up." It was a book about Shakespeare.

"Are you studying English literature?"

"Is it that obvious?" She smiled.

"No, but people don't normally read about Shakespeare for fun. I am Andrew by the way, and I'm delighted to meet you," he replied. He offered his hand, which she took.

"I'm Kim. Pleased to meet you, too."

Kim was also trying for a business degree and was actually in her final year. She was from Hong Kong and had no family here, but she had a large family back home. Her father was a tailor who had a successful business catering to Westerners, making their shirts and suits, and he was funding her education. Now that Hong Kong was a part of China, there were many opportunities for English speaking employees, as China was growing more influential in world affairs. Like her family, though, Kim regarded herself as British, and she was proud to have a U.K. passport.

For his part, "Andrew" told Kim that he was in Berkeley because he'd had to meet a client there earlier that morning and had gone into the bookstore on a whim. He admitted to living in the city across the bay, but he had no family nearby. He was an only son, and his parents lived on the east coast.

Kim joined Andrew for an open air lunch from the Brazil café truck, enjoying each other's company and their food and mango smoothies. Although older than the students around them, Andrew fit in nicely with the crowd. When Kim asked him to join her for dinner, it was with reluctance that he declined. He told her that although he wasn't dating anyone at the moment, he had some commitments to his clients that he couldn't get out of, but that he'd love to see her on Sunday, if she was available.

She said she was, they exchanged numbers, and Andrew said he'd call, although Kim said she'd call him if he forgot. They finished their long lunch, exchanged kisses on the cheeks, and shared a good hug. They went their separate ways.

CHAPTER FIFTEEN

GEORGE WAS EXCITED

AT THE prospect of Alec bringing another of his gorgeous women home. He felt the old stirrings of thrill that he thought were behind him. This arrangement was better than Stanford, in most ways. He'd always been fearful of getting caught by a stray fingerprint or an unseen witness, or by the victim remembering something about him. He did miss the adrenalin surge of following the victims and taking them in their own abodes, but he could live without that. Just as he had for most of the years since.

College had been hard for George despite his inherited intelligence, as he had to study so much to keep his grades high. It all seemed so easy for his brother in comparison, but it nearly always is harder for a younger brother. Neither of the brothers were very popular, but Alec had his looks to be a favorite with the female students, if not the male. George didn't have that though, so he ended up creating his own excitement.

It had started for him with one rejection too many, just a casual hello and how are you doing in a café. The girl in question had yelled aloud, "Are you hitting on me?" Before joining her friends and laughing at his audacity. He paid her back for humiliating him a couple of weeks later when he followed her back to her room from a party she went to with one of her friends.

He knew she had casual boyfriends, but this particular night she went home alone to her room, staggering a little from the alcohol she'd drank. Her friend had been the same, so he didn't think to escort her to her door. George hadn't been invited to the party, he never was. But he knew about it and was hiding in the shadows, watching the comings and goings. He'd been home the week before and had picked up his dart gun and tranquilizers, so he was ready for his opportunity.

Dressed all in black with a ski mask rolled up, he followed them both home, keeping to the shadows wherever he could and avoid- ing the few others walking the campus in the early hours. As soon as her friend had said a slurry good night, he moved in closer to his quarry. She was a cheerleader. She thought she was a big wig on campus, as she fraternized with all the jocks. She was very attractive. Blonde, big-breasted, and long, beautiful legs. Way out of George's league.

He knew where she lived and that she had a single room, so he pulled down his mask and hurried ahead of her on the other side of the street before he darted into her dorm. She lived on the first floor, and he was thankful that no one was around. He waited quietly in a dark alcove by her room. He didn't wait long, as he watched her walk unsteadily in her party attire of stilettos, short skirt, sleeveless top that displayed her cleavage, and smudged red lipstick. She carried a tiny clutch bag, and she rummaged in it for her key. As soon as she managed to put it in the keyhole, he blew his dart into her back, just below her hairline. He ran to prevent her from falling and took her weight as he opened the door and bundled her inside.

He closed and locked the door behind them, then he quickly found the light switch and flicked it on, happy to see the room was empty apart from her bed, desk and chairs. Her clothing was scattered everywhere. George picked her up instead of dragging her, and he gently placed her on the bed before checking her bathroom, which was empty, although messy with underwear, make up, and junk.

Returning to her bedroom, he had never seen a sexier sight. Her white skirt had ridden up to expose her tiny, frilly white panties as she lay on her side, and she looked to be bursting out of her red top. She was sleeping peacefully, totally oblivious to her dilemma.

Her bed, like everything else, was a mess, he'd never seen a room in such disarray before. But despite his excitement, he was careful with his hands. He didn't want to leave any prints around.

The pink drapes had been drawn, and that must have been her favorite color, as there had been a lot of pink around the room. Even her sheets had been in the same color. She also had a lot of Stanford paraphernalia around, including her cheerleading uniform and pom-poms.

He removed his mask but left the lights on, which were just a couple of table lamps. He took his phone out of his pocket and snapped some photos. The new phone he had with the built-in camera was his new favorite toy. He locked her door and found her phone, which he put on vibrate before he wiped it down and put it back in her clutch bag.

He removed the condoms from his pocket and put them on her nightstand with his phone. Then he took off all his clothes and left them in a tidy pile. He undressed her, starting with her shoes, which he tossed away. He kissed her feet and stroked her smooth legs before he removed her skirt and top, letting his hands roam over her body. He put on one of the condoms before taking more pictures, he was already aroused. After he put the phone down again, he laid her on her back. Then he opened her mouth so that he could feel her breath and tongue around himself. He came shortly afterward, but left the condom on until he removed her underwear. He took his time, and snapped more pictures. He went down on her with his mouth and got hard again. He replaced the condom and raped her, moving her body around at to experience different thrills. Although she was unconscious, he imagined he felt her move with him in arousal. He thought he was in heaven.

After he finally came again, he got some towels from her bathroom, which he placed under her body. Then he washed her from head to toe, even turning her around to wash both sides. He didn't wash himself, he liked her smell on his skin and wanted to keep it for a little while. After he washed her and had taken yet more pictures, he put her towels back into her bathroom and covered her with a sheet and blanket. He put his used condoms in a small plastic bag he brought with him, dressed, and prepared to leave.

Making sure he wiped everything down, he started her computer, opened Word, and typed, "Thank You for last night" in big script. He left the words displayed on her screen. He wiped the keyboard down, and he took a last look at her before leaving the door unlocked but closed.

As he carefully made his way back to his own room, disposing the used condoms on his way, he felt like the happiest man in the world.

There had been others in and around campus since that first time. He always used the same method. At first he thought he'd like them to be conscious. But he found out that he didn't want them to fight him, which they did. The girls had rarely reported the rapes, perhaps they thought boyfriends had come over and they'd had sex.

He never tried to speak to the cheerleader again. Sometimes he'd smile at her when he'd recall the evening, and she'd look at him funny but with the same disdainful look as before.

Other victims had reported it, but he'd always been very careful not to leave anything for the police to pursue. Despite these precautions, though, he'd been questioned once by the police, quite intensely. That had made him stop.

Now he was getting the old feeling back, and he liked it. Real life was better than his pictures and movies, but these treasures were important to him. He was careful with his computer storage. He didn't want Jane to stumble upon them if she used the computer. He also didn't want to stop her from using his computer if she needed to, because that would be a sure sign he was hiding something, and she might snoop.

He couldn't wait to see who Alec would bring home next and leave for him.

CHAPTER SIXTEEN

SHORTLY AFTER

CHRISTOS LEFT HER home, Ruth received a most unexpected call from her husband, Jason. Although Ruth no longer wore her wedding or engagement rings, she and Jason hadn't formalized their divorce, as neither of them had particularly wanted to do that. She knew that Jason had been seeing other women, just as she'd been seeing other men. But they'd been together since high school, so they'd never experienced being with other partners until the last few years. Sometimes they talked on the phone or said hello on Facebook, but that was about it, and it was always with respect and understanding.

"Hi, Jay. How are you?"

"Hi, Ruth. I'm good, thanks. How are you?"

Jason didn't sound down or troubled. He sounded quite upbeat really, and Ruth wondered what he wanted.

"Very well, thanks," she replied, smiling at the memory of last night's sex session. "So, what's up?"

"Oh, nothing much. I just wondered if you'd have lunch with me today. If you're not busy, that is, or if you don't have other plans."

Since they had split, they'd both been very careful not to intrude into one another's private lives, so they were ultra polite. Ruth had taken the call in her office, so she had her calendar in front of her, and apart from a call to a client this morning she was free. This was a good time of the year for her time wise. Once it got to January then she'd be very busy for four months, with barcly a spare moment

"Umm, sure. That will be fine. You want to meet somewhere?"

"I'll come to the house. We can walk, if that's okay, I thought we'd go to Allegro Romano's."

Allegro's was a very good restaurant and was just around the corner from Ruth's.

"You'd better make a reservation, they're always packed. What time will you be over?"

"I'll be there around 11:30 am, and I'll call them right now. Be good to see you, Ruth."

It puzzled Ruth most of the morning, as she went about eating her breakfast, showering, and putting on unflattering black slacks with a purple v-necked pullover before dealing with her client. She stayed barefoot until she left the apartment.

Jason rang the doorbell at 11:30 prompt. He was in his business attire of navy suit, black shoes, white shirt, and striped tie in a lighter blue with white. He was the same age as Ruth, but he was a little paunchy nowadays from sitting at a desk too long. His graying hair was receding but still combed back like in the old days. It was much shorter now. He had blue eyes, no facial hair, and a strong chin. He was tall and still quite handsome, around 6'1".

Ruth greeted him warmly with a kiss on the cheek, which he reciprocated. She put on her white raincoat, and she was ready to go.

"Change of plans I'm afraid, Ruth. I forgot that Allegro's only opens for dinner, so we'll have to go elsewhere."

"I should have realized, Jay, I go by there often enough. So where do you want to go?"

They were still standing on the doorstep, and she thought to herself that maybe she could rustle something together and invite him inside, but he offered a suggestion.

"Let's go to Miller's."

Miller's East Coast Deli was a favorite of the locals of Russian Hill, very reminiscent of the delis on the east coast with its atmosphere and friendliness.

"Sounds good, let's go. You're looking well Jason, the best I've seen you in a long time."

They weren't holding hands, nor did Ruth put her arm through his. Yet they looked like a man and a woman who knew each other as they walked along.

"Thank you, Ruth. As always, you look great."

"Thanks, Jay, but you're being way too kind. It's not like I'm dressed particularly well or have all of my make up on, but thank you anyway."

"I meant it." Jason still retained his Chicago accent, which made Ruth think of her relatives back there, ones she missed and hardly saw.

"Have you been back home lately?" Asked Ruth. They both understood where home was.

"I actually went back there a couple of weeks ago. I had to go to the corporate office and was able to stay a few days, visit family and some of our old friends. It was a great trip. You should go back more often, everyone was asking about you and they miss you. They want to see you more."

Ruth missed them, too. Although she was very curious to know more about his trip and who he'd seen, she didn't want to get homesick, which she knew she would if he started talking about her family and old friends.

"I know it, Jay. I miss them so much, but I never seem to have the time. Whenever I think about booking the flight, something seems to come up, and then I don't book it. I will soon, I promise."

"You should go ahead and get it booked, then block off your calendar. You won't regret it."

They'd already reached Miller's, and on entering the deli were delighted to get one of the last remaining tables. Another couple of minutes and they'd have been sitting at the counter or waiting for a table to empty, probably half an hour. Both of them had been here before so they basically knew the menu, but they went through the rigmarole of looking through it before giving their order. Both went with the matzo soup, and a half sandwich on wheat roll, Ruth with a corned beef and Jason with pastrami. Ruth also had a side of coleslaw, and Jason went with potato salad, and they knew they'd share these. Both drank water.

They both loved delis. They reminded them of home, of Chicago, and of the one they used to frequent with their friends and family, sharing jokes and sampling all the different offerings.

Their soup came fast from the charming waitress, and they added some Parmesan to it.

"So Jay, do you have something you need to talk to me about?" Ruth asked in a friendly way. She wondered if he finally wanted a divorce or if they had money problems or something. She'd noticed he still wore his wedding band and thought it sweet of him.

"Well." Jason put his spoon down. "I've been thinking things over for quite some time now, and I owe you a huge apology. I hope that one day you will forgive me, because I am very sorry."

Ruth put her spoon down, seeing in his eyes he was earnest and genuinely contrite.

"Why do you owe me an apology, Jay? You haven't done anything wrong." She spoke quietly, not wanting their near neighbors to overhear.

Their sandwiches came and were left to the side of their soup bowls. The deli ran on a fast turnover, so they always got food to the table quickly.

"Yes I have, Ruth, and you know it. I was silly, stupid, and totally naïve, and I will regret it to my dying day." Jason spoke in a low voice, and he saw that Ruth was about to interrupt. "I need to say this, Ruth. Otherwise it's something else that I will regret. I should never have left you, and I still love you with all my heart!"

After going through so many different scenarios, Ruth hadn't once considered this comment, and all she could do was sit and stare as he picked up his spoon to finish his soup. She saw his face relax, it had obviously been a relief to him to get this off his chest. She was stunned.

Finished with his soup, he put it to the side and replaced it with his sandwich, taking a bite, chewing, and swallowing before saying anything further.

"For some reason, Ruth, I got it into my head that I really wanted to be a daddy. I know we'd talked about it, but whether it was the guys at work talking about it, or seeing families together or whatever else was in my head, I was wrong. There wasn't even another woman when I left you, just this ridiculous thought that I should be someone's daddy, and that the only way I could accomplish that was to leave you. I couldn't have been more wrong. I know this is probably not what you wanted to hear from me, but I had to let you know. It was driving me crazy."

Ruth hadn't returned to her soup and was still unable to say anything. She'd never stopped loving Jason.

She'd thought she was moving on now, but she let him carry on talking.

"I know you are probably seeing someone, Ruth. I understand that, because you are still very beautiful and very wonderful. Sure, I'd like us to get back together, but I'm under no illusions here. I did you wrong, and you can probably never forgive me for what I did to you. If this was the other way around, I'm not sure I could forgive you, so I understand. It's just been weighing on my mind, and I needed to tell you. And I hope you understand that."

Jason went back to his sandwich, and Ruth finally found her voice.

"Wow Jay, you know how to curb a girl's appetite." She smiled, looking at her half-eaten soup and untouched sandwich. "When you left me I was, frankly, devastated. I thought for sure you'd found another woman, one who could have children, despite your saying not. I did understand after a time that you were having paternal feelings, and I couldn't blame you for that because it's not like I never had maternal feelings. Sure, I'd make snide comments about our friends' children and their behavior, but I always thought the comments were cruel because we didn't want to have children and that was my reaction. I learned how I could live through life without having any children, happily, and without regret. Maybe we also had some wild oats to sow. Neither of us saw anyone else before or during our marriage, so maybe we needed time apart. At the moment I am seeing someone, I don't think it's serious on his part, and I'm not sure how serious it is on my end, but I am seeing him. This is a bombshell, Jay."

The waitress came back over to enquire if everything was okay with the untouched sandwich and to ask if they wanted anything else. Ruth apologized and said that the soup had filled her but that she wanted to take the sandwich home, along with the coleslaw and the remaining potato salad. They didn't want anything more, so the waitress left the check and took away the sandwich to box it up for Ruth. Jason put his credit card on the check and finished his sandwich.

After the check was sorted and they left the deli, they stood a moment on the sidewalk.

"You need to get back to work Jay, and I need to think for a while. I can make my own way home from here. We need to talk some more, though, so can you come over tonight after work?"

"Course I can, Ruth. Be happy to."

"Don't start getting any ideas, Jay. We just need to talk. Come over after work, and we can sit down. Don't bring anything, we'll just talk for an hour or so. Okay?"

"That's fine Ruth, just an hour or so. I'm sorry if I've screwed up with your mind. I didn't mean to."

"I know, Jay. I'll see you later."

She didn't kiss him, just left him standing there watching her walk away toward her home, before she turned the corner and he went the opposite way back to his office.

CHAPTER SEVENTEEN

ALEC WAS AWAKE EARLY THE

next morning, excited about tonight's date with Jenny and hopefully, its conclusion. After a breakfast of cereal, shredded wheat, he put on his scruffy clothes and an old discolored overcoat and headed over toward Ruth's house. He wasn't suspicious of her in any way. He just liked to keep alert, and he so enjoyed his spying role.

He found a small store down the street from her front door. The store didn't open until 10 am, so he made himself as comfortable as he could on the concrete step, looking for all the world like one of the homeless.

He'd been there for at least an hour when he was flabbergasted to see some guy emerge from her front door, and he couldn't help himself from saying aloud, "What the fuck?" The balding guy was wearing some dark blue suit that to Alec's eye needed a pressing. "Who the hell are you?" he spoke aloud again, getting a weird stare from a passerby.

The guy on the doorstep paused for a second before he stepped back onto the doorsill and kissed the bath robed Ruth. Her hair was all tousled, and she still looked half asleep, but she had a look of contentment on her face as she kissed him back, warmly, with feeling.

Alec had stood up as soon as he saw the guy emerge, but he stayed where he was in the shop doorway. He was fuming. This guy was losing his hair, had a bit of a belly, was older than he, and he'd just been having sex with Ruth. Alec had no doubt about that, he knew that look. He was raging, and all he wanted to do then and there was run up and kill them. With savagery.

Ruth closed the door, and the guy headed toward Alec on the opposite side of the street. After he passed, he went up a side street, and Alec heard a beep as he unlocked his car with a remote. Alec was still standing in the doorway as the guy got into his BMW and drove away, leaving Alec cursing as he couldn't follow him to his work or home, as he had no wheels with him.

This was a new experience for Alec, as he had never seen any of his prospects with another man. And it was so blatant. His mind was whirling, and he wished now that he had asked Ruth to go away and never be seen again. He remained in the doorway until the proprietor showed up and, surprisingly, very politely asked him to leave.

He left for home. Alec removed his coat and hat before entering the apartment entrance, saying hello to the doorman and two elderly people who disembarked the elevator he got into.

He knew he had to calm down. He had a date tonight, so as soon as he got inside his apartment, he swallowed a couple of tranquilizers, which he knew would not only calm him but would also make him sleepy. Right now he needed to sleep and to think rationally.

CHAPTER EIGHTEEN

RUTH SAT IN HER KITCHEN,

eating her breakfast and reflecting on what had transpired. Jason had come over straight from work as promised. They'd sat down with just some water and talked. They'd talked about everything, like they used to do when they were first married. She'd let him talk about his trip to Chicago and the gossip about everybody. How they all looked, how some had aged and others hadn't. Who had divorced or were having affairs, how many children they had.

Seeing the time slip away, Ruth had made them some dinner, and Jason had helped with the cooking and cleaning up. Ruth had opened some wine. They'd drank and talked more, but mainly about themselves and what they'd learned from being apart.

Jason had confessed quite readily that he'd had a relationship with a divorced woman with children. He'd said that at first, he had enjoyed it, eating meals with them, helping with homework, taking them to their activities and encouraging them. Going on vacation, even admonishing them when they did wrong.

Then he'd gotten tired of it, especially when he'd had to keep repeating to them his instructions or advice. Then he'd hated the tantrums if they didn't get their own way, or they refused to go to bed and then didn't want to get up in the mornings. He'd disliked the stress everything caused, such as being unable to go out whenever he'd wanted unless a babysitter could be found. His car had been piled with rubbish from sodas to fast food joints.

Since he'd gotten out of that relationship, he'd calmed down and had learned his lesson. How stupid he'd been to have left Ruth in the first place.

Ruth, for her part, had learned how to function independently. How to deal with all manner of folk, how to enjoy sex more, and how much confidence she had in herself. On the downside, she missed confiding in someone, having someone to share in her successes and failures, and just having someone, "there."

For the both of them, it had been a comfortable night. They weren't trying to impress each other, nor had they felt the need to lie about anything. They were the same couple who'd just had a separation.

When Ruth had asked Jason to stay the night, it was like going to bed with an old friend. It was comfortable, rather than exciting like it was with Christos, and not as thrilling, but Ruth was happy this morning. She felt vindicated.

She'd have been even happier if she'd known that Jason had possibly just saved her life.

CHAPTER NINETEEN

IT TOOK ALEC A WHILE to get some sleep.

His rage prevented the tranquilizers from working quickly, but he finally dropped off, and when he awoke he felt much better and far calmer. It wasn't like him to get angry, and he admonished himself for doing so, knowing full well that another episode like that could get himself into a ton of trouble.

He still had a couple of hours to waste before seeing Jenny, so he started to think of her as he roamed about his apartment, switching on the TVs and making himself a turkey salad sandwich, along with some coffee.

Jenny was getting ready for her date. She had packed her small case with jeans, boots, sweater, tops, a negligee, skirt, blouse, and new underwear from Victoria's Secret. Apart from horse riding, she didn't know what else Robert had planned, so she hoped she was prepared for anything. Her case just needed her toiletries once she'd finished preparing herself for tonight. She felt like she'd gone over every pore of her body with the tweezers and razor, and as she lay in her hot soapy bath, she checked her legs again for smoothness.

Once out of the tub, she wrapped herself in a soft pink towel. While she was still damp, she practically covered herself in lotion, liking how her skin smelled and felt to her touch. She applied some antiperspirant and then set about her hair, but as it was short these days it took her only minutes. Yesterday she'd had a manicure and pedicure, so her nails and feet still looked perfect as she carefully applied make up and perfume. She could barely remember the last time she had taken so much care of herself to go on a date, but she liked Robert very much and already knew she wanted to spend more time with him.

She sipped some water as she readied herself, finally putting on her tiny underwear and short, black and white dress. The dress, too, was new. The black panels on the sides gave the wearer an hour glass figure, which in Jenny's case only accentuated it. She'd seen a couple of movie stars wearing the same type of dress, and after she'd seen one and tried it on, even the price tag didn't put her off. Finishing her packing, she got out a couple of coats from her wardrobe, her long black coat for the evening and a much more practical fleece jacket for riding. Fairly satisfied with her selections, she wheeled the suitcase to her front door with the coats and awaited Robert.

Alec was almost out of his door after finally showering and shaving, dressing almost entirely in different shades of blue. The only items that weren't blue were his black shoes and the beige silk pocket handkerchief in his blazer.

As he'd be out for the evening, but more importantly taking his car, Alec took two phones with him. One, of course, was "Robert's" phone. But he also had his own phone, which he put on vibrate. If something happened with the car, he didn't want to use the pre-paid phone, as eventually that could lead to questions. He also had his wallet, keys, and a small bag containing a change of clothing for tomorrow. He didn't need toiletries, he had enough at the farm.

After checking he'd left nothing on to cause a fire, but not setting the alarm, he made his way to the parking garage to get his car. He'd only recently traded in his old car, a Mercedes E-Class Saloon, for a used Range Rover Evoque Prestige. It was barely used when he'd purchased it, but he abhorred buying a brand new vehicle because the value decreased by thousands just by driving it away.

The apartment building promoted a car valet service, and Alec had used it after returning from the farm the previous weekend. They'd done a good job, and he was more than happy when he opened the car and could not smell Rebecca. He'd actually enjoyed her smell on his way back to the city, but he didn't want to keep smelling her scent, and he doubted if Jenny would like it.

In his trunk he kept a survival bag, and he deposited his phone in it. The bag was only for emergencies, and it included some warm clothing, a blanket, a small shovel, some flares, warning signs, and a first aid kit. He put his small bag on top of it, closed the trunk, and got into the driver's seat. He liked this car. He felt tall while driving it, and it handled superbly for its size. There weren't that many of them around either, which he also liked.

The car was white with a black interior, leather seats, and teak panels. No trace whatsoever of Rebecca. Starting up, he put the car in drive and rolled away, pressing the button on his rear view mirror to open the garage door as he approached the exit, then drove down the hill toward Jenny's place.

No parking spots were available outside of her building, so he pulled into one down the street. After putting the car in park, he called her to let her know he'd arrived.

She answered quickly, obviously seeing his name on her phone. "Hi, Robert. Are you on your way?" She asked with a hint of anxiousness.

"Hi, Jenny. I'm outside your building, but I have to double park. Can you meet me outside please?"

"Oh, okay. There's never any parking outside here. I'll be right down." Alec hung up and put the car in drive again. He double parked outside her building, leaving the car running as he got out of the car and opened the trunk, happy to see her coming out the building with her case and jacket. She wore a coat and waved to him as she exited the door.

He went to greet her, giving her a hug and a kiss on the lips as he took her case and jacket, putting them in the trunk. He helped her into the passenger seat and admired a flash of her legs as she climbed into the car. As he closed the door, someone honked their horn at him for double parking, and he held up both hands as if to say, "What the hell else could I do?"

After he got back into the driver's seat and put on his seat belt he said, "You look great, Jenny. I hope I wasn't late."

"No, you're on time. I was ready earlier than I thought I would be. I was like, what do I do now that I'm ready? You look very handsome Robert. I am so looking forward to this weekend. Where are we headed?"

"Over to the East Bay. It should be fun and a little different than it is on this side of the bay."

Jenny didn't look ill at ease, and Alec could see that she'd taken a lot of time and trouble to get ready. Her nails were pristine, her long crossed legs were enticing, and her make-up was perfect.

"I've barely been out of the city since coming here, apart from a trip to Napa. And then I couldn't really drink, because I was alone and driving. But it is beautiful up there."

"I'll have to take you to Tahoe and back to Napa. The northern coast is spectacular as well, you'd love it there, and then there are the redwood forests. You will have to come on more weekends with me."

This was more than she had expected to hear, and she was overjoyed. A smile radiated from her happy face.

"This is a great car. Is it new?" she asked, looking around the interior.

"Almost, it had a few thousand on the clock when I got it. I like it too. It's nice to sit high."

"It's a lot higher than my Mini, it's a nice change from that. But I do love being able to zip around in my car and park anywhere."

"Your car is perfect for San Francisco. I can barely go anywhere in this without having to find a car park, and that is expensive. But I usually walk around town, so I don't need a car that's nimble."

By now they were heading over the Bay Bridge toward the bright lights of Oakland to their right. Their turnoff was immediately after the Oakland turn, and they were able to maintain a good speed.

"Traffic is good." Jenny commented.

"It is, at this time of night. An hour or two earlier, we would hardly be moving. Why don't you find a radio station so we can listen to some music?"

She leaned over to turn on the radio and find a station, settling on The Mix, which played tunes from the present back to the '80s.

"What kinds of music do you like, Jen?"

"Oh, some hip hop, but also things like Lady Gaga, Rihanna, and Bruno Mars, stuff like that."

"I kinda go for Usher and Pink, but I like the old bands like U2. This station is perfect for me, good choice."

"Thank you, Robert. I like this station and its variety. I hope it's not too loud for you."

"No, it's good. Wait until later; we won't be able to talk at all."

"It's been ages since I danced. I'll be, like, lost!"

"You'll be fine. But be warned, I have two left feet."

"I'm sure you'll be fine. It's not like you have to break-dance or anything."

"Good job I don't. I'll just shuffle around you. We're almost at the restaurant."

The restaurant was Ottavio, a family-run Italian kitchen. It wasn't too expensive. Alec didn't want to appear foolish with his money, and so far everything he'd said to her seemed to be what she wanted to hear. A big part of his stalking was to discover what made his prospects tick, where they liked to shop and dine, their hobbies, their tastes, and so on. The game for him was to act so much like his prospects that they almost regarded him as their long lost best friend. It was so much fun for him.

They parked fairly close to the restaurant on a side street. Alec helped her out, and they made the short walk. He'd noticed before hand that she was wearing a simple gold chain and cross that he had seen before and resolved to ask her about it.

They were shown their table straight away, and Alec held her chair and took her coat. He almost whistled at her dress. "Wow, Jen. You look fabulous, that dress is amazing!"

She thanked him and sat down, pleased with herself for purchasing it. He sat opposite and asked the host for a bottle of Pinot Grigio.

"I can barely take my eyes off you, Jen. You look stunning."

She smiled like a Cheshire cat and felt his eyes on her, along with the eyes of about a dozen other guys.

As soon as their wine arrived and was poured, Alec made a toast. "To the most gorgeous woman in the Bay area. I am so glad you are on my arm this evening."

Jenny blushed and smiled some more, taking a sip of her wine after they clinked their glasses.

"Will you be able to drink much, Robert?"

"No, a couple of glasses is all. I'll have some champagne with you when we get to the farm," he replied reassuringly, knowing full well she wouldn't countenance him driving drunk or impaired, nor would he.

"Good, I can barely wait."

"Me either. Let's order dinner, suddenly I'm famished!"

She giggled, and Alec realized that Ruth was almost forgotten now, and that he was set for a most memorable evening.

The biggest features of the restaurant were the murals that adorned the walls with scenes from Italy. They were very impressive, and it almost made them feel like they were in Sicily or elsewhere. They had mozzarella marinara for an appetizer, then a seafood cannelloni and a penne al pomodoro con pollo, which they shared. The food was very good, and they thoroughly enjoyed it. Alec had a coffee at the end of the meal as Jenny finished off the wine. After Alec paid the check with cash, they left the restaurant, hand in hand. Helping her into her seat again, Alec kissed her, delighted when she instantly pushed her tongue into his mouth and probed around. His hand found her knee, and he was surprised when she stopped her kiss, but smiled when she said, "Now let's dance. That comes later!"

He took her to Redux Lounge, a club in Walnut Creek, He only drank water, while Jenny had a couple of glasses of Chardonnay but mostly drank water. She did like dancing. Alec wasn't much of a dancer, but he greatly enjoyed watching her thrust and sway her body around, even more so during the slow dances when she'd push into him, eliciting many envious glances from the other guys.

Jenny had retrieved a tiny clutch bag from her case before they entered the club, and when she went to freshen up, she took it with her. Alec waited at the bar and ordered another glass of wine and a water.

As the bartender served his drinks, a busty, tanned, long-legged brunette came to the side of him and whispered in a honey voice, "I know you're with someone, but give me a call some time. I think we'll have a lot of fun." She slipped a piece of paper into his hand, and he looked at her. Even in the dim light she looked better than good, and her skin glowed from perspiration. She didn't wait for a reply as she saw Jenny approach. She swayed her hips seductively as Alec watched and admired her walk away.

"Do you know her?" Jenny asked, with a hint of jealousy and annoyance.

"No, no idea who she is."

With the noise of the music, they were almost yelling.

"What did she want?"

"She wanted to know if we wanted company tonight. She thinks you're hot!"

"What did you say?"

"I said I agree, you are hot, but that you are the only one I want tonight, and I don't want to see you with a woman."

Jenny wrapped her arms around his neck and gave him a long lingering kiss. "Thank you, Robert. I think we should go now, I need to kiss you a whole lot more."

They had a couple more sips of water and wine and then left the club, holding each other tightly as they retrieved the Range Rover and drove to the farm, not that far away.

As soon as he pulled up, he ran around to the passenger door and took her around the waist as she stepped to the ground. Her coat was unbuttoned, and he kissed her. She let his hands roam her legs as she pressed into him, feeling him get hard yet again.

He pulled himself away and said, "Let's go inside, have some Champagne."

He got their luggage out of the trunk and led the way, opening the door and leading her upstairs to his bedroom, flicking the light switch with one finger that lit one of the bedside lamps. Dropping the bags in the middle of the room, he turned around and saw her close the door. She had already put her coat on a chair. He walked back and grabbed her waist again, but this time she had her back to him. She didn't try to move, she pressed her buttocks into his groin and moved it from side to side, softly moaning. His hands went to her hips, and he moved them up her side, fondled her breasts, then let them move down again to her legs. He was nuzzling her neck as he lifted her dress and stroked her thighs, feeling her legs move further apart as he went to her crotch. She was wet with expectation.

His mouth found her zip. He stopped kissing her and slowly pulled it down, admiring her skin and underwear as he did so. By now she had a firm grip on his manhood and was trying to pull his zip down. He turned her around so that they could kiss again. As they kissed, she found his buttons and undid them. She unbuckled his belt, and his pants fell around his ankles as she grasped his penis again. He felt a little stupid with his pants where they were, so he pushed her back and undressed entirely in front of her, stopping her when she attempted to do the same, then smiling as he slipped down her dress to expose her underwear.

She slipped out of the dress but kept her heels on. She motioned for him to lie on the bed. He did so, and she faced him from the front of the bed as she removed her bra, holding the cups until they were unfastened, and then let them fall. Her breasts were small, like half grapefruits, but her nipples were hard and erect. She turned around and removed her tiny white panties that matched her bra in style and color. She rotated her buttocks like a stripper. She was unexpectedly very erotic but she kept her shoes on and turned around to him, climbing onto the bed with her knees.

"I need you right now, Robert. You have kept me waiting way too long. We can play later," she whispered, and he wasn't about to complain.

Quite unexpectedly, she stood up before squatting down on him, guiding him into her very wet vagina, her hands clasping his knees as she rode him into ecstasy.

CHAPTER TWENTY

THEY LAY FACING EACH

OTHER but barely apart after they had both come, just touching and feeling each other, getting their breath back.

"Thank you, Robert. That was even better than I thought it was going to be. I just couldn't wait any longer," she murmured, kissing his neck.

"No, thank you, Jen. I was bursting, and you are wonderful," he replied, finding her lips to kiss again.

"Do you want to sleep now?"

"I think we need a glass of bubbly now, don't you think?"

"That'll be nice. I'll just use the bathroom."

"It's over there." He pointed.

"I'll be right back."

"Me too," he replied.

He didn't bother to put anything on. He wasn't shy, but he was amused when she put on her panties and bra.

When he returned with the Champagne and glasses, she was still in the bathroom, and he heard the water running in the sink. He poured the bubbly and sat up on the bed to await her, not taking a drink until then.

Apart from her dress, she looked like she had at the restaurant, although she had removed her shoes. He could now admire her underwear. The bra gave her a little uplift and cleavage, and the panties barely covered her modesty. The frills were tiny but effective, and she had great legs.

She sat next to him, and he handed her the glass, making a toast.

"To more wonderful evenings like this one!"

"Cheers to that. I'm still pulsing."

They both took good drinks.

"I was admiring your chain and cross earlier. Is it a family heirloom?"

"Thank you," she replied, fingering the necklace. "It belonged to my nana."

"What do you like for breakfast, Jen?"

126

"Oh whatever, just toast and coffee usually."

"I'll make us breakfast in bed. Do you like cream and sugar?"

"Cream or milk, but no sugar. Are you going to sleep now?" She sounded disappointed.

"No." He climbed over and straddled her. "I want to play with you now and savor your fabulous body. Would you mind if I tasted your skin with champagne?"

"Mmm, that sounds good. Will the champagne tingle?"

"It will where I intend to put it," he replied mischievously, pouring the remains of his glass over her proud breasts and bending over to lick off the champagne, unhooking her bra at the same time.

CHAPTER TWENTY ONE

ALEC LEFT THE FARM AROUND

midday the following day, ecstatic at how the evening and morning had unfolded as he reflected on his memories. He had an idea about what his brother would do to Jenny, but he'd never ask him, as he didn't really care. He just knew that another man would never ever be able to sample the delights, the unbelievable loving of Jenny ever again.

When he returned to his apartment, he'd email the photos he'd taken to himself, look through her messages, maybe send a general text to cancel any appointments she had, and then dispose of both phones.

He was also thinking of calling Ruth to finish their relationship. Unfortunately, he couldn't get rid of her now as he should have done, but then he wasn't trying for a 100% success rate. He was very happy as he drove back to San Francisco.

At the same time, his brother was also extremely happy, and as Jane wouldn't come near the farm this weekend, he'd be able to take his time enjoying the gorgeous Jenny, as Alec had named her.

He already had her strapped down, so he thought he'd call Jane to put her mind at ease and erase any possibility of her calling him and perhaps ruining a moment.

"Hi, Jane. How are things?"

"Hi, George. I was just thinking of calling you. Is everything okay there? Do you want me to come over?"

George heard a little hopefulness in her voice.

"No, it's okay, Jane. Since Alex is here, it gives me a chance to catch up on a few things, because it gets a bit embarrassing to be in the house when they're parading around in next to nothing."

"Maybe I should come over, George, sounds like fun." Jane could only imagine seeing George's brother in next to nothing, but she was also aware that whoever he was with was probably a model or something.

"Come over tomorrow night, Jane. They'll be gone by then."

"Is this another of his super models?"

"Actually, I haven't seen her yet. I saw Alec at breakfast time, but she was still in his room. I worked in the office for a while and then came over to check the farm equipment and do some little repairs. So are you coming over tomorrow night?"

"Yes George. Do you want me to bring anything?"

"No, we're fine. It'll be nice when we have our own place and I don't have to worry who I might bump into when Alec comes over."

"You mean you worry about bumping into a gorgeous naked model parading around the house?"

"I think you know what I mean. So what time will you be over?"

"Around four or five. I don't want to eat late, I have a busy Monday morning."

"Okay, I'll see you then. I love you, Jane."

"I love you, too. See you tomorrow."

George hung up, not at all bothered about his lies to Jane. His mind whirled with how many hours he'd have with Jenny and the time that was now set in his mind that he'd have to start the clean- up.

CHAPTER TWENTY TWO

AS SOON AS ALEC GOT back to his

building, he arranged with the doorman for his car to be valeted. Once he got into his apartment, he called Kim to confirm for the following night.

She sounded very excited to hear from him and although he offered to pick her up, she said she'd meet him at the restaurant. Andrew had somewhere in mind, and he told her he'd call her back as soon as he'd made the reservation.

He obtained a table at the Zatar Restaurant, a tiny, eclectic Mediterranean place. Kim knew where it was, just down the street from her, and they arranged to meet at 7 pm.

Then he called Ruth, but as his temper had totally abated now, he changed what he'd been going to say. He'd planned to tell her that he'd met someone else who had his same interests and was his same age, and that he'd no longer be able to see her. Instead, he told her that he'd planned to surprise her yesterday morning with some pastries and champagne, but as he almost got to her door his phone rang, and he'd had to dash off to see a client. He gave her the time that he was there, which was the exact time that she was at the doorstep, and said he'd call again soon.

When he told her that, he could almost hear her brain working through its gears as she silently recalled the time Jason had left her house. The only thing she could say was a lame "Okay." Alec was smiling as he finished the call, imagining the shock on her face after being found out.

Then he retrieved Jenny's phone from his overnight bag, along with the prepaid phone he'd used for her. He had a myriad of email addresses, for which he was very thankful for his memory. The names and web addresses were easy, but the passwords to access the accounts were all different. He supposed that most people used the same password all the time, but that was a dangerous thing to do, and he didn't need to do that. He was amazed, though, that even from a prepaid phone he could take photos and email them, which he did but only to himself.

Logging onto his computer and then a different email account, he made sure he received the photos. He wasn't into trophies, but he did like a naked photo of the victims to look at sometimes, just to refresh his memory. Once he looked at the picture, everything else was as clear as day in his recollection.

He then moved the pictures to a folder, deleted the email, and emptied the trash. He left his laptop open and on the sports page as he went to check Jenny's phone.

She had some messages. From what he could tell, most seemed to be from clients. But her mother wanted a return call and, although it wasn't urgent, she wanted to chat. He also found a couple of other messages that could have been from anybody and Facebook message updates.

He went through her calendar and sent texts to her clients to say she'd be away for a few days but would reschedule them next week. He then found her photos and was shocked to find a couple of himself from the club. He hadn't known she'd taken any, but with all the flashes there'd been in there he would never have suspected. Thankfully, they hadn't come out too well, and though he could recognize himself, he thought it highly unlikely anyone else would. Besides, she might not even have sent them anywhere and he checked the sent emails and couldn't find them.

She'd also taken some photos of herself in her silhouette dress, and these he sent to himself. There were other photos but nothing of any interest to him.

Then he went through her other apps. Although she was a part of a few social network sites, the only one she had posted on recently was Facebook. She mentioned Robert a few times, and commented on Thursday that she was going on a date with him, for which she'd bought a new dress and spoiled herself. In reply, her friends had made remarks like "Go girl!", "Don't do anything I wouldn't do," "About time you got some," and "Keep us posted."

Alec made a new comment. "Great night with Robert, the dress was well worth the money! Just got home, Sylvia wants me to go camping with her. Will try to post but away for a couple of days."

Satisfied, he disabled both phones. He'd trash them in the morning on his way to the Embarcadero.

CHAPTER TWENTY THREE

ALEC WAS AWAKE EARLY

SUNDAY morning. He looked forward to seeing the walker again, and as he'd lost three prospects in just the last week, he had a busy week coming up. At least he'd remembered to retrieve the note he'd been handed in the club. She could be another prospect.

He'd reuse the phone he'd had for Ruth. There was nothing to hide there, and he could also use the same name. It wouldn't matter.

The weather wasn't looking that great today. It was cold, and rain was threatening. As he got ready, he hoped her fitness regimen overrode any inclement weather. He'd dump the disabled and broken apart phones on his way down there, and hopefully he'd get home in time for most of the 49er game.

He didn't dress any differently than the last time, which he didn't like doing, but he wanted her to recognize him. He would know her anywhere, she was very distinctive, and if she was walking there wouldn't be a huge crowd to shield her from view.

As he left the building he realized that it was colder than he thought it would be, so much so that he jogged a little to warm up. He thought he felt a sprinkle or two on his face as he made his way down California Street, and he was doubtful if he would see her.

He found a couple of different trash cans to dispose of the phones, and having done that he continued on to the Embarcadero, which, not surprisingly, was very quiet.

Having gotten warm, he slowed down to a brisk walk, keeping his hands in his tracksuit top pockets to prevent them getting cold and wet.

He was almost at Pier 39 and thinking that this was just a good workout day when he spotted her coming directly toward him. Suddenly it wasn't so cold and wet any more as he saw her smile and grimace at the weather. Even in the chill of the bay, she looked good in her skintight, sky blue running suit and matching cap. Alec thought she deserved more admirers than she was getting today.

"Hi," she said brightly as she approached. "I thought it would be too cold for you today."

"It is, but I needed the exercise. And I was hoping to bump into you, despite the weather."

"Then it's a good job I came out."

"You're not saying that you hoped to bump into me, are you?"

"Not at all, what on earth gave you that idea?" She gave him a huge smile.

Her eyes were watering and her nose was running a little. He felt his eyes and nose doing the same, so he suggested that maybe they should find a little shelter and get some warm fluid down them. She readily agreed, so they walked together quickly and found a coffee shop, which was almost empty.

"Oh, that's better," she said as they entered.

"It certainly is," he replied. "What can I get you?"

She looked up at the chalked menu above the counter. "I'll have a cappuccino and some toast, please."

"Okay. If you sit down, I'll order it."

"I'll go and use the bathroom first."

He watched her walk away before ordering. He was going to have a blueberry muffin with his latte. He took off his cap and ruffled his hair.

She wasn't gone long, the coffees weren't ready yet. But when she returned, she looked as fresh as a daisy.

"You look great," he complimented her, as she took a seat at a table.

"Amazing what a little hot water does for you." She smiled.

"My turn. The coffees should be ready in a minute, they're already paid for."

Alec hurried to the rest room. His nose felt like it was running like a stream. He did there as he supposed she did and took a hot wash in the bowl, feeling his skin warm up back to almost normal again. He returned to the table to find the coffees and food already there. She was putting jelly on her toast.

"That's better," he said. "I took your advice with the hot water."

"You look as handsome as ever." He could tell from her eyes that she meant it.

"I'll always take a compliment from a beautiful woman such as you, but let me introduce myself. My name is Christos. And to whom am I having coffee with this chilly morning?"

"Christos? That sounds Greek. Is that where you're from?"

"No, it's just a name my parents gave me. But I believe my ancestors may have come from there."

"Well Christos, a pleasure to meet you. My name is Aisha."

She held out her long delicate hand to be shaken, which Alec gladly took.

"A very lovely name, and a pleasure to meet you, too."

She was a beautiful woman, and Alec enjoyed looking at her. He knew there would be no shortage of suitors for her, although he suspected that many would be put off by her elegant beauty. Most men didn't approach women such as this, they thought they weren't good enough or more probably, rich enough. Alec had no such hang-up. He had both things going for him, and he was never deterred.

"You don't seem short of confidence," she commented, her voice cultured and warm, but not too strong.

"Should I be?" he asked lightly.

"No, I actually like it."

They drank their coffees and ate their food, and Alec bought them an extra cup. They went through the normal routine of boy meeting girl by telling each other who they were, although, of course, Alec lied throughout.

Aisha was a paralegal who worked in a soulless cubicle for a law firm downtown. Most of the work was boring and the paperwork was endless, but it paid exceedingly well and they had great benefits. Due to that, she was able to maintain a one bedroom apartment just off the Embarcadero, and although it didn't have a bay view, it was still very nice, and she greatly enjoyed it.

She was from Sacramento, went to U.C. Davis, and had lived here for three years since obtaining the position with the law firm. Her family still lived in the capital, both parents and two little brothers, and she saw them on holidays and various other times, when she had time.

Some of the lawyers had asked her out, but all of them were married, and she didn't want to find herself in the middle of a company scandal, so she'd always declined. She'd been out with a couple of other paralegals and also guys she'd met while out, but nothing had been serious or even long-lasting.

Alec spun his usual story, the only partial truth being the business advice he gave and the enjoyment he got from sport.

When he asked her out for lunch some time during the week, she accepted without hesitation, and they exchanged phone numbers and email addresses, putting the numbers into their phones there and then.

Reluctantly, they went their separate ways, although Alec knew he could probably have prolonged their time together. He didn't want to rush her. He liked his strategy, and so far it had worked, so why change?

CHAPTER TWENTY FOUR

JANE ARRIVED AT THE FARM

around 4:30 pm and found George in high spirits, at least for him. Even when he was happy, his face was expressionless. But today he was positively smiling. She knew the 49ers had won today, the TVs were still running the highlights. But they'd won before, and it hadn't elicited this response, so she wondered what had happened.

"You seem happy, George. What's the occasion?"

"I don't know. It's just been a good day, I suppose. I thought we'd have a burger tonight. I've made a salad, there's some potato salad as well in the fridge, and I've just lit the barbecue."

"So you had a good weekend?"

"I suppose so, how was yours?"

Jane just couldn't get over him smiling, it was almost uncanny. Sure, she'd seen him smile a lot of times, but he just seemed so happy, like all of his dreams had come true all at once.

"Mine was pretty busy. I worked yesterday at the clinic and did some paperwork today. We were swamped yesterday."

"Really?"

"Yes. Dogs with fleas, cats with infections, snakes with cuts, it made me realize why I prefer the large animals. It was like a zoo in there."

"That's funny, Jane. Sorry you had a tough day. Are you hungry, or do you want to wait for a while?"

"Let's have a glass of wine first, let me relax a little."

George opened some Cabernet and poured them both a drink, taking both glasses into the family room so they could take a seat on the couch and he could catch up on the football. He was well aware that the Sunday night game was starting very soon.

"So how was Alec?" she asked as she sat at the other end of the couch.

"I didn't really see him. He arrived late Friday night, slept in Saturday morning, went out again that night, and left late this morning after sleeping in again. We kind of saw each other from a distance, and we waved, but I didn't want to intrude."

"So he didn't even introduce you to his latest super model?" asked the indignant Jane.

"He never had the opportunity, really."

"Oh please, George. The least he could have done would have been to let you meet her. What was she like? It was a different one, wasn't it."

"I think so, but I only saw her from a distance. About all I could see of her was that she had long, wavy, black hair and was tall. She looked good from a distance though."

"Like I said, another super model. You think he'll ever bring the same girl more than once? It's time he settled down."

"I doubt that's going to happen. You know what he's like."

"Yes George, I know what he's like. Would you like another glass of wine?"

"I'll get it. Do you need anything else?" asked George as he headed back to the kitchen.

"No, but I'll take an Advil if you have one, it'll stop the headache before it comes."

"I don't think we have any down here, but I think there's some in Alec's bathroom cabinet. Go and help yourself while I check the barbecue and get us some more wine."

Jane headed upstairs to find the Advil, thinking she'd be walking into a bedroom that would be a total mess. Instead, it was immaculate, with not a thing out of place. It was so disconcerting that she even went over to the king-size bed to see if the bed had just been fixed or if the sheets had been changed. The sheets were fresh. She walked into the bathroom and that was the same, fresh towels, nothing out of place. Finding the Advil, she helped herself to a couple and poured herself some water to wash them down.

Returning to the bedroom, curious now, she looked in both nightstands. She didn't find much apart from a plentiful supply of condoms, ribbed for the utmost satisfaction according to the wrappers. Well at least he's careful, she thought. But there was nothing in the trash cans. They were empty, with not even a used tissue inside.

She headed back downstairs.

George was back on the couch, and he'd refilled both their glasses. "Did you find any?" He asked.

"Yes thanks, they were right where you said they were. Did your housekeeper work this weekend?"

Jane sat back on the couch. The game had just started on the TV, so they both looked at the screen.

"Who? Marita? No, she never works here during the weekend, you know that."

"I didn't think so, but Alec is very tidy."

"I know, he always has been. He makes me look like a slob. Are you ready for a burger yet?"

"Yes I am. Let's go and get them on."

They moved back into the kitchen, and George took the burgers out to the barbecue while Jane got their plates out, along with the salads. She sliced a tomato and an onion. George came back in and got buns, slices of cheese, and mayo.

Jane poured herself another drink and wondered if Alec had actually been there that weekend, or if George was seeing someone else. She had smelled an expensive scent in the bedroom, but everything else was too perfect.

They had dinner in the kitchen, watched the game on the small screen, and drank more wine. Later, George made love to her. Jane thought he was very intense in bed, but still happy in his expression. For some strange reason, it felt to her that he was making love to someone else.

CHAPTER TWENTY FIVE

ALEC TOOK THE BART OVER to

Berkeley. Because he was early, he took his time, waiting inconspicuously just along the street from the restaurant in hopes of seeing Kim approach. He waited a few minutes. When he checked his watch at 6:55 pm, he spotted her walking alone down the street toward the restaurant.

Like him, she wore jeans and a jacket. But unlike him, her jeans were skin tight above her heeled ankle boots. She, too, wore a jacket, red compared to Andrew's blue, and her top was black while Andrew's polo shirt was white.

Berkeley wasn't really a dress-up town. With all the students on campus, it would have been suicide for restaurants to impose dress codes, so they were both casual for dinner tonight.

He met her at the entrance, and they exchanged kisses on each other's cheeks. "Andrew" complimented her on how wonderful she looked before he led the way into Zatar's. A few people milled around, folks who didn't have reservations and hoped to be walk ins. But

Andrew had a reservation, so they made their way through the small crowd.

Zatar's was an eclectic Mediterranean restaurant, tiny, and very cozy. It was also organic, and they provided much of the produce themselves. It was always busy.

On being shown to their table, which was very close to the adjoining tables, Andrew ordered a German lager, and Kim told the host to make that two. The restaurant only served beer or wine, so there was no possibility of ordering a cocktail, but it only added to the distinctive feel of the place.

Andrew praised Kim to the hilt, how she looked, how he'd missed her, and how much he'd been looking forward to this evening. Kim told him how handsome he looked, and that she, too, had been looking forward to this evening.

They ordered their meals of grilled leg of lamb with cumin and a fish tagine, and they shared a bareka appetizer. Filo pastry stuffed with chard, kale, feta, and fresh herbs. They also shared dessert. Cardamom ice cream with dates and walnuts.

Unusually for Andrew, as he was called this evening, he asked the server to select the wine himself, as he wasn't familiar with any of the wines on offer. This actually wasn't a strange request in the restaurant.

They prided themselves on offering obscure wines from small vineyards in Europe.

The meal was spicy, fragrant, and quite fresh, very enjoyable for both.

Kim had touched Andrew often during their meal, with her feet and hands, and her eyes never wavered from him to look at other diners or to see who entered the door.

Andrew wondered how he was going to avoid going home with her, although he did have a good excuse with the Bart service stopping before midnight, when disaster struck. At least, for him it did.

"Hi, Kim. I didn't know you were coming here!"

One of her friends had come in, had seen her, and had made a bee line over. Kim looked up as Andrew turned around.

"Hi, Jill. Are you with Ben?"

Kim stood and gave her friend a hug, waving at Ben who was still at the door and trying to get a table.

"Yes, but who is this dreamy guy you're with? It's no wonder you've kept him quiet. We'd have been stealing him from you."

Jill's eyes were firmly on Andrew as she said this, and he stood to meet her. She was quite attractive, with a nice shape. But she was a little plain in looks, and she hadn't done anything special to come out this evening, which she acknowledged.

"If I'd known I was meeting you, I'd have done something to myself."

Andrew gave her his best smile and held out his hand for her to shake. "Very pleased to meet you, Jill. I'm Andrew, and you don't need to do anything to yourself."

Jill gave him a hug instead of a handshake, and looked around at her friend. She opened her mouth and flicked her tongue.

"Okay Jill, you can let him go now before you suffocate him."

Andrew was amused at Jill for pressing herself at him, even with her boyfriend just yards away.

"You know me, Kim. I'm all talk, I don't mean anything. I belong to my darling Ben."

Andrew wasn't sure about that comment, he'd been on the other end of her hug.

"Yes, I know you, Jill, and I love you for being you. Listen, we're about to leave, so if you want our table you're more than welcome."

"That's a great idea. Let me go and tell Ben."

Jill rushed away as Andrew and Kim took their seats again.

"Sorry about that, Andrew. I didn't know she was coming here, and she can be a little overpowering."

"That's okay. This is a small town really, and you're bound to bump into your friends. I'll get the check." Andrew signaled the server for the check. "This has been a lovely evening, Kim. We'll have to do this again, if you'll allow me."

"You're not thinking of going home, are you?" Kim held his hand again.

"I will escort you home, if I may."

"Of course you may, Andrew. I have some wine back in my room, which I was hoping to share with you. Or I could make you some coffee," she said with more than a hint of hope.

"Don't you have a roommate?" he asked.

"Yes, but she won't be back tonight. I have you all to myself." Meeting Kim's friend was a total disaster for

Andrew's plan with Kim, but not all was lost. He could still have a great evening.

"Then let's go. Maybe I could have some wine and coffee."

The check came, and Andrew paid with cash. They said hello to Ben and good night to the couple as they left the restaurant, holding hands tightly.

"Did she come on to you?" Kim asked.

"She kind of pressed her body against me."

"I thought so. What did you think?"

"I thought that I wished it had been you."

"You'll get your wish in about 5 minutes, Andrew," and he saw from her eyes and her sly smile that she wasn't lying.

CHAPTER TWENTY SIX

HE DIDN'T RECOGNIZE THE SAN

Francisco 415 area code and wondered whether to ignore the ringing. They could always leave a message.

"Hello."

"Hello, Mr. Young?"

"If this is some sales pitch, then don't waste your time. I'm not interested."

"No Mr. Young, this is not a sales pitch. My name is Elizabeth Ferris, and I have a modeling agency in San Francisco. The reason I'm calling you is that I hope you know where your sister Rebecca is."

"My sister? I have no idea where she is. I haven't seen or spoken to her for ages. Is there something wrong? And where did you get my number?"

Both of the callers could hear each other's consternation.

"I don't know, Mr. Young. About a week ago she sent me a text to say that she had an assignment in Las Vegas for a few days, but I've heard nothing from her since."

"She's probably having fun then, but the last time I heard from her she was in L.A. Has she been working for you?"

"Yes, for quite some time now, and this is very unlike her. She is one of my most dependable models and, quite frankly, I'm worried."

"Have you called her?"

"Yes, repeatedly. The phone goes immediately to voice mail, and I can't leave any more messages because the file is full."

"Have you called whoever she's working for in Vegas?"

"I've called everyone I know there, and no one has even seen her. Now I think that she never actually went there."

"You think that maybe she went there with a guy and is just having fun?"

"I'd like to think so, Mr. Young, but like I said, this is so unlike her."

"Are there any other numbers you could call? You've obviously got mine. And please, call me James or Jim, if you prefer."

"Like I said, James, I've called everyone I know, and I got your number from her employment form. You are Rebecca's only contact in an emergency."

"You think this is an emergency? Oh God! Does she have a roommate or a number where she lives?"

"She lived alone in an apartment, but she only had a cell phone. I called her building, but no one has seen her recently. You were basically my last hope."

"Oh Jesus, no! She's all I've got left, even though we don't speak much. What do you think we should do? Should I come out there?"

"I really hate to say this, but I think we should report her missing, see if the police can find her. I can't think of anything else we can do."

"God, I don't believe this. Nothing could have happened to Becky, surely. So you think I should call the police?"

Elizabeth heard the panic in James' voice. He was almost crying, and she was glad that she didn't have to make calls like this more than this one time.

"I'll call them James, there's probably more that I can tell them than you. I really just wanted to let you know and see if you agreed. As you haven't heard from her, then I think that's all we can do."

"She wasn't depressed or anything, was she, when she went to Vegas?"

"No, she was actually in a very good mood the last time I saw her. She didn't say anything, but I suspected that maybe she'd met someone special."

"So there was a guy? Any idea who he is?"

"Like I said, James, she didn't say anything. It was just my woman's instinct that thought that. I'm hoping there is a guy, and they're in a hotel room in Vegas having a ton of fun."

"Me too, Elizabeth. Me too. So you'll call the police?"

"Yes, right now."

Elizabeth went on to give James her telephone numbers and told him to call at any time. She also let him know where her agency was located and said that he'd find her there when and if he came to the city.

He was still very distraught when she hung up, and she felt awful that she'd had to leave him in that state, but that was the situation. At least now they had each other to share the disappearance of Rebecca and help each other.

Finding the number for the missing person department at the San Francisco Police on the web, she called and gave as much information as she could to an officer, who was obviously filling out the form. He told her that a detective would call her back as soon as possible to follow up.

Surprisingly to Elizabeth, she was called back within an hour by a Detective Garcia, who went through all the information she had given a little earlier.

Although the detective sounded young and nice, she also seemed thorough to Elizabeth with the questions she was asking. It made her feel hopeful.

The detective asked if it would be all right if she swung around for a photograph of Rebecca later in the day, after she'd checked a few things. Elizabeth told her that would be fine, she'd look forward to her visit.

Putting the phone down and heading for the file cabinet to retrieve Rebecca's photos and information, she glanced in one of the many mirrors at her reflection. She thought she looked haggard. With eyes puffy and skin blotchy, this wasn't her best day. Overall, she still looked good for her age, 45 now, and thanks to her old modeling figure and eating habits that stemmed from that time, she was still trim and lithe and could still carry her long black hair. She'd seen other women of her age who looked stupid with long hair, and as soon as she thought she looked too old, she'd chop it off. She had lines on her face now, but didn't want to do Botox yet.

Her cheekbones were still high and pronounced, and she had good teeth. Her only regret that she thought she saw in her reflection was that she hadn't married and had children.

Easily finding Rebecca's file, she marveled at how beautiful she was, and what a great figure she had. She'd been featured in so many magazines it was unheard of, and because she was so dedicated she always stayed in demand. Of course, there were slow weeks. But during those times Rebecca could always find work elsewhere if she so wished.

Elizabeth left the file on her desk as she went about her business. Arranging shoots, calling models and photographers, and returning calls from advertisers.

It was almost time to close the office when Elizabeth got a visit from Detective Garcia. Elizabeth's assistant, Tina, announced her arrival.

"Send her in, Tina, and that'll be all for today. Have a good evening."

"Thanks, Elizabeth. I'll see you in the morning."

Tina sent the detective through after telling her that she hoped she'd be able to find Rebecca safe and well.

Elizabeth got up from her desk as the detective entered and walked around to meet her. Her office walls were covered with framed magazine covers of her models and herself when she'd modeled, but it was a very feminine office. She obviously liked the color yellow, it dominated the room but was broken up by the cherry wood of the desk and chairs. The flower arrangement on the desk was huge and practically covered half the desk.

Elizabeth was tall and towered over Detective Garcia, who was stocky and could probably look after herself. She had a pretty face enveloped by short black hair, a brown complexion, and smooth unblemished skin. She wore a grey pinstriped pant suit with a white blouse and very low heels. As a comparison, Elizabeth wore stilettos, a knee-length fitted skirt in emerald green that matched her shoes, and a frilly blouse in her favorite yellow with long sleeves. Unlike the detective, she also wore a lot of jewelry, including pearls around her long, elegant neck.

"Hello, detective. I am Elizabeth Ferris, and I hope I have you on a wild goose chase."

"Good afternoon, Ms. Ferris. I hope you're wasting my time also."

"Take a seat, detective, and is there anything I can get you?"

The detective sat down on the couch. "No, thank you. Do you have the photo of Ms. Young?"

Elizabeth got the file off her desk and took it to her, sitting down on the other end of the couch.

"She's very beautiful," the detective commented, with only a trace of Hispanic in her strong voice. "Have you thought any more of where she could be?"

"I can barely think of anything else, but I have no idea."

"You said you'd spoken to her brother. Did he have any idea?"

"No, and that was an awful phone call to make. I don't know how you do it all the time."

"It's not something you ever get used to. Do you still have the text that Ms. Young sent you?"

"Yes."

"Let me see it. Then forward it to this number, if you will." She handed over a card with a number circled.

Elizabeth handed over her phone, and the detective read the message.

"Is this a normal thing for Ms. Young to do, to go off and do work elsewhere?"

"No, but we were quiet, and she is always in demand. So I didn't think it that odd. It was only after I didn't hear from her again that I got worried, and she knew there was work here this week."

"You called everyone you know in Vegas?"

"Yes. No one has even seen her."

"I know we went through most of this on the phone earlier, but I need to be sure of all the facts as we know them, and talking to you face to face is a big help. Do you know if she was romantically involved with anyone?"

"She didn't discuss it, but I suspected something. She was more radiant."

"So you think it's possible she may have gone somewhere with someone."

"Yes, but even if she had, she was dedicated to her work and would have called me. I have no doubt about that. Do you think something has happened to her?" This was very distressing to Elizabeth. She'd tried not to think of something bad happening to Rebecca, but her silence was worrying.

"I can't say yet, Ms. Ferris, but the longer she remains missing, then more the likelihood something has happened to her. I was able to get access to her apartment, which looked undisturbed, although she did have some clothing on her bed. It looked like she'd thought of packing them but had decided against it. I also bumped into her neighbor, who wondered why I was in her apartment, and he told me she was only going away for the weekend. She'd asked him to keep an eye on her apartment, and he hasn't seen her since.

We've taken her computer, and hopefully there'll be something in there that will give us a clue, but that's all that I learned from there. She was probably picked up, as her car is still in the garage. Right now, I don't think she was going anywhere for longer than the weekend."

"But what about the text?" asked Elizabeth.

"I don't know. Her neighbor was adamant that she said she was only going for the weekend, so maybe she changed her mind. But her phone has not been used since, and as we can't get a trace on it, it's probably turned off."

"Oh God! I should have called you a week ago!"

"You weren't to know, Ms. Ferris, and she may well be just living it up in Vegas. It's something we have to check before we can do anything else.

We'll be checking the computer, of course, but until I hear back from Vegas or something occurs here, then there's little to go on or to check up on. I'll keep you updated, but if you hear anything, the slightest thing, call me straightaway."

The detective left with copies of Rebecca's file and her photos, and Elizabeth was very distraught, wishing she'd been more personal with Rebecca about her private life.

CHAPTER TWENTY SEVEN

ANDREW HAD SPENT

THE NIGHT with Kim. It had reminded him of being back in college and trying to sleep in a small bed, not to mention wearing the same clothes as the night before.

He'd awoken early, and Kim had made them some toast and coffee, and then she'd jumped his bones again before he'd left and she went to class. He promised he'd call her, and when he left her room, he got some knowing looks from the students who were hurrying to and fro.

Back at his apartment, he showered and changed, replenished the condoms he'd used that he kept in his wallet, and wondered about his next move. He needed more prospects.

He thought he'd take the Muni, part of the San Francisco Public Transportation, to the de Young Museum of Fine Arts in Golden Gate Park. He hadn't been there for a long time, and it was always a great place for him. Even if he didn't meet anyone, he liked the peace and reverence it offered, and although he wasn't an admirer of abstracts or sculptures, he did like impressionism and most other forms.

It was quite mild in the city with a small threat of showers, so along with his normal wear of one of his myriad of sport coats, he also wore slacks, slip on loafers, and an open-neck shirt. He put on a white trench coat and a dark blue fedora that matched his shoes. It didn't take long to reach the museum on the bus, and he enjoyed public transportation, as he was a great people watcher. He loved to observe all the different people and try to guess what they were and the things they liked. He never spoke to anybody, unless he had to, but he listened to conversations when he could and do a lot of critical appraisals of their attires.

He was deep into a conversation that was going on behind his seat with two middle aged women who were talking about a friend of theirs whose husband was a total jerk. Seemed he was out of work, drinking beer all day long, not doing anything to help out, and then criticizing their friend for being stressed and not very loving.

The two women were saying that their friend should throw his fat ass out the door or cut off his beer money and cigarettes. It was all very interesting, and he was disappointed that he reached his stop before he could find out more.

After entering and paying his $25 fee, he removed his hat and coat and paid the cloakroom attendant. He roamed around. The museum had a special exhibit of over 100 Picasso works, and he was very interested, as it was mostly his earlier pieces.

What he really liked was to see the original work and all of its brushwork, and he often wondered how they could do such marvelous paintings when up close it was difficult to distinguish the complete scene.

The museum was by no means empty, but it wasn't so busy that you couldn't sit in the various rooms and admire the art, losing yourself in the scene before you.

It was in one of the rooms where he was doing just that, totally immersed in the painting, that he was surprised when someone spoke to him.

"It's beautiful, isn't it?"

He looked to his right and found her sat beside him, her black stockinged legs crossed beneath her dark gray suit, a flowery scarf tied around her neck under the collar of her black blouse. Her light brown hair was scraped back from her head and tied into a bun at the back, and her glasses were small and oblong. She was probably in her late thirties, looked like a librarian but on a way better salary, as he could tell the suit was costly and her adornments were expensive. She even smelled wealthy.

Physically, she was in shape, not as good as a model but not overweight, and her back was ramrod straight. Her face was a long oval, with attractive smooth skin and large green eyes beneath her glasses. She obviously took her time with make-up.

"I love this painting. I think I've been gazing at it for about half an hour now," he replied.

She had her hands resting on top of her knee as she leaned forward a little, her purse between them on the cushioned seat. She made no attempt to hide her wedding ring as he watched her out of the side of his eye, as she looked at the painting and swung her crossed ankle in lazy circles.

"Did you like the Picasso's?" she asked, in a slightly husky voice.

"I did," he replied, "although I wasn't keen on the sculptures. I'm glad I came and saw his work though, it wasn't what I expected."

Without changing position, she turned her head around to look him directly in the eye. She wasn't a shrinking violet. To Alec, it seemed she could go to a board room meeting or to an evening reception without having to change the slightest thing about her.

"This is my second visit to this exhibition, as it wasn't what I expected, either. I thought there'd be more of his abstract work, but this is enlightening. I've really enjoyed it. Do you mind if I ask you a personal question?"

Alec gave her his best slightly amused look. "Not at all."

"You don't appear to be with anyone. But are you being joined, or are you meeting someone for lunch?"

She'd neither flinched nor looked embarrassed when she asked this. She was obviously a confident woman and was used to asking awkward questions.

"No, I am alone today."

"Would you care to join me for lunch?" She smiled and half laughed, as Alec admired her dental work. "You must think me very brazen," she continued, smiling, "but I'm quite hungry, and I don't wish to go home just yet or dine alone. I'd love for you to join me for lunch."

"Do you wish to stay here, or can I take you elsewhere?"

"Here is fine. If we go elsewhere, I'll no doubt get gossiped about, but I don't see any of my acquaintances here. I also have a driver, and that would make it doubly awkward. So let's eat here, please."

As they made their way to the museum café, Alec thought she was forthright because she no doubt had staff. Either at her place of work or at home. After ordering their food, Alec paid with cash. She offered to pay but made no fuss when he said he had it, and they sat in the café and ate their salads and drank their Chardonnay.

"Cheers." Alec took a sip of wine and asked, "So who am I having a most enjoyable lunch with?"

"Actually, this may sound very underhand and suspicious, but I don't wish to tell you, nor do I wish to learn who you are. Is that rude?" she whispered.

Alec looked around. The tables were occupied, so he kept his voice down as well.

"It sounds more exciting, more erotic even, than suspicious. If I may be so bold, it sounds like you may have more than an innocent lunch on your mind."

She played with her glass and took another sip, glancing around and letting her eyes smile.

"Are you gay?"

"No." He was amused now.

"Do you think I'm attractive?"

Alec looked her over. He wanted her to be in no doubt about his answer, and he let his eyes drop to her breasts and back to her eyes again. "Yes, and very sensual. You are a very sexy and desirable woman."

"You know that I'm married?"

"I see the ring. Are you unhappy?"

"For the most part, I am. I feel like a prisoner sometimes. My husband makes a bunch of money, and I can spend as much as I wish. But he always seems so suspicious of me, yet I always think he's shafting his assistant. He used to be all over me, but now he always says he's tired, yet he reeks of her cheap perfume. I need my own excitement and, to be frank with you, as soon as I saw you come into the museum, I've been as horny as hell. Does that shock you?"

"I'm flattered."

"Oh, I think you have a lot of women friends. I'm under no illusion there. It oozes out of you."

Alec smiled at her. It was rare when a woman was so brazen with him, but when it occurred, he liked it. He found it refreshing and intoxicating. He emptied the remains of the wine into their glasses.

"I do have my fair share of women, and I'm fortunate that they are also beautiful, just like yourself. It is very arousing, though, when someone like you comes along. Right this moment, I can think of nothing better than taking you right here, or around the corner, or in the back seat of your car."

She looked at him very closely now. Her tongue slowly licked around her lips, and she took off her glasses to give him her full attention. She looked around again to make sure no one but he could hear her. "As much as I'd enjoy a quick fuck right now, what I really want is a day with you, alone, with no distractions. I think you could do that, I know I could, if you're there. Give me your number, and I'll call you. I'll tell you when I can get away, and if you can do the same, you'll find out why my husband never used to get bored with me. I'll also tell you when I call what I want to do to you. Can you give me your number?"

"Only if you promise to tell me everything you want to do to me and let me reciprocate."

"If you like, I can call you early tonight. He won't be home, and I need a bath. So I could call then, if you're not busy."

"Give me your phone, and I'll type in the number."

She retrieved her phone, selected "New Contact," and handed it over, her fingers playing with his a little as she did so.

Although they had coffee and flirted some more, they both wanted to return to their respective homes to continue the heavy conversation on the phone. Alec was trying to imagine her naked in the bath, so he was taking in her every curve, and she did the same with him. It was a very intense museum lunch.

Alec waited inside as she left, and her driver opened the rear door for her and drove her away. He walked to the bus stop shortly after.

He didn't get into another overheard conversation, he was too preoccupied with the lunch he'd just had and what was upcoming later that day.

CHAPTER TWENTY EIGHT

JAMES FLEW INTO SAN

FRANCISCO later that week. He didn't think he'd be able to help much, if at all, with the search for his sister, but he couldn't stay at home and worry.

He'd managed to train as a realtor, which wasn't perfect, but without taking out a huge student loan or parents to fund him, it was the best he could do, and he quite enjoyed it.

He held no animosity toward his sister. She'd done what she could have done and more to help him, and he was convinced that had she stayed home, then life would have been even worse. He knew she'd have taken him with her if she could, and when she eventually got to the stage where she could do more, he was quite independent and didn't require it.

Now that she was missing, he was missing her like crazy and desperately wanted to be there when they found her shacked up with her new husband, and he could tell her off.

He'd told his boss what had happened, and she had ordered him to go to San Francisco. To not worry about his job, that it would still be there when he returned, no matter how long he was gone.

After arriving in San Francisco, he had no idea what his next move was, as he'd never been here before and didn't know anyone. Except his sister and Elizabeth.

Like Rebecca, he was blonde and blue eyed, good looking. He wasn't married or going strong with anyone yet, he wanted to be more successful first so that could wait. He was, though, determined to be unlike his parents. He didn't know where they were now or if they were alive, so contemptuous was he of their parenting.

After standing on the sidewalk for a while outside the airport, he hailed a taxi and went to the only address he had, the modeling agency.

After the cab charged him way more than he could afford, he made his way into the office of the agency, where Elizabeth's assistant was situated.

He introduced himself and asked if Elizabeth was available. After he sat for a few minutes, she came out and greeted him very warmly, giving him a big hug, a few tears, and telling him how much he resembled his sister.

Elizabeth took James into her office and, unusually for her, offered him a drink. She had some malt whisky that she very rarely opened, but this was a time she needed it. James was so alike his sister that she couldn't help but cry.

"I haven't heard anything from the police since we last spoke, James."

"That's a pity, I was hoping she'd be found. Do you think they'll let me look around her apartment, see if I can find anything?"

"Oh, I'm sure they will. Where are you staying, James? You have your luggage here, haven't you checked in yet at your hotel?"

"No, I've still got to find somewhere. Can you recommend anywhere fairly cheap?"

Elizabeth inched closer to James on the couch they'd be sitting on and clasped his hand, tears still in her eyes.

"You know what, James. I feel terrible about Rebecca and not knowing more about her, so I would like to make it up to you a little, if I may. I have a spare room, and I'd be delighted if you would stay with me, for as long as needed. Please James, do this for me."

James had more or less resigned himself to finding some fleapit of a hotel, so this was a godsend, although he didn't like being a charity case. "That is very kind of you, Elizabeth, but I can find a hotel, I'm sure, I don't want to impose on you."

"James, listen to me. I'll be offended if you don't take up my offer. I need you to stay with me, okay?"

"Okay Elizabeth, that's very kind of you. I'll be more than happy to."

"Good, that's settled. Tomorrow we'll call the police and see what's happening and if you can go to Rebecca's apartment. Tonight, I'll cook us a meal, and we can have a drink or two and talk. You wait here, and I'll be back in a minute."

Elizabeth's assistant Tina waited as she tried to overhear the conversation from the adjoining room. And as soon as Elizabeth emerged, she was ready.

"Something you need Elizabeth?"

Tina was a great assistant, yet she also could have been a model, if she'd wanted to. She had a great figure for lingerie but didn't like posing, and the thought of undressing in front of a bunch of people horrified her. She liked the other side of the business, the nitty gritty of it all, and she liked being Elizabeth's assistant. She also liked Rebecca, who wasn't besotted with her looks and figure like some of the other models, and she was easy to get along with.

"I need you to do me a favor, Tina, that's not part of your usual work."

"Whatever you need, Elizabeth."

"I need you to go and get me some groceries. I've persuaded James to stay with me, and I told him I'd cook tonight. The only problem is that I have nothing in the apartment, so I'm going to need a few things, if that's okay with you."

"That's no problem, Elizabeth, but what do you need? To be truthful, I didn't even know you could cook."

"I can't, Tina. You know me, but it sounded good when I said it, so I need something easy to cook."

"Well, pasta is easy, and chicken or fish are hard to ruin, so you could start there."

"Whatever you say, Tina. You'd think a woman of my age could cook something. It's quite pathetic, really."

"You know, Elizabeth, I really like Rebecca, and I'd like to help in some way. Why don't I get the food and help you prepare it? I don't have any plans tonight."

"You'd do that? Oh, thank you, Tina. You can teach me to cook a little, but you must stay and eat with us. Okay?"

"Okay, I'll keep it really simple. And if you really have nothing in your refrigerator, I'll get a couple of things for breakfast that James could have."

"You're a lifesaver, Tina. Use the company card to buy whatever you think fit and leave whenever you need to. Thank you."

"You're welcome, Elizabeth."

When Elizabeth returned to her office, James was standing in front of one of Rebecca's posters.

"Does she like doing this?" James asked, feeling a little uncomfortable looking at the photo of his sister in the briefest of underwear.

"Yes, she does. I don't know how well you know Rebecca, but she used to do the fashion runways. For the most part she liked it, although she didn't like the cat fights and the constant pressure to remain thin. Doing the lingerie was such a relief to her, she felt she could eat healthy again and remain slim, rather than waif like."

"No, I don't know her well, and right now it's my biggest regret. She used to look after me, and when she left she wrote to me. But like an idiot, I never wrote back. I didn't want to keep making her feel guilty for leaving me, so with nothing much else to say, I said nothing and didn't write back."

Elizabeth stood with him and put her arm around his back. "Rebecca has never really spoken about her childhood, and to my regret, I never asked. I feel guilty as well, James. It's not just you, and we need to deal with it somehow. Just don't ask me how."

James put his arm around her back and his hand on her waist. "We have to find her, Elizabeth, and then we can deal with it. I need to know where she is or what happened to her, and hopefully it's a better outcome than I'm thinking right now."

Elizabeth unhooked herself from James and told him she needed to make a few phone calls, so he could relax a while before they made their way home.

James sat down on the couch and got his phone out of his pocket, pressing buttons.

"I believe that Rebecca's phone is turned off, if you're trying to call her. The police were trying to trace its whereabouts."

"I guessed as much, you can't even leave a message. I was trying to reach my boss in Florida to let her know I got here okay but hadn't found out anything yet,"

"Yes, of course."

Tina popped her head in to say she was leaving, and after Elizabeth did her calls and typed a few things into her computer, she said that she was ready to leave.

James led the way out, carrying his luggage. Elizabeth followed behind, checking the security of her office and turning off electrical switches and lights, then finally setting the alarm as James waited outside.

She had her coat on, a purple wool knee length garment, and she had picked up an umbrella. She rarely walked anywhere without an umbrella in the city. It was always liable to rain at the most unexpected time.

Elizabeth lived on Sacramento Street, which was a climb, and she commented to James that walking up and down streets like these were great toning exercises for the models, so she was always encouraging them to walk whenever possible.

James wasn't used to it, so when she announced they'd reached her apartment, he was a little out of breath, and his shins ached a little.

After climbing more steps into her apartment building, he panted, "I need to get in shape."

"It's only when you come here that you realize that."

They arrived at her front door. Elizabeth opened it, and she led the way inside, talking as she did so.

"Come on in, James, and make yourself at home. I'll show you to your room first, then give you a quick tour of everywhere else, which won't take long as the apartment is not that big."

Like her office, her apartment had a lot of yellow in the décor, but she'd made if very homey with lots of cushions, thick rugs, cashmere throws, large armchairs, and a couch. Her walls were covered with flowery scenes, either still or as a landscape, and she had a couple of tapestries. Lots of books were scattered around, and the beds were wide and frilly.

James' room had a small, flat panel TV facing his bed. Elizabeth had a larger one in her room, and she also had a large walk in closet and big bathroom.

James's bathroom sufficed. It was nicer than the one he had at home, and it contained way more towels and toiletries.

As he looked out of her living room window, a small park was directly opposite, and Grace Cathedral was to the right.

"Would you like some wine, James?" she shouted from the kitchen.

James headed to the kitchen, which was quite large, as it also incorporated the eating area. She had a simple farmyard wooden table with four upholstered swivel chairs that could be used to watch the large flat screen TV. James suspected Elizabeth used this room more than the others, as she also kept her laptop on the table, along with various loose papers.

The kitchen side was very modern and very clean, with nothing lying around like dirty dishes or empty food packets.

"As you can see, this is my office away from my office. Glass of wine?"

"Yes please, that would be very nice."

Elizabeth poured him a glass and brought it to him, "To finding Rebecca."

They clinked glasses and sat at the table.

"What are you cooking, Elizabeth? We could go out, if you prefer."

"No, we'll stay in. I hope you don't mind, but Tina is coming over to help."

"No, that's great and very kind of her."

"She's a gem. So, what do you do, James? Tell me about yourself."

James talked about his upbringing, his job, and where he lived. He thought he was doing fairly well as a realtor in a terrible economy. Miami and Fort Lauderdale were having a lot of foreclosures and short sales, so under the circumstances, he was doing okay. He'd even managed to pick up a place for himself on the inland waterway for a virtual steal, as its owners had gotten into trouble with losing their jobs. It had been taken by the bank, but as there were thousands of properties on their books, they were selling them off for a pittance. The awful thing about it for James was that if the bank could have done that for the previous owners, they could have kept their house. The system didn't work like that.

He thought he'd eventually make partner or go alone, but he wanted more experience first. And for the same reason, he wanted to remain single.

He drank socially and not to an extreme. He didn't smoke and wasn't interested in drugs. But he wanted someday to buy a boat for his dock and to have more fun in his spare time.

The doorbell rang, and Elizabeth answered the intercom, pressing the button for the front door to open.

"James, can you go down and help Tina with the shopping bags, please?"

"Of course." He got up and set out for the door.

"I'll go and change out of my work clothes while you do that. Leave the door ajar, it'll be okay."

He took the elevator down to the front door to find Tina struggling with several bags, and he grabbed most of them out of her hands.

"I went a little crazy with the shopping. I was imagining a bare refrigerator and an empty larder."

"You even managed to get changed and do all this shopping as well."

"Thanks for noticing." She smiled. "You lead the way, I haven't been inside before."

Tina had changed from her office skirt and plain long-sleeved top to form fitting jeans, different black heels, a loose black belt with a big buckle, and a pink tee shirt. Her short black hair was wavy and went all ways, intentionally and very effectually. She was very attractive, not as tall as some of the models but not tiny either, around 5'6'' in her stockinged feet. She was wearing an unbuttoned black coat that came to her hips, and she had a slight sheen from carrying the groceries.

James led her into the kitchen and helped put the bags on the counters. Tina took off her coat and checked the refrigerator and pantry as James unpacked the bags. What she needed for dinner she put to one side, the rest she put away. As she did so, she told James what everything was.

As she finished putting things away, Elizabeth returned in pajamas and apologized for doing so, saying she wanted to be comfortable and relaxed.

"Thank you again, Tina, for doing this. Where do we start? Would you like a glass of wine first?"

"Yes, please. If you can tell me where you keep your pans, we can get the water boiling for the pasta."

Elizabeth poured Tina a glass of wine and topped off the glasses of hers and James's. Then threw the empty bottle into the trash can.

"I'll look for them," replied Elizabeth after disposing of the bottle.

"Don't you cook much, Elizabeth?" asked James, watching her open all the cabinets.

"As you can see from all my fumbling around, no I don't. In fact, never."

"Well, I can help out there. I've been cooking for myself for years."

"I may hold you to that, James, but you're our guest tonight, so Tina and I will do dinner. You go and sit down out of our way and chat with us when Tina isn't throwing stuff at me for not listening to her."

James had quickly gotten to like both ladies. They were so nice and kind to him, and he thought that Rebecca was very happy here in San Francisco.

It wasn't the time or the place, but he was attracted to Tina. He thought she was lovely and was sure she had a boyfriend, she had to.

Elizabeth was attractive as well, older than he preferred but a very nice lady who probably got a lot of dates.

Tina and Elizabeth, with a ton of encouragement from James, made a spaghetti Bolognese with grilled chicken and garlic bread, and it turned out very well. Elizabeth was thrilled to have cooked, and Tina showed her how to keep on top of the dishes as she cooked so that the kitchen wouldn't resemble a bomb zone after finishing their meal.

They stayed in the large kitchen area to eat and drink more wine, talking about Rebecca a lot, but also little things about themselves here and there.

Nobody at this stage wanted to talk about the possibility of Rebecca not being around any more. They wanted to cling to the hope of finding her safe and well, but the more time passed without hearing from her, the less likelihood of it happening.

Despite this, they managed to have an enjoyable evening. After Tina went home, refusing James's offer to escort her, he and Elizabeth went to their separate beds and, unknown to each other, both watched the local news.

CHAPTER TWENTY NINE

ALEC WAS MEETING AISHA TODAY for lunch, and he was feeling very good.

The woman from the museum had called him from her bath, and for the very first time, Alec had phone sex. He couldn't wait for her to call again so they could arrange a long, private meeting.

Yesterday, he'd been to the City Lights Bookstore again and had met another married woman. She wasn't as forward as the lady from the museum, but she was bored and craved attention. Her name was Chelsea, and he'd introduced himself as Gregory.

Chelsea was a young bride. She'd eagerly told him that her husband was much older than she, but since they'd gotten married, he wasn't as much fun and worked way too much. She didn't want to leave him or embarrass him in any way. She still loved him, but she wanted a little excitement in her life, which ultimately would help her husband.

Gregory could see right through her. Her husband was a sugar daddy. She didn't have to work any more. She could buy what she wanted, but she wasn't ready for a monogamous relationship. Her husband would probably remain happy with her if she allowed him sex once a week and would be affectionate to him when they went out.

She didn't look old enough to be married and was totally out of place in the bookstore as she strutted around in her mini skirt and fur jacket, with blonde big hair halfway down her jacket. She'd been so out of place and so noticeable that Alec was unsure whether to approach her, as it seemed that everyone had seen her tottering around.

She seemed to follow his movements, so when he'd gone to a quiet corner of the room and he'd seen her browsing, he moved beside her.

"Is that interesting?" he asked.

She'd turned and given him her full attention. The heavy mascara on her eyelashes had fluttered, she licked her ruby lips, and her blue eyes had twinkled.

"Why yes, it's very interesting." She looked at the title for the first time.

Alec had been very amused. The reason the corner was quiet was because it was the foreign language section, and she'd been looking at a Russian book.

"Do you speak Russian?" He asked her.

She looked again at her book, giggling.

"I don't know why I picked this up, I can barely read English."

She put the book back on the shelf and had looked awkward for a moment.

"Would you like to join me for a coffee?"

"Yes thank you, that would be nice," she said, smiling.

He went to get some regular coffees, and she sat down on one of two armchairs. He watched her sit and had admired her long legs and panties as she crossed her legs. The panties had been the same color as her beige skirt.

When he returned, he got the same show as she re-crossed her legs. When he put the coffees down, she'd unzipped her jacket to reveal her breasts that were struggling to be contained.

If she dresses like this, he thought, her older husband is probably under pressure to perform when he gets home. So he stays late at the office and hopes she falls asleep.

When he got to talking with Chelsea, however, she'd been frank about her marriage, but she hadn't been as forward as the "librarian." Really, she was lonely, as she didn't know anyone as a friend. She'd actually been quite nice to talk to.

Gregory had given her one of his numbers and had asked her to call him if she'd like to join him for lunch one day.

He left the store and had waited undercover for her to emerge. It hadn't taken long, and he'd been disappointed but not surprised when she'd hailed a cab and rode away. The heels she'd worn were way too high to walk up any hills.

Chelsea had called this morning, and they'd arranged to have lunch on Friday. She wanted to arrange it and had said she'd call again to tell him where.

Alec wore a suit today for his lunch with Aisha. He knew she'd be smartly dressed, and he didn't want to look awkward. He was meeting her at Sinbad's, on the Embarcadero, which he thought she'd feel safe in, as it was inside her "area." Close to work, near her home.

He had a good idea where she worked and waited on the street for her to emerge. He was keeping a close eye on the time so that if he was wrong, he'd still be able to make it to the restaurant in time.

He was about to leave when he saw her emerge from a building with a female friend. She looked very business like in her light gray suit. As he walked behind her, he was able to admire her wiggle and her delightful shape as she moved along. Her highlighted black hair was to her shoulders, straight, and parted down the middle. Her legs were beautifully shaped and formed.

Her friend was larger than Aisha, white, about the same age, but more worn looking. She went in a different direction at the end of the first block after giving Aisha a peck on the cheek.

Alec didn't try to get ahead. Instead, he got closer. If she saw him, he'd be able to say that this was his direct route from home, and he wouldn't be lying.

Aisha was confident in herself, though. She was used to being looked at, so she wasn't worried if anyone was looking at her and never felt she was being followed.

As she entered the restaurant, he was right behind and called her name. "Aisha, I was afraid I was going to be late."

She turned around to face him, smiling and looking as gorgeous as she did in her running suit. "Hi, Christos. I just got here myself, great timing."

She came over and gave him an unexpected hug. She smelled very nice.

"You look great, Aisha. Work clothes make you look even better than your exercise clothing."

"Well thank you, Christos, and you clean up well, too. This is a nice treat for me. I usually just have a sandwich or something."

Christos checked in with the host, and they were seated with a nice bay view. Neither wanted a drink, Aisha because she was working and Christos because he was pretending to be working. As they took their seats, Aisha commented that she'd never been here before, yet it was so close.

Christos said it was his first time as well, which elicited a sly smile from her.

They ordered quickly, French onion soup and Shrimp Louis for her, clam chowder and grilled halibut champignon for him.

Aisha hadn't had a good morning at work. As usual, the lawyers wanted the information they had requested minutes before, yesterday, and it had been stressful. The thought of having this lunch had taken her through the turmoil, and she was glad he'd asked her out.

Christos told her he'd had a client that morning who'd refused to listen to his advice, so his whole morning had been a waste, He would have to see the client again that afternoon to continue his advice, and hopefully he'd finally listen. And if he didn't, his business would go bust. He went on to tell Aisha that he'd been looking forward to seeing her again since the weekend.

She felt very comfortable with Christos. She was more used to guys being overt with her, grabbing and trying to kiss, looking at her lasciviously He kept his hands to himself, didn't ogle her body, spoke to her like a person, listened to her, and didn't push. He was just what she needed, and when he stated that he'd like to take her out to lunch again, Aisha was delighted. Christos was a terrific and very handsome guy who wasn't trying to rip off her panties at the first sign of encouragement. She liked that, but eventually she'd force him to do that, just on her terms.

He offered to walk her back to work but she declined, stating that if he was seen, then she'd have to field questions about him. So she made her way back to work alone.

Alec went home and changed. Now that he was sure of where she worked, he'd follow her home tonight to see if he could learn anything. This was a good day for him.

CHAPTER THIRTY

ELIZABETH

CALLED DETECTIVE GARCIA THE following morning to see if she'd learned or discovered anything. There was nothing new, and they were still looking at the computer.

Elizabeth asked her if it would be okay for Rebecca's brother to go over to her apartment and have a look around. The detective said it couldn't do any harm, it might even help, and she said she'd call the apartment building to ensure he was let inside.

Although Tina had bought some breakfast food, James did as Elizabeth and just had cereal and coffee. Although she did very little grocery shopping, Elizabeth did buy Cheerios and coffee. She also used a Keurig machine now, that she really liked, as it was easy and not messy.

Elizabeth offered to accompany James to Rebecca's apartment but he declined her offer, saying he needed to spend some time alone there. He also pointed out that Rebecca would probably get upset if she came home and found her boss rummaging through her belongings. It was understandable to Elizabeth. She didn't particularly want to go there, it felt a little ghoulish to do so.

She drew a little map for James. It wasn't far at all, and he was easily able to find her apartment. The superintendent had been told that he would be coming and readily let him into the apartment. He told James that she was a great tenant, always paid her rent on time, was never a bother, and that he hoped she would show up soon and they could all have a laugh at her disappearance.

On entering, James realized that his sister was obviously doing very well. He could tell that over the years she'd discovered how to be neat. She liked modern décor, there was a lot of stainless steel and glass, but it was tempered with Persian rugs that softened and warmed the whole apartment. She also liked abstract art that James couldn't make head or tail of.

She'd kept the walls white, which with the steel and glass felt clean and very light. She had a double sided gas fireplace, and because she had the rugs on the hardwood floors, it didn't feel cold.

It was only a one bedroom apartment, but it had a good view and was quite large. James cringed at the thought of how much rent she was paying.

The kitchen was quite large, with modern appliances and an island worktop that had all her pots and pans hanging over it. He could see that she used them though, and when he opened her French door fridge, it was full of food. Lots of fruit and vegetables, yogurts, and mainly healthy food, apart from some chocolate. She'd always liked her chocolate cold, so it was no surprise to find it there, and he supposed it was her one indulgence.

A small round table and a desk were between the kitchen and the living room, presumably where Rebecca ate and did her paperwork. The desk was untidy compared to everything he'd seen so far, and there was a space where he thought her computer may have been.

Going back into the living room, he opened doors to see what was inside. He found her washer and dryer in one, a full bathroom in another, and the others were storage.

A flat screen TV was above the fireplace and a Bose cd/radio player was on one of the three glass tables, with cd's below.

The entrance was to his left, and she had a couple of coats hanging on the pine coat stand next to the full-length mirror. To his right was an open door to her bedroom.

To the right of the bedroom, by the window, was a single armchair that faced him. The crimson fabric matched the fitted carpet. She also had thick, fluffy white rugs scattered throughout the room. The queen-sized bed was covered with a crimson and white comforter with matching pillowcases. Some of her clothing was also on the bed.

What really surprised him and made him a little tearful were the photographs all over the walls of himself, his sister, and their parents from better days. He didn't even know these photos existed, and he took his time looking at them.

Two openings at the other end of the room entered her bathroom and dressing room, and they were also interconnected. Her bathroom was the same size as her dressing room, and it easily contained her tub, glass shower cubicle, double wash basin, toilet, and dressing table, with lots of lights and a stack of make-up.

Her dressing room was well arranged. He could smell the cedar, and all her clothes were hanging or folded neatly into drawers. She had another floor-length mirror in here, along with a cushioned foot stool on casters that had some of her clothes on it. A wheeled laundry bag with three compartments was almost full.

Although she had luggage items above her shelves, it was impossible to determine how much she'd taken or what. So if she'd told her neighbor she was only going away for the weekend, then that's what they had to believe. He felt very sad.

James went back into the bedroom and began to look through her two mahogany nightstands. She didn't really have anything out of the ordinary, books and magazines, a remote control for another flat screen above the fireplace, an alarm radio clock, tissues, aspirin, lip salve, eye shades, notepads, and pencils. Much to his discomfort, he also found her vibrator, feminine pads, birth control pills, and condoms.

He went through everything he could see, even looking under the bed to find something useful, to at least give them a clue. Not finding anything, he went back to her desk and went through it, finding a few receipts and business cards that he put to one side and some sticky notes with telephone numbers, so he put them with the cards. He was a big proponent of modern technology, and he always put everything on his iPhone or laptop. But now he felt frustrated because his sister was almost the same.

That being all he could find, he went to the kitchen. Feeling a little peckish, he opened the fridge and found some whole wheat bread and sliced turkey, so made himself a sandwich, which he ate at her table.

She had a shelf full of water bottles in the fridge, so he took one of them as well. When he finished, he opened her dishwasher and found it was half full of dirty dishes that looked like they'd been rinsed, so he added his plate and knife to the contents.

Getting back to his search, he went through her storage areas. Along with the vacuum, dusters, and polishes, he found a heavy box and was overjoyed to find it full of journals.

He took the box to her table and went through them. They all had the years inside the cover. He was distraught to find the last one dated 2010.

He kept the two journals from the year she'd left home and put the box back, browsing through the books back at the table.

They weren't very good reading for him. They detailed her departure from home and her agony at leaving him with their addict riddled parents. She wrote about how she had to get away before going down the same road.

He put the books back in the box and went looking again, hoping she didn't have the current journal with her, but not finding one anywhere.

He sat on her armchair in the bedroom and thought about what he'd read, and he let his arms dangle over the armrests. He hadn't seen it as the chair was angled toward the window, but he felt a bulge on the side. A pocket was on the chair, and in it he found two journals for 2011.

Scrambling to her final entries, she'd written in her very neat writing that she'd met this most gorgeous man, who she felt she was developing feelings for. He was taking her away for the weekend, where she fully intended to let him take advantage of her.

She was very excited about this guy, Brad. She detailed all the clothing she was taking to seduce him. In her journal she wrote about him for a while, the fancy restaurants where he'd taken her. Yet he hadn't tried to go to bed with her, and he'd made her feel special, worth waiting for.

He was some kind of business consultant. He was obviously wealthy, and she was so glad he'd answered her ad in the Gazette.

So who and where was Brad?

CHAPTER THIRTY ONE

ALEC WAS LOOKING

FORWARD TO going to the Stanford game at the weekend, but the 49ers were playing out of town again. He called George to make sure he was going so they'd meet at the usual place. He also needed to tell George that he wouldn't be at the farm that weekend.

Stanford looked like they were going to have another good sea- son despite the coach leaving, and they'd already won their previous games by emphatic scores. He didn't think they'd win the National Championship or anything, but he was confident of a great season.

Checking his phones, he found one message from Kim, who wanted to see him over the weekend, but the "librarian" hadn't called. He was anxious to get together with her. Her phone call had been so intense, and he loved how forward she was.

Ruth also left a message. She was worried about him and wanted him to return her message, she needed to explain something that he may have misconstrued. He deleted it.

Earlier that morning, he'd bumped into one of his lady friends in the elevator, and she had asked if she could come to his apartment on Sunday, while her husband was at the Raider game. He'd thought that sounded good. He could even watch the game while he was doing the guy's wife, so he agreed.

He called Kim to tell her he'd be out of town for the weekend but that he'd call on his return.

He then called Aisha to say how much he'd enjoyed her company, that he had to go out of town for the weekend, but maybe they could have lunch again on Monday. She was disappointed it couldn't be sooner but accepted his invitation, and he said he'd call again to tell her when and where.

That done, he checked the Sports Channel to see what was happening and then went on the internet.

Going to the Missing Persons page on the San Francisco Police Department website, he wasn't surprised when he saw the posting for Rebecca Young. He was surprised, though, when he saw the new posting for Jenny Charles. He thought that wouldn't be posted for several days, if at all.

He looked at the two photos. The one of Rebecca was very good, but the photo of Jenny was awful, and he wondered if they would make the connection. They were both young, both blonde, both beautiful. He thought the police would, but didn't think they would have much to go on, at least for now.

He made two more calls, one to his accountant and one to his lawyer.

He met Chelsea at the Naked Lunch, which was close to the City Lights Bookstore. As he didn't know which direction she'd be coming from, he couldn't wait anywhere to see her movements.

Gregory was dressed casually in designer jeans with a brown sport jacket and a white shirt with light blue and brown crossed lines. The weather was very agreeable and pleasant. They didn't take reservations, so he waited outside. He was glad to see she was on time, as the line would get long soon.

She was a little more demure in her attire today after the bookstore. He spotted her in time to admire her walking toward him, smiling, her long hair bouncing above her horizontally striped, black and white boat neck cotton dress that was mid thigh length, black stiletto heels, and a plain crimson unbuttoned cardigan. She liked to swing her hips as she walked, which attracted a lot of admirers.

As she got near and went to kiss his cheek, he also noticed she wore less make up and looked all the better for it. Her more natural cosmetics enhanced her young, unblemished face.

"You're looking very beautiful today, Chelsea," he complimented her, exchanging her kiss.

"Thank you, Gregory. That's very kind of you. I went to the beauty salon yesterday and took their advice, and I'm glad I did, I feel like a new woman. I guess I was wearing way too much make- up."

"You look great, and even your hair is better."

"Yes, they thinned it out some, cut some of the length, and did some highlighting. I'm very happy with it."

He could see she was. The apples on her cheeks were more prominent on her roundish face as she smiled.

"We'd better order our food before we have to stand in line for half an hour. Do you know what you want?"

"Yes, I've been here before. I'm going to have the seared tuna sandwich and the cinnamon iced tea."

"Okay, why don't you let me get it? If you grab a table, I'll get our lunch."

"I thought this was my treat."

"You can do the next one."

Chelsea was happy to hear that, and she gave him another kiss on the cheek before she left the line and took an outside table, somewhere that they could enjoy the nice day.

Gregory wasn't long, but as he made his way to their table, he saw that the line now was as least twice as long as it had been. He put the tray on the table, and Chelsea helped him take their lunch off before he put the empty tray on the one empty seat at the table. Sitting down beside her, he was happy to see she was angled toward him, giving him another view of her long legs.

"What did you get, Gregory?" she asked as she unwrapped her sandwich.

"I got the Foie gras sandwich, along with the cinnamon iced tea."

"That was a bit rich for me the last time I came here, but it's very good."

Gregory took a bite, and it was indeed very good. Just right for his tastes.

"Were you at the bookstore again?" he asked.

"No, I was browsing the shops. I'm not keeping you from work, am I?"

"No, but I do have to speak to one of my clients this afternoon."

She looked a little disappointed at hearing this, and Gregory regretted saying it, but now that he had, he'd have to adhere to it.

"If you need to go I'll understand," she said forlornly.

"No, I have time to eat." He smiled. "I refuse to rush away from your company."

She was happier now, and as they ate and drank, she told him how much she'd been looking forward to seeing him again, how nice and charming he'd been, and how delightful it was to be in his company.

Gregory knew full well she wanted a fling, some excitement in her life to make up for the boredom, and he played her along, gazing into her eyes, touching her arm in a fleeting movement, accidentally meeting her hands. Her attention was all on him. She never turned away, and he kept her engaged.

Eventually, after sampling each other's food and finishing their well enjoyed lunch, they had to leave. Gregory hailed her a cab. After he opened the rear door for her, she gave him a very close hug and another kiss on his cheek before saying, "Can we do this again on Tuesday? My treat, and don't rush away afterwards."

"Here again?"

"No, I'll let you know where. Thanks for today Gregory, it's been wonderful."

"My pleasure, Chelsea. I'm sorry that I have to work this afternoon, but Tuesday will be good. I'm free, as far as I know."

"Keep it that way," she teased, kissing him again as she climbed into the cab and closed the door, telling the driver where to take her when she was out of Gregory's earshot. They waved to each other as the driver pulled away from the sidewalk, and Alec headed home.

CHAPTER **THIRTY TWO**

GEORGE WASN'T TOO

HAPPY TO learn that Alec wouldn't be at the farm over the weekend. The last couple of weekends had been great, and he'd been really looking forward to the upcoming one. It made his life with Jane way more exciting, and the rush he got from the weekends was practically addictive. He could barely wait for his next fix.

Via his computer, he was able to relive his recent experiences, which was very gratifying to him. But after suppressing the urges, which seemed like an eternity ago, he now wanted another beautiful woman on his table.

He'd been thinking about how he could keep them around longer, but he had nowhere to do so. Yet he'd seen some news recently about people called "Doomsday Preppers." He was thinking of adopting some of their activities, except for a different purpose.

The Doomsday Preppers stockpiled guns, ammo, water, and canned food, as they were afraid that America was heading toward Armageddon, and they wanted to survive. They also built underground bunkers as shelters and for stockpile storage, which is what he was most interested in.

George had broached the subject with Jane, which didn't go well. She thought they were gun loving, paranoid idiots. He couldn't really argue, but he did wish he had a cellar beneath the barn. The difficulties didn't dissuade his thoughts, such as being soundproofed or having plumbing and ventilation. An underground holding area would be ideal for his needs.

He resolved to see if he could make other arrangements now that Alec had said he wouldn't be there this week, and he went searching on the internet to see what he could find, without revealing his identity or using a credit card.

CHAPTER THIRTY THREE

JAMES CALLED ELIZABETH

TO TELL her what he'd found and that he was leaving his sister's apartment. She told him she would meet him back at home and that she would call Detective Garcia with his news.

After making his way back, he let himself into her apartment with the key she'd given him, and he found Elizabeth already home, sitting at the kitchen table while she waited.

Without even taking off his coat, he handed her the journal to read, to see if any of the contents could jog her memory in some way.

"I called the police, and the detective said she'd be over shortly," she stated, taking the journal.

"I'll show you where it starts getting interesting," he replied excitedly. He leaned over her and flicked through the pages. "This is when she meets this guy." He pointed with his finger, letting her read as he took off his coat, which he deposited back to his room.

On his return, she was still reading, and he sat beside her, trying to read again the words he'd seen earlier.

"She said that this guy replied to her ad in the Gazette," she commented without looking up.

"What is that, a local paper?"

"Yes, but it's only monthly. It's called the Nob Hill Gazette."

"Why did she put an ad in the paper? Doesn't seem like her. Did you know about it?"

"No, this is the first I've heard. I had no idea. She said in the journal that she was lonely and only seemed to meet the wrong men."

Elizabeth continued to read, her excitement at the find waning as she read that Rebecca was going away only for the weekend and she learned about the small amount of luggage she was taking.

"Have you any idea who this Brad is, Elizabeth?"

"No, no idea. Whoever he is, Rebecca really likes him, and as she also says he's wealthy, then maybe he whisked her away somewhere," she replied with hope.

"Well if he did, they're still in the States, as her passport is still in her desk drawer."

Before Elizabeth could make another comment, the door bell rang. She paged the detective into the building and opened the front door for her, waiting as the elevator hummed upward.

"Hello, Detective Garcia. How are you?"

"I'm fine, thank you. How are you and Mr. Young?"

She entered the apartment, and Elizabeth closed the door behind her, answering as she did so. "Okay I guess, under the circumstances."

"I understand. Where is the journal?"

"It's in the kitchen with James. Just go on through."

The detective led the way forward and introduced herself to James, who handed over the journal, telling her where he found it. She sat down to read it. Elizabeth and James quietly watched and waited.

"Do either of you know who this Brad is?"

They shook their heads and said no.

"We'll do what we can with the little she's told us, and we can also follow up on the ad she placed and the restaurants she named. Maybe we'll get lucky. Can I keep this journal for a while?"

James told her that yes, she could.

"We haven't found anything on her computer to go on. She does have a Facebook account, and her friends are nearly all in L.A. We've contacted them, but no one has seen or heard from her. Rebecca's last message was that she was going away for the weekend, but we have no details.

Her phone still hasn't been used since the text message, and the fact that she hasn't contacted anyone is really troubling me, as she doesn't seem to be the type of person to disappear. She also doesn't have a drug or mental problem that I know of, which can lead to some people to fall off the radar."

The detective continued.

"She hasn't used her credit cards for purchases of any kind, so it doesn't seem likely they were stolen or lost. It's not looking good, I'm afraid. I should also tell you, as it's already on our website, that another very attractive woman has been reported missing. We don't know yet if it's connected in any way to Rebecca, but I thought I should tell you myself before you heard from somewhere else.

Like I said, this new case may have nothing to do with yours. It's still too early to tell, and the only similarity to yours is that she is blonde and beautiful."

Elizabeth and James were stuck for words. They were basically being told to prepare for the worst possible news regarding Rebecca and that whoever took her away may have also have taken someone else. It was too awful to contemplate.

The three of them were silent as they sat at the table for a while. Detective Garcia read the journal some more before eventually getting up.

"We'll look into the information from the journal, and hopefully we'll get a break somewhere. Is there anything else you can tell me?" The detective remained very matter of fact. She was used to this, and no matter how trying, she couldn't get involved personally.

Elizabeth broke the silence. "Is there anything we can do?"

"Ask your other models if they know this Brad guy. She says he's very handsome, so maybe he dated one of them some time. Anything would help. We'll look into the restaurants and the Gazette, and maybe we'll get a photo or something or a credit card slip. I'll let you know. I've got to go now, but call me if you need anything or just want to talk. Okay?"

She looked at the two of them. They gave her a nod. She knew it was hard for them right now, and she gave them a nod in return before letting herself out.

Detective Garcia was sure that Rebecca Young was dead, probably murdered, unless she'd gone to Tahoe and fallen off a cliff or something. She made a mental note to have someone check the ravines for crashed vehicles.

CHAPTER THIRTY FOUR

ALEC MET GEORGE AT THE bar

before they made their way to Stanford for the game against UCLA. A sell- out crowd was expected, and now that they'd demolished the old stadium that was way too big for the fan base, and constructed a new one, it made for a more enjoyable experience.

As was normal for them, they would take the Bart to the stadium, which meant they'd both be happy. Alec could have a couple of beers, and George wouldn't have to drive in heavy traffic.

George still sported his old worn Stanford cap along with a wool jacket. Alec's cap was fairly new, although his leather jacket was quite aged.

Alec had been on the phone that morning booking a restaurant for Monday lunch with Aisha, after which he called her to meet at Annabelle's Bar and Bistro on Fourth Street. He'd never been there, so he wondered what it would be like.

He'd also received a call from Chelsea, who wanted to confirm their date on Tuesday. She insisted on arranging it herself, saying she'd call again to let him know where.

There had still been no call from the "librarian," and he'd ignored yet another call from Ruth.

George had also been busy. He'd created another email address for himself. After looking through the personal listings on craigslist and at various escort agencies, he'd searched for the words "local hookup" and found a huge area of different sites promoting casual sexual encounters.

He was extremely surprised yet delighted that women would post pictures of themselves. He'd thought that they could possibly be hookers, but he didn't really care about that. Finally, he'd arranged to meet "Cindy" at the Luna Ristorante in Concord at 7 pm.

He certainly didn't think that Cindy was her real name, just as the name he gave her, Michael, wasn't his. He was just hoping that she looked somewhat like her almost-naked photo. He hadn't tried to deceive her with his own looks, he'd even made himself seem worse than he actually was in comparison to his brother. She had not been deterred, so he was excited about the evening to come. George surmised that Alec got way the better deal from their parents in the looks department, although that wasn't their fault. He just wished that he'd been luckier.

Alec had called George and told him about the Missing Persons website. He'd said they had nothing to worry about but had advised George to stay careful. Alec was under no illusion about what would or could happen, and he certainly wouldn't lay all the blame at his brother's door if he was ever accused. In fact, he would do the opposite. George was of the same opinion.

They talked about it very quietly in the bar and on the train. The brothers also discussed what to do with their assets and holdings so that no one else but them could lay their hands on their wealth.

Alec told George he'd already set the wheels in motion and that he'd receive some calls about that this coming week. They both resolved that if anything happened, they would say absolutely nothing and ask for their lawyer, pledging that they would never drop each other in it with the police.

That out of the way, they thoroughly enjoyed the football game, especially as Stanford won 49 – 19.

George didn't need to go home before meeting Cindy. The restaurant wasn't overly fancy and just by changing his jacket to a sports coat and removing his cap, he looked quite presentable. If she did look like her photo, he was ready with a wad of cash, should she ask for it. His blow gun was behind the passenger seat, hidden under a blanket.

Picking his truck up at the Bart station, he headed for his date. He parked down the street from the restaurant and was inside early to make sure he didn't know anyone who was dining. Satisfied, he relaxed a little and waited, ordering a bottle of Chianti Classico in the small, cozy, and dimly lit room.

He spotted her as soon as she stepped inside the door. She wasn't as beautiful as the women that Alec attracted, but at least she hadn't lied with her photo. He was more certain now that she was a hooker as he caught a glimpse of the knee length black boots with stiletto heels, fishnet stockings, and short black skirt under the long red leather coat that kind of gave her away. But she didn't look wasted on drugs, and he waved to her so that the host wouldn't have time to think of an excuse to throw her out.

Thankfully, the dark room prevented too many stares, and he ushered her to her seat quickly. Her smile revealed even, well cared for teeth.

Sitting back down opposite her, he took in her looks a little better. Her blonde hair was flat and parted on the left, bangs to her eyebrows, the rest hanging down to her collar. Her blue eyes were framed with a light blue eye shadow, with mascara on her lashes, and her lipstick was a dark blue that matched her long fingernails.

He figured she was around mid-20s. Her jaw was wide and not very angular, her nose was long and thin, and she wore a gold ring in the right side of her nostril. She wore a lot of rings, costume jewelry to his uneducated knowledge of it.

Beneath her coat, she wore a tight, red, high necked zippered top that he discovered was long sleeved when she slipped off her coat. She wasn't as slender as Alec's women, with thicker arms and legs. Her breasts were large and struggling to be contained within the tight red shirt.

"Hi, Michael," she whispered just loud enough for him to hear. "Glad you made it." Her voice was like butter dripping off a hot knife.

"Hi, Cindy," he replied. "You look much better than your photo."

"And you look way better than your description. You don't do yourself justice."

The server came over with some crusty bread, a dipping dish of olive oil and balsamic vinegar, and two glasses of water. She poured the wine and then left, saying she would be back shortly to take their order.

"Here's to a great night," saluted Michael.

"Before we do that, Michael, I need to tell you something." She was whispering but bent down a little toward him. "I think you do realize that I will need some recompense for anything we do after dinner. So will you swear to me you are not a cop and that you are not recording me?"

"I swear I'm not a cop or recording you. So, what are you saying?" Michael had adopted her whispering tone.

"A blow job is a hundred, a quickie is three, and all night is a thousand. You can see the goods if you wish." She proceeded to pull down her zip very slowly, and her right foot found his crotch.

"No need for that." He bent closer. "I'll go with the thousand. You want me to pay now?"

"Give me half now and the rest in the morning. I have somewhere we can go. It'll only cost $40, and I'll take it off the price. Okay?"

"Can I drive us there? I don't want to leave my car outside all night."

"Sure, it's too far for me to walk on these heels anyway. Give me the half and I'll make a quick call, then I'm all yours." She smiled, getting another smile in return.

His cash was in hundred dollar bills, and he was able to retrieve five of them without opening his wallet.

"Cash? That's nice, it's nearly always credit cards these days."

"I prefer to pay for everything with cash. I find it easier still."

She kept her foot on his crotch, rubbing him, feeling him get hard. She made her call, just a simple message.

"It's me. Got the money, usual room please, see you in the morning." She hung up and put her phone back in her purse. "You are in for the best night of your life Michael."

"I know that, Cindy. Let's order our food and get out of here."

The server returned and they ordered, baked chicken breast with tomatoes, basil and mozzarella for her, and veal with prosciutto, sage, white wine, garlic, and cheese for him. The food was very good, and she especially enjoyed it, saying it was nice not to be rushed for a change. She kept playing with him under the table, not all the time but enough to make him want to get her alone. He paid the bill with more cash, and they left hand in hand. He took her to his cleaned truck.

He opened the passenger door for her, and she let him kiss her and fondle her before he handed her the seatbelt. He opened the rear door behind her, saying he'd left something there, and before she could feel any fear or react in any way, he had a dart in her neck and she was unconscious, sleeping on his front seat.

He reclined her seat. If anyone saw her, it would just look like she was naturally taking a nap. Seeing no one was around, he jumped into the driver's seat and drove away very calmly.

Reaching the dark farm, he drove straight to the barn, where he unloaded the still sleeping Cindy and carried her to his table. Very slowly, he undressed her, taking photos and running the video as he did so.

Once she was naked, he got a towel from a closet and carefully put it under her. The steel was cold, and he didn't want her to feel it.

He undressed himself, then touched and kissed her. Finally he climbed onto the table and raped her, telling her as he did so that it was a bonus that she was asleep. It was much better that way.

CHAPTER THIRTY FIVE

IT HAD BEEN A GREAT weekend for Alec.

Not only had Stanford and the 49ers won, but the Raiders had been beaten by the Patriots, which had really made his Sunday afternoon.

Monday morning he surreptitiously followed Aisha from her home to work. She'd been alone the whole time, and he knew she hadn't spotted him.

He left her workplace and went home. He needed to shower, shave, and change clothes for their lunch date. Hopefully the rain would stop.

He called Kim. She didn't answer, so he left her a message, saying he'd missed her over the weekend but that he was successful with his client, which partly appeased him. He asked if she was busy for the upcoming weekend and said that he'd like her to come over to the bay on Saturday night.

Although the liaison yesterday during the football game had been most enjoyable, he still didn't think it was as good as when he took women to the farm. At the farm he was making love to them for the very last time and it made the sex extra special. Alec really liked being their last intimate memory.

He had no idea what George had been up to since they'd gone their separate ways a couple of days ago, and if he had, he wouldn't have approved unless his brother had taken all precautions to remain anonymous.

His chat with George had cleared up any concerns, so Alec called the accountant and lawyer again to ask them to contact his brother, and to find out from them how the asset transfers were going. They were setting up offshore companies that would seemingly have no link whatsoever with him and his brother, and the company would own everything but would in no way be liable for anything the brothers did. Other assets were being scattered far and wide, and it would effectively make them appear to be employees of a remote company, with no savings.

The day was chilly and wet, so he'd gotten out one of his wool pinstripe suits today. He paired the grey with a white shirt and grey tie with discreet white spots. Very business like.

He topped off his suit with a Burberry trench coat and took along a black, golf size umbrella.

He waited for Aisha to emerge from her office along the street and head toward the restaurant. Like the last time, her friend came out the door with her but went the opposite way. Aisha held aloft a pink umbrella that concealed her face as she walked toward him, and he turned around to hurry ahead.

He was standing in line to check in when she joined him, removing her wool maroon coat and shaking off the raindrops as her umbrella dripped by her side.

"Hi Christos. Good to see you." She stood on her toes to kiss his cheek.

"Hi, Aisha. Good to see you, too. You look terrific."

She did look good in her pink wool suit. The jacket was single- breasted and buttoned to her neck. The skirt came to her knees, and it hugged her figure beautifully. It wasn't a cheap item of clothing.

Aisha had a good enough eye to see that Christos was dressed very well, and she knew that the Burberry slung over his arm cost as much his suit.

"You look good too, Christos. As always, it's hard to match the quality of your clothing."

"Oh, that's not necessary, Aisha. I only dress like this for very special occasions, and meeting you is extremely special."

"Your flattery will get you everywhere, Christos."

"I'm hoping so," he replied with a sly smile. As the line had now gone, he checked in, and they were shown to their table.

They ordered the flat iron steak and frites for Christos, and Aisha had the grilled king salmon. Neither of them had any alcohol. Aisha looked stunning today, and Christos didn't hesitate in telling her so. She wasn't like some of his latest dalliances, she kept quiet, accepted his compliments with a smile, and didn't attempt to detail any desires she might have. The food was delicious, very flavorful, and very fresh, and Christos was glad he'd chosen this place. He'd heard about Annabel's but had never been here before.

He talked about work and asked how her fitness regime was doing, but he was really indirectly trying to discover if she'd spoken about him to anyone.

He finally went along the route of asking about her friends, if there were many or just one in particular, or if she was in touch with her family much. He paved the way for her by saying that he didn't have any close friends, just a whole lot of acquaintances, yet he really wanted to tell them all that he'd met this gorgeous woman called Aisha and couldn't wait to be in her company.

She finally opened up. Her private life was private, and she wanted it to remain so until such time that they were "going steady." She didn't like sleeping around, and she was thankful that he hadn't pushed her. She really liked him, but she'd also been burned a couple of times. So she was careful now, didn't want to be hurt again. But if he had patience, then she assured him she was well worth the wait.

He didn't doubt it and asked her out to dinner on Sunday night.

"Can I ask why Sunday and not Friday or Saturday?"

"Very simple answer, Aisha. If I take you out on Friday or Saturday, I will either want to take you home or be invited into yours for the rest of the night. On Sunday, I have to be up on Monday morning as do you, so it's easier to just say good night."

She laughed, heartily but not loudly, and it was a contagious laugh.

"So what's so funny?" asked Christos as he giggled.

"I appreciate your thoughtfulness, Christos. If you'd asked, I may have gone home with you this afternoon."

"You tease me, Aisha. I don't think you would. So, dinner on Sunday night?"

"Definitely. Will I see you Sunday morning walking?"

"Maybe, I'll be out there. I'll call you when I get the dinner reservation."

"Okay. Now you can walk me back to work."

CHAPTER **THIRTY SIX**

ELIZABETH,

JAMES, AND FOR THE most part Tina, had spent almost the whole weekend in a virtual daze, sober and drunk. No one had heard from Rebecca, and the inevitability of her fate was very slowly sinking in. It was a terrible situation for them all.

Elizabeth and Tina had been recalling everyone they knew to see if anyone had forgotten anything, the slightest thing, as it might help in some way.

James didn't know what to do apart from go back to his sister's apartment and hope that he'd be able to yell and hug her at the same time, when she returned. Instead, he went through her things again, hoping he'd missed something vital that would lead them to Rebecca and Brad.

None of them got anywhere.

After having way too much to drink on Friday and Saturday, no one was feeling particularly well on Sunday morning. Tina suggested they get out and show James the nicer side of the city. They rode the cable cars, went down to the wharf, took a boat trip around the bay, dined in Chinatown, and managed to raise a smile or two, which was a huge accomplishment.

That night, they went to Tina's tiny, cramped apartment, and Tina made them dinner. They sat in her living room and ate with the food on their laps. Elizabeth resolved to give her a raise.

It was a much better evening than the previous ones. They all needed the change, and James resolved to stay until the following weekend. If nothing had been heard from Rebecca, he'd arrange for her things to be shipped, and he'd go home until something happened.

Elizabeth said she would pay for the shipping, and she also said she'd give James any salary or money owed to Rebecca.

CHAPTER THIRTY SEVEN

CHELSEA CALLED

GREGORY EARLY TUESDAY morning and asked him if he was still free for lunch, which he confirmed. Gregory also added that he didn't have any clients until the following day.

She didn't make any comment on that, but he suspected that she sounded a tad happier as she told him to meet her at the Grandviews Restaurant at 11:30 am.

Gregory didn't know where the restaurant was. He'd never heard of it, so was surprised when she said it was on the 36th floor of the Grand Hyatt Hotel on Stockton Street.

"Sounds good, Chelsea. I can't wait. I've missed you the last few days. Are you well?"

"I feel great, Gregory. I can't wait to see you. You know where it is?"

"Yes, I've gone past it many times. I'll see you later."

"See you later, Gregory."

Gregory had indeed gone past the hotel many times, but he'd also been inside a couple of its rooms as well, with some visitors to the city. He had never been to the restaurant before, so he was curious about it.

Alec showered and shaved, liberally applying skin lotion, cologne, and deodorant, before dressing in stone-colored chinos, a matching shirt, a dark brown wool jacket, and brown shoes. Checking his wallet, he picked up his keys, Gregory's phone and left his apartment.

It only took him ten minutes to get to the hotel. After checking his watch, he entered the lobby, located the elevator, and pressed the button for the 36th floor, which signified it was the location of the restaurant.

As the doors opened, he immediately saw Chelsea sitting in a little lobby by the entrance. Beaming, she stood up, and he gave her a hug. She put her mouth to his with a very welcoming kiss.

He pulled off and admired her from head to toe. "Wow, Chelsea, you look stunning!"

She wore a wine colored scoop neck dress. Mid-length and sleeveless, it clung to every curve. She also had matching toe less sandals and a tiny clutch bag.

"Thank you, Gregory. I got it especially for today. I'm glad you like it."

"It's amazing, it really is." He looked her over again before putting his hands on her waist and leaning in to kiss her again on the lips. "But don't you have a coat?"

"I had the hotel hang it up. Are you ready to eat?"

"Yes, I suddenly feel famished."

"Then let's go."

She led the way into the restaurant, and he admired how she looked from behind. After checking in, the host escorted them to their table, which had a magnificent view of the city, and held out the chair for Chelsea.

Once seated, she immediately ordered a bottle of Champagne, a good one that was moderate in price.

"So what's the occasion?" asked Gregory.

"Just being here with you is all," she replied with a sly smile.

"You are too kind. I don't know which view is better, the city or you. I think looking at you is much better."

"Now you are being kind. This is fun, Gregory. I'm glad you came."

"I wouldn't have missed this for the world."

The Champagne came, and it was expertly opened without a pop, just a little hiss. Once it was poured, the server said she'd be back in a couple of minutes to take their order. Chelsea raised her glass to make a toast, and Gregory raised his in anticipation.

"To a glorious afternoon."

Gregory looked at her a little bemused, and she answered his look by opening her tiny bag and producing a key card.

"To a glorious afternoon," he concurred, as they clinked their glasses and took a sip.

He leaned in toward her, taking in her perfume and the wetness of her lips.

"Do me a favor, Chelsea. Don't order anything that will take long to prepare. I need to get you to the room in a hurry."

"I won't, Gregory. But I enjoy it when you look at me. It feels like a long time since someone did that, especially someone that I want to look at me."

"You are very easy to look at, Chelsea. In fact, I'm ogling, not looking. I'm imagining peeling off your dress and discovering what lies beneath, bit by bit."

Chelsea smiled some more, blushing a little at his words.

"Then you won't mind if I do the same with you? And you will let me undress you, bit by bit?"

"I look forward to it. In fact, you can start here if you wish."

"I'll just undress you with my eyes for now. I think we should order our food right away. I want to go to bed with you."

Gregory signaled the server, and they ordered their food. The Champagne was quickly consumed, but they didn't order another bottle, as Chelsea said she had one on ice in the room.

Within 30 minutes they had finished a delicious lunch, and Chelsea had insisted on signing the check to her room, as this was her treat.

They held hands tightly as they walked to the elevator. The room was only two floors down, and she kissed him wetly for the brief trip. As the elevator doors opened, she took his hands off her hips and pulled him toward their room, giggling like a schoolgirl as she fumbled with the door card. Once inside the room, she quickly put the "Do Not Disturb" sign on the door.

Gregory grabbed her as they stood just inside the door. His hands went everywhere as they passionately kissed, and she pulled her head back.

"Gregory," she panted between kissing his face, "as much as I want you right now, let's slow it down. I want to unbutton you one button at a time."

"Okay."

He took his hands from beneath the hem of her dress and led her to the king-size bed, standing with his back to it. "Undress me, Chelsea, and take as much time as you want."

CHAPTER THIRTY EIGHT

ALEC FELT LAZY THE

FOLLOWING day, and he wanted to sleep late. But Maria was coming, so he had to get up. After spending all afternoon and some of the evening in the hotel room, he was worn out. But it had been worth it, he'd had a fabulous time.

He didn't know what to do about the weekend. Yesterday had been almost as good as a final night with a prospect, but George needed to know his plans sooner rather than later.

Maria arrived before he got showered and dressed, so he had her clean his office first, then the kitchen after he ate. He hadn't planned on going anywhere today, so he'd just vegetate for the rest of the day and snack and watch some sports.

He felt much better after showering and shaving, Chelsea's smell was no longer in his nostrils and on his body. After putting on a clean pair of pajamas, he got more coffee and took it to his office. He heard the washing machine spinning, which was a distraction, so he closed the door and turned on his laptop.

Since the weekend, he'd been thinking he might have to make a hasty exit from San Francisco, and he needed to think about where to go. He was also concerned about George, the only family he had.

If something happened, he didn't want to disappear and leave George to fend for himself. He didn't care what George was doing to his prospects after he left them. He could guess, but the important thing was that George was taking care of it. In fact, George could have had him arrested, but he didn't, and Alec thought he owed it to his brother to take care of him.

He would have to talk to George and get him prepared, just in case. Alec looked online at some places where they could go. Knowing several languages made it easier, but Alec was aware that George hadn't kept up with his language skills, so he thought it might be best to either go to a place where folks spoke English or Spanish. It would certainly narrow the options, although Alec had no desire to go to Eastern Europe or the East.

He continued to search online, noting what was available and where. He certainly wasn't thinking of purchasing anything, just looking and learning. He spent almost two hours looking at various places and prices that wouldn't make a huge dent in their finances.

Feeling hungry, he went to the kitchen to make himself a sandwich. He heard Maria working in his bathroom, and the washer and dryer were still in operation. After he put together his sandwich and grabbed a bottle of water from the fridge, he returned to his office.

Although he already had all the TVs on, he checked out the ESPN website as he ate and read a couple of articles on upcoming football games, including his beloved 49ers.

Finishing the turkey, tomato, and lettuce sandwich, he went to the Spruce restaurant website, got the phone number, then called and made a reservation for two at 7, Sunday night.

Using the Christos phone, he called Aisha. When she didn't answer, he left her a message.

Switching phones, he called Kim and was a little surprised when she answered on the second ring.

"Andrew? Where've you been? I was worried."

"Sorry, Kim. It took longer than I thought, and I should have called you. Are you okay?"

"Yes, I'm fine." She sounded annoyed.

"You sure? You sound a bit annoyed."

"Well, I was worried, Andrew, when I didn't hear from you, I thought I wasn't going to hear from you again."

"Oh Kim, I'm sorry. After our night in Berkeley, how could I not want to see you again? I'm still recalling it whenever I close my eyes."

"So when can I see you, Andrew?"

"If you like, you can come over to the city on Saturday night, and we can go out and stay at my place. I'll come and get you, if you want."

"That sounds good, but you can come here if you prefer. My roommate will be out of town again."

"I just thought that since my bed is bigger, we could actually sleep in it."

"Who wants to sleep?" She finally laughed, and the tension was noticeably gone from her voice. "I know I said I would come over to you the next time, but I have a lot of cram work to do for Monday morning. If you come here, I'll sort out the room so you can sleep. But only a little."

Alec laughed too, although he was a little annoyed. If he'd known this was going to happen, he wouldn't have called her.

"Okay. I'm going to the Stanford football on Saturday, so I'll come directly to your room after the game. I don't know what time it'll be, but I can call you from the Bart when I'm on the way."

"Okay, Andrew. I'll wait for your call. This is going to be fun."

"I know it is, Kim. I can't wait to see you again."

"You too, Andrew, and I'm glad you're okay. I'll see you on Saturday."

Alec put the phone down, wishing he was taking her to the farm.

If he hadn't met her friend, he would have insisted. But this would be his last time with her, yet he was thinking of not going.

He called George and told him that although he'd wanted to bring someone over this coming weekend, it had fallen through. But since they had games to attend on both days, maybe it was for the best.

George didn't sound disappointed. He looked forward to the football games and thought it best that his brother wasn't coming over. He didn't say anything to Alec, but he needed to appease Jane, who was still annoyed that he wasn't around on Saturday. There was no way he could keep Jane away this coming Saturday.

Alec asked George if he still used the old computer or if he'd upgraded it in the last few years. When George said he was using the old computer, Alec said that he'd get him a new one and would transfer all his stuff the next time he was at the farm.

Alec also told George what he'd been doing that morning and shared his belief that if something unexpected happened, then they would have to move fast and without hesitation. George agreed, but he wanted to know what he needed to do, so Alec explained everything to him. George especially wanted to know what would happen to the farm, as it was very special to him. Alec thought it would be a good idea if he promoted one of the farm hands, or shepherd if that's what he preferred to call them, to farm manager.

He also told George that within a week, all of the farm workers, along with George and Alec, would receive checks from a different source that to all intents and purposes would be completely separate from them. They would just be employees. But whatever happened, the farm was staying under the ownership of the brothers.

As far as Jane was concerned, if nothing happened, then Jane would be none the wiser. If something did happen, then George wouldn't be able to contact her if they got away.

As far as the new house was concerned, George would continue with their plans. If no questions were asked about any women, then the money for the construction would be available.

George said he'd immediately get his essential stuff together and be ready for flight. He'd check his passport and be ready to go, if needed.

Alec told him he'd only need a carry on bag, not to worry about clothing or mementos or anything, as they wouldn't lose anything. It was all taken care of.

The call was finished, and they agreed they'd see each other at the bar before the game.

Alec took his plate and empty water bottle to the kitchen where he disposed of the bottle and put his plate in the empty dishwasher. He thought other dishes had been in there but realized that Maria had obviously emptied it. He was drained after his conversation with his brother, so he opened a bottle of wine and poured himself a glass.

He was almost back in his office when he heard one of the phones ringing. Knowing which one it was, he hurried to it. "Hello."

"Is this the man I talk dirty to from the gallery?"

"Yes, it is. Is this the librarian?"

Alec had mentioned to her that she resembled a prototype librarian, and she liked the analogy.

"Yes, and you're overdue."

"So when would be a good time to pay my dues?"

"Friday at 8 am. I'm being dropped off at the Huntington Hotel. Can you make it?"

"Even better. I live next door."

"No, you don't."

"Yes, I do. Go inside the hotel, and I'll watch for your car to leave. Then I'll come and get you."

"You promise?"

"I promise. I have to go where your fingers went during your bath."

"What are you doing right now?" she asked seductively.

"Apart from thinking about you? Nothing."

"I'm lying on my bed. What are you wearing?"

"Me? I'm in my pajamas."

"At this time of day? Why?"

"I'm having a lazy day. You're lying on your bed, what's your excuse?"

"I'm lazy, and I needed a nap. Can you handle me?"

"Whatever you give me," responded Alec.

"I'll give you everything on Friday, and it's a lot. Have a big breakfast, 'cause you'll need it. What's under the pajamas?"

"Nothing. What are you wearing?"

"What color are they? I'm wearing a white bathrobe over my black bra and panties. My panties are high cut, wet, and my breasts are trying to burst out of my push-up bra, the nipples hard and protruding."

"Give me a second."

"You coming already?"

"No, my housekeeper is here. I need to close the door."

"You sure you don't want her in on this?"

"I'm sure. Just a moment. They are a plain light blue."

"Nice. You sure about Friday?"

"Definitely. So is your bathrobe closed?"

CHAPTER THIRTY NINE

DETECTIVE

GARCIA WAS AT A loss. Although other missing people were on the files, the two blondes didn't seem the type to voluntarily vanish. They both had jobs and made good money, and they had no signs of any drug, alcohol abuse or mental illnesses.

The second one, Jenny Charles, had been reported missing by her parents in Los Angeles when they were unable to contact her and she had failed to call when she'd promised. It was so unlike her that they called her apartment super to check on her. After finding her apartment empty, they'd called the police.

The only thing that the detective found was a posting on her Facebook page saying she was going on a hot date with some guy called Robert. Garcia actually found a number for him. But his phone, like hers, was dead.

Jenny had also left a text message that she was going camping for a couple of days, something her mother rubbished, as Jenny hated camping.

Both investigations were going nowhere, so a couple of uniforms were taking their pictures around to random spots in hopes that somebody remembered them, as well as going to the restaurants they'd mentioned. Normally, people only remembered the ones who stood out or made a commotion of some sort, so it was all a long shot.

Walnut Creek also had two missing person's cases, a blonde and a brunette in the same age group. Garcia didn't think they had anything to do with these cases. The blonde was a prostitute, not half as beautiful as the others, and she had a history of drug use, although only minor. Walnut Creek was dealing with it themselves. They thought the ex-husband was good for the brunette. The blonde had probably run from her pimp, but Garcia would keep an eye on both cases.

What was really galling to her was that even in this age of Twitter, Facebook, MySpace, iPads, and cell phones permanently attached to ears wherever you looked, people still went missing. She knew that it was mainly because of privacy, not everyone wanted the whole world to know what they were doing for 24 hours a day, but it was still annoying.

She also was aware that because of the social media absence, both women were probably dead. No bodies had been found that fit their descriptions, and she had no idea where to look. For all she knew, both women could be 50 yards away from their homes, waiting to be found.

The worst part was dealing with the relatives, folks who wanted answers and results, not the shrug of the shoulders and the shake of the head. They couldn't understand that the police needed clues or leads and that if there aren't any, then it was almost impossible to find someone. It was all black and white to the relatives, find their loved one, preferably alive. But if not, dead, and then we can deal with it. For the family, there was no such word as lost, that only happened to the family pet.

She had struck out with Vegas. Garcia also couldn't find reports of any wrecked vehicles in any canyons, no washed-up bodies with the description of the victims, no reports of any other bodies that might have been them, no sightings, no credit card usage, no phone calls, no anything. The PO boxes had been a dead end, and they hadn't had any success with the restaurants. The cases were so lacking in everything that she thought someone was being clever. But eventually, either he would make a mistake, or she would get lucky.

CHAPTER FORTY

JAMES WAS GOING BACK TO

Florida tomorrow morning, Sunday. He'd been making arrangements all week with a company that would pack everything in Rebecca's apartment on Monday, and they would transport everything, along with her car, to Florida. He had a friend who had storage units, and because James gave him inside information on property from time to time, he was giving him free space.

It was all very depressing for James. In his wildest dreams, he'd never envisaged doing this. To add to the pain, his sister was still missing.

Elizabeth and Tina had been a huge help to him, but they were suffering as well. Although he knew he could stay longer if need be, he thought it best for everyone if they could all continue their lives, and so he'd decided to go home. His boss had been very understanding. He wouldn't forget the kindness he'd been shown, he just wished Rebecca could be found.

If she'd gotten lost hiking or sailing, or had at least been seen somewhere, then a search could have been organized, and she might have been found. In his own mind, he agreed with the view of the police that she was likely dead, purposely or accidentally, but hadn't yet been found. Of course, someone might be holding her against her will, in which case he would be forever grateful but also guilty in thinking the worst.

James really felt alone now. It wasn't as though he'd been in regular contact with Rebecca, which he now regretted, but she'd always been there in the background. He'd taken her for granted for too long, and now she was probably gone before he could make it up to her.

Their parents were unaware of the happenings in San Francisco. James didn't even know where they were now, probably on the street begging and stealing for even more drugs and alcohol to fuel their addled brains. He didn't think he'd try and find them. It would be too depressing, even if they were at the same stage as they were when he last saw them. Even then they barely knew who he or his sister was, they just wanted money for themselves and their supplier, because they owed him money. His parents had continued to deny they had any kind of problem. They wanted no help, apart from monetary. They weren't that old, but even then they looked aged and haggard, their bodies wasting away from the constant self abuse. If he wanted to find them, he knew he could probably contact the police, who were always arresting them for possession, intoxication, or theft.

At least he and Rebecca hadn't gone down the same road, which would have been easy with all the substances that were always lying around. His sister had been very influential in that. Her determination to want her own life and success in doing so made her a superb role model for him, and he followed her example and created his own life, with no help whatsoever from his parents.

Elizabeth and Tina were sad to see him go. Despite the situation, he'd been nice to have around, and it had been especially true for Elizabeth, who wasn't used to having house guests. They both escorted him to the airport for his flight home, and they all had tears coursing down their cheeks as they hugged each other goodbye at the security terminal and promised to keep in touch.

CHAPTER FORTY ONE

IN HIS OPINION, ALEC'S WEEKEND only got better as it went on. It hadn't started as well as he thought it would with the librarian, and he'd been so looking forward to that. In his view, she was way better at phone sex than in person.

He'd had a haircut, pedicure and manicure on Thursday. Friday, he'd watched the librarian's car make a u-turn after dropping her off. He stepped outside to get her and took her to his apartment, making out in the elevator. But despite her hot underwear of black basque and suspenders, she was cooler in his bedroom than he thought she'd be, and he was disappointed. He also didn't like the huge eagle tattoo on her back.

She wasn't as uninhibited as the girls he'd taken to the farm, or even Chelsea. And although he'd had a good time with her, it wasn't what he'd expected. He'd even thought for a brief moment that it might have been his fault, as he was always more focused when it was their last night on earth. But when he remembered Chelsea and his other ladies, he dismissed that thought very quickly.

Chelsea had called him Saturday morning before the game, and they'd tentatively arranged to meet mid-week. She was going to call again on Monday or Tuesday.

He'd met his brother at the bar on Saturday, and they'd had a good chat. The Cardinals beat Colorado 48 – 7, and on Sunday they both went along to Candlestick Stadium to see the 49ers beat the Buccaneers, 48 – 3.

Before the game on Sunday, he'd gotten up early and had followed Aisha as she'd left her apartment for her walk. But he had to be careful, as she kept looking around, probably looking for him before they went out to dinner that night. He'd managed to avoid her by staying well back and on the opposite side of the road.

As he made his way home, he came across a striking redheaded woman sitting on a low wall as she tried to regain her breath. Initially, he looked at her and passed by. He turned around after a few yards. She was still struggling and now was bent over. He retraced his steps.

She wasn't well dressed or wearing expensive clothes, just grey sweat pants, white socks and trainers, a blue sweatshirt, and a white baseball cap with a pink ribbon motif. It certainly wasn't her attire that drew his attention. What did attract him was her striking face, green eyes above a narrow thin nose, wide lips with a little pout, a clear complexion that was free of make-up. Her hair was pulled back from her face, and the only part of her hair that he could really see was just above her unremarkable ears and the long red braid hanging out the back of her hat.

She was sitting down, but despite the baggy pants he could tell she was slim and tall, with thin wrists and ankles. She had no rings on her long hands, and her nails were cut and not manicured.

She was obviously hurting when he asked her if she was okay, still bent over and holding the back of her legs on the calves. She didn't even look up when he spoke, just mumbled that she was fine. So he asked her if she had cramp and if there was something he could do.

She lifted her head up and he saw her pain, but she managed to give him a smile of sorts, and said she'd be fine after a minute or two.

She had a nice voice, warm and a little soft. Her smile brought out the lines at the side of her mouth. She was in her mid-30s, he thought. She had no bags under her eyes, no double chin, but she had experience lines on her forehead and around her striking eyes.

As he moved to leave, she apologized for her bad manners and thanked him for asking about her wellbeing.

"You're welcome. Are you sure you're going to be okay?"

"I think so. It's just a bit of cramp, and I overdid the running."

"How far did you run?"

"Not far. I'm not used to running, is all. I don't think I'll be doing it again." She smiled.

"You need to stretch out your legs. I could help you, but it will hurt."

"More than this?" Her eyes showed her pain as she clutched her calves.

"More, but only for a few seconds. You want some help?"

"Go for it," she implored.

He had her brace herself on the wall. Doing one leg at a time, he stretched them out by holding her toes down. The pain slowly dissipated from her face.

"God, that was terrible," she confessed. "Now they just ache."

She was rubbing her legs, the cramps were gone.

"I'm afraid they will for a while. You should take a bath with lots of Epsom salt. That will help some."

"Thank you, sir. I'm very grateful."

"Please, I'm glad I could help. And it's Alan, by the way."

"Thank you, Alan. I am Sinead. Pleased to meet you."

They shook hands and talked a little more. She only lived down the street on Taylor, yet this was the first time they had ever seen each other. Alan told her he lived on Jones, which was in the next block.

He eventually helped her to her feet. She wanted to thank him in some way, so he suggested she buy him a coffee one day. She thought that was a good idea and asked for his number, so he gave her one. She gave him hers and said she'd definitely call him later.

He watched her gingerly walk away down Taylor. When she was a safe distance, he followed, noting the building she entered but not approaching, just in case she looked out the window when she got inside.

She did call, and she left him a message while he was at dinner with Aisha.

He walked down to Aisha's apartment and hailed a cab while he waited outside, calling her once the car was there. It was a chilly evening, so he wore an overcoat over his dark blue pinstripe suit and open necked, plain, light blue shirt.

He only had to wait a few moments. She breezed out with a huge smile on her face and immediately gave him a hug and a kiss on the lips. She wore a long blue overcoat with a matching purse and high heels. She'd highlighted her high cheekbones and had used black eyeliner and pale pink lipstick. She looked divine, and he wasted no time in telling her so. She thanked him, gave him another kiss, and commented on how chilly it was. He saw her into the waiting cab before going around the car to get in on the other side.

He'd already told the driver where they were going, and as they moved away from the sidewalk he held her hand, and she nestled into him, both quickly warming up in the heated car. They discussed their weekends on the route. He mentioned his sporting weekend but nothing else, and she said she'd been shopping, cleaning, and walking of course, in the morning.

It wasn't far to the restaurant. They were going to the Spruce, one of his favorites, but she said she'd never been there, so was excited about it.

He paid the cab driver with cash after they disembarked, and he led her inside. The host took their coats, and Christos admired Aisha's sand colored, halter crochet dress that came to her knees. When she turned around, he saw it was backless, displaying her well defined spine and flawless ebony skin. Because it was crocheted, he could also catch glimpses of her skin beneath. It was very sexy, very enticing.

As they were shown to their table, he whispered into her gold ringed ear that maybe he should cancel his work schedule tomorrow, which brought another big smile along with a very suggestive wink.

Although he'd been here before and regarded it as a favorite, it had been many months ago, and he wasn't known by any of the staff. Besides, it was a dark place, with velvety fabric walls, dark woods, and high ceilings, very cozy and romantic. Aisha loved it. The bar on the other side of the glass screen was busy and vibrant, and the clientele were young and smartly dressed.

Once seated, they had cocktails, and Christos ordered gruyere cheese puffs. Then they ordered their meal. Beet salad followed by the Liberty Farm duck for her and blue cheese salad followed by the rib eye steak for him. He also ordered a bottle of Bordeaux.

It was difficult for Christos to avert his eyes from Aisha. She dressed up well, and his gaze kept dropping from her sparkling eyes, to the plain gold chain around her slender neck, down to her breasts. He kept apologizing to her, but knowing she enjoyed being looked at, as she hadn't dressed like this to be demure.

The food was divine. They went through another bottle of Bordeaux, held hands across the table, and played a little footsie. He let her talk as much as possible, as his chatter was, well, mainly a lie. They spent most of the evening there, taking their time, not being rushed by the server, enjoying each other in the wonderful ambience of the restaurant.

He paid for the meal and the cab with more cash, careful to remain anonymous with a standard tip for the server and driver. He'd been told a long time ago by a waitress he'd dated that the only diners she remembered were the ones who over tipped or the ones who stiffed her. She told him that most servers kept an eye on the door to spot their most favorite patrons, as well as the ones they disliked. He'd remembered that advice and always stuck with it.

Aisha wanted him to stay over when the cab dropped them off, and he declined with great reluctance. He wanted her to be a special night, so he made the excuse of having an early client.

Instead, he said he'd take her out for lunch on Wednesday and, if she liked, they could go to his friend's farm on Friday and spend the weekend there, hiking and riding. No one else would be there. It would just be the two of them, very casual but very romantic. He told her to think about it and let him know on Wednesday, but he'd call beforehand to let her know where they'd have lunch.

She asked him inside again and gave him a taste of what he was missing with a very hot and moist kiss before they bade each other good night. He walked away after she entered the apartment block entrance.

He followed her to work the next morning, and when he returned home he called Sinead to accept her coffee invitation for Tuesday, 10:30 am at the Gallery Café on Mason Street.

Changing phones, he made a reservation at Bix on Gold Street for lunch on Wednesday, then called Aisha to inform her and to tell her how much he'd enjoyed their previous evening and that he couldn't wait to see her again.

He was a little unsure of what to do with Chelsea. He wanted to see her again, for a few hours at least, but he didn't want to bring her to his apartment. He knew that if he took her to a hotel, it could create a situation. Hotels normally wanted credit cards to book their rooms, and although he had some fake IDs to go with his aliases, he didn't want to use the fake credit cards he had. He foresaw a situation where he would check in with one name and then, when he was using another name, someone would address him using a different name, or even his real name.

He thought he'd go down to Fisherman's Wharf and get a motel room, but he decided instead that he'd talk to Chelsea when she called. She might want to book a room herself somewhere. He didn't want an angry husband confronting him and making a scene if he found out, but he also wasn't bothered about her marriage. She'd find some other lover after him, but he didn't want to get in the middle of something.

He saw that he had a message on the Christos phone that he didn't listen to. It was probably from Kim, who would be pissed that he didn't show up on Saturday. He'd dispose of the phone after the weekend, and he checked to see if he needed to buy more.

CHAPTER FORTY TWO

GEORGE'S

WEEKEND HAD ALSO GONE well, although he missed having a defenseless beautiful woman on his table.

Jane had been over for the entire weekend, amusing herself when he went to the football games, but also excited about the building plans. She'd even thought that having a basement was a good idea, not for stockpiling, but for extra space. Jane said that they could make it into a game room for the children.

She'd picked out the spot where they could build, and as there was already a track that went by there from the main road, that would eliminate the cost of having to do a new one. Her spot was by some trees that would give the backyard some shade, and she wanted the rear of the house to face the mountain. She thought it was perfect, a flat part of the hilly farm with good natural drainage, hidden from the road, and with a great view.

She didn't want a huge home, but she did want one big enough for themselves and a couple of kids. A spare room or two, a large kitchen for everyone to be able to move around and sit in, a big family room, and a study they could share as an office. Lots of bathrooms, of course, a big porch on the front, and maybe a swimming pool and spa in the yard.

She'd taken George to the spot she'd picked out when he got back from Stanford, and he'd agreed with her assessment. It was a great place for a house.

George wanted an adjoining garage for maybe three vehicles, and he wanted the house to be two stories with a basement. George also wanted the attic to be utilized, as he didn't like wasted space. He wanted to learn about using solar power to reduce the electric bills and said that he'd rather spend money on having great insulation so that they weren't using a lot of wasted energy.

Jane was thrilled that he was contributing his ideas, and she kept showing him designs from magazines that she'd picked up that she thought were perfect for all the different rooms. George went through them like a good fiancé, showing lots of interest and expressing his dislikes of certain things. Like tiny areas for laundry with no room to move, uncomfortable looking furniture, or colors he didn't like.

He realized that having a basement for his own use wasn't going to happen, but he'd probably be able to have his own man cave, and he'd be happy with that.

When he made love with Jane over the weekend, he found that she became a collage of herself and the other women, and he enjoyed her more. She thought he was more in love with her and was being more attentive.

He didn't object, though, when Alec informed him that he would probably be there that next weekend. He even asked Alec if he wanted some shopping done before he arrived.

CHAPTER FORTY THREE

CHELSEA CALLED

GREGORY ON TUESDAY morning. She wanted to see him again as soon as possible but had some bad news. Her husband was taking some time off, and they were going on vacation to Europe, leaving on Sunday for London. She'd be out of town for three weeks.

Gregory said he'd miss her while she was gone but that he wanted to meet up with her before she left. He voiced his concerns about her making hotel reservations, as her husband would no doubt find out.

Chelsea explained that he never got suspicious, as they were always booking rooms for their relatives whenever they came into town, even at times when they didn't see them. In fact, she'd been told by him to do that, as he didn't want their relatives and friends staying with them. He preferred that they be in a good hotel. As long as she used the same American Express card, then no one asked about it. And if they did, she would say so-and-so came to town.

Gregory told her he was busy Wednesday, but Thursday was free if she could manage to meet up then. She said that would be great, she couldn't wait.

She wanted to go to the InterContinental Mark Hopkins on California Street. It was one of her favorite hotels, and she said she'd call him with the room number when she checked in. She didn't want to have lunch. She wanted to make the most of their time together, so she encouraged Gregory to eat before arriving.

After some small talk with her, he made his way to the Gallery Café to meet Sinead. He was about as casual as he could be, wearing black jeans, a white tee shirt, loafers, and a short black wool coat to repel the chill of the day. He didn't see her inside, so he waited outside the front door.

He knew the direction she would come from if she was coming from home, so that's where he was looking when she came up unexpectedly from his right, carrying some shopping.

"Good morning, Alan. I hope I'm not late."

He turned around. Her hair was blowing a little in the wind, and like him she was casually dressed, wearing blue jeans with a thick, white, cable knit sweater. Her hair was more of a copper color than red, parted down the middle of her head, straight and long. Her eyes were happy and sparkling.

"I've just got here. Thanks for the invite."

"It's the least I could do. Come on, let's go inside and out of the cold."

She led the way, and it gave him the chance to admire her figure, or at least her legs.

"What would you like, Alan?"

He looked at the menu and went for a large cate au lait. She chose a medium white mocha, and neither wanted anything to eat.

She found a table, and they both sat down with their drinks once they were made.

"It's nice to see you, Alan, and thank you again for the other day. I didn't think I'd ever walk again." She had a nice smile.

"I'm glad to see you on your feet again. Cramps are awful, and in both legs at the same time, I can only imagine."

"It was my own fault. I hadn't done any exercise for ages and thought I'd go for a jog, but I went way too far. I had to walk up California, and when I got to Taylor I couldn't move any more, so I saw the wall and sat down. That's when you came along, so thanks."

"It's the hills, they're killers. I sometimes don't know which is worse, going down or coming up."

"Well, I appreciated your help, Alan. So what do you do, do you live nearby?"

Alec gave her his stock answer about the business advisor and said he lived on Jones Street, just as he'd said when they'd met. She'd caught him on a good day, as he had no calls this morning, but his afternoon was full until the early evening. He was careful not to start complimenting her looks. He didn't know where this was headed or any of her personal details, and some women don't like being admired by strangers. He asked her what she did.

"Well, apart from making a fool of myself in public," she laughed, "I'm able to work from home doing research for a couple of authors." She saw the look from Alec and went on, "You won't have heard of them, they're not best sellers, but in their own fields they are well known. Their books are not cheap, but they need a lot of facts and figures. I do the facts, and they do the figures. It's mainly for college textbooks, so the students have to buy the books to get their degrees. But they are boring to me and probably are to everyone else as well."

"I read some business books. Is your work along those lines?"

"No, it's more science and math. Even the research is boring. I can barely make heads or tails of it, but they seem to like what I do."

"Well that's good to hear. So they don't do book tours?"

"Actually they do, but they don't do bookstores. They go to the different colleges and sign books there, usually in the libraries."

"How long have you been doing this?"

"A few years now. I started doing it when the two boys were in middle school and I was at home getting bored. At first it was a little part time thing. But when I got divorced, I needed more hours, and they were able to give me them."

That was a lot of information for Alec in one explanation, and he quickly absorbed it.

"You just have the two children?"

"Yes, they're in high school now. Do you have any?"

"No, I'm afraid not. No children and no wife." He was trying to read her looks, as well as trying to keep his own thoughts to himself.

"Have you been married?"

"No, it never quite happened for some reason."

"Perhaps they think that other women will throw themselves at you. You are very good looking, you know."

She was complimenting him now, so he thought he could change tack a little.

"No, women don't throw themselves at me, I'm afraid, but thank you for the compliment."

"I'm sure you've heard it before, but you're welcome."

"I have heard it before, but I see something different in the mirror than they do, I suppose. You yourself are a beautiful, very striking woman, but I doubt if you admire yourself in the mirror, and it's the same with me."

Her look had changed now from amusement to a certain embarrassment, now that she was being openly complimented.

"You've caught me on a good day. You wouldn't say that if you saw me first thing trying to get the boys up for school. But thank you, it's much appreciated."

He thought that she'd be looked at a lot, but maybe working from home and having two boys curtailed her from going out much, if at all.

"I can only tell you what I see, Sinead."

"Is that why you stopped to help me?"

"Actually, when I stopped, you were looking at the sidewalk with your head bent over. You were wearing a cap and baggy clothing. For all I knew, you could have been a 60-year-old hag," he lied and smiled, happy to hear her laugh in reply.

"That's true, Alan. This is a nice change for me. Can we do this again sometime?"

"I'd love to. I enjoy your company."

They chatted some more as they drank their coffee. When Alan said he'd call her, she looked very happy and said she would look forward to hearing from him.

After they went their separate ways, Alan watched her rear for a while, wondering if he could leave two boys without a mother.

CHAPTER FORTY FOUR

BIX WAS A TWO-STORY restaurant. At

night, it was a romantic jazz venue, with a pianist playing a grand piano. By day, it looked like an old saloon transported from the 1930s to the present day, a speakeasy almost. You'd be almost forgiven for thinking the FBI would be breaking down the doors and arresting all the occupants.

Aisha arrived wearing a brown stone, slim-fitting suit. The skirt hugged her skin to just above the knees, and the one-button jacket flared out at the waist. Beneath it she wore an ivory halter neck top. Her brown heels accentuated her finely toned calves.

Christos had been on her tail for a couple of days, seeing her with the office friend having a simple lunch from one of the many trailers in the city and going to the movies with the same girl last night.

"I'm glad you don't work in my office. I'd never get any work done," he greeted her, in his usual sport coat and trousers.

"If I was in your office," she smiled, "I wouldn't want you to work."

They kissed before heading inside. She was delighted with the choice of venue and wanted to return for dinner some time.

"We can come next week, maybe Friday night," he replied.

"I'll look forward to it. I like jazz."

"Me too, but more the old time stuff rather than the modern."

They sat down on the lower level, but the place was almost full. When they looked up, all the tables seemed to be taken.

They ordered quickly, Christos knew she had to get back to work, and they settled on soup with half a sandwich each, only drinking water.

Christos asked her if she'd been doing much since he'd reluctantly left her the other night. She said she'd been to the movies to see Dolphin Tail, which she'd thought was a cute and happy film, which was a change from all the blood and gore.

He told her he'd been very busy with clients, even at night, which wasn't his usual routine with them. It was very rare when he had to speak to them at night, but they were from Hong Kong, so it was difficult to speak at any other time because of the time difference.

He didn't push her on the upcoming weekend. He waited for her to hopefully open the subject, and she did.

"So, where is this farm you're taking me to?"

So simple, so easy.

"On the East Bay, it's not far. It's very peaceful, and you'll love it. I'll take you walking up the mountain, or we can ride, then light a fire. We can watch the flames and drink some nice wine."

"What will I need to bring?"

"Something to walk and ride in, like jeans and boots, casual clothing, whatever you feel comfortable in."

"Anything sexy?" She whispered.

"You are sexy whatever you wear, very sexy. Something that's quick to remove and very brief," he whispered back.

"Do you want to come over to my place when I finish work today?"

"That would be wonderful, but I want to wait until Friday. I'll pick you up at six at your building."

"Okay, Andrew. I'll be waiting. You sure about tonight?"

He laughed and wondered about it. Friday would be superb.

He escorted her back to work and kissed her goodbye, then headed to the Apple store on Stockton Street and bought a Mac Book Air for his brother.

After he returned home, he deposited the laptop in his car and caught some scores. He changed before he headed back downtown to follow Aisha home after work. She picked up some groceries on her way, so she was probably staying in for the evening. After waiting around for a couple of hours, Alec felt hungry, so he picked up some carry out Indian food on his way home, where he remained.

Chelsea called early the following morning and gave him her room number, saying she'd be waiting.

Heeding her warning, he made himself a large breakfast of bacon, eggs, and several pieces of toast before he dressed in jeans and a tee shirt. He'd showered on waking up that morning, so he checked his wallet for condom supplies, slipped on a brown leather jacket, and made his way to the hotel.

It didn't take him long to get there. It was practically next door, and the day felt cool but fresh, perfect weather for the city.

He walked into the hotel as he normally did, which was like he owned the place. After finding the elevator, he headed to Chelsea's floor, and, to his knowledge, no one had even glanced his way in the foyer.

As the elevator door opened, he saw the sign signaling the direction to take for her room. Counting down the numbers, he came to a door that already had the "Do Not Disturb" sign hanging on the handle. He knocked, and it opened almost immediately.

She held back until he entered, then embraced him as the door silently closed as she led him to the window. She was dressed in a red bandage low cut dress that came to her mid thigh, it was strapless and seemed to only be held up by her breasts. She wore black stilettos, so she wasn't that far below his tall frame, and she held out a glass of mimosa, which he took as he admired the view of not only her, but also of the Golden Gate Bridge and the bay.

"You look stunning, Chelsea. Here's to an exhausting day." He toasted and she smiled, catching his innuendo.

They drank, and Chelsea pointed out the tray of coffee and cookies before she put down her glass and wrapped her arms around his neck.

Gregory slipped off his jacket and threw it over a nearby chair, deftly keeping hold of his drink as he did so. After taking another swig, he put it down next to hers and wrapped his arms around her waist, pulling her groin to his own and kissing her, their tongues probing one another's mouths.

His hands went down and under her dress, and after he felt her bare outline he pulled off from their kiss.

"No underwear?"

She shook her head no and pulled his head toward her own.

Gregory said, "Great minds think alike."

She smiled some more before his lips got to hers, and he felt her undo his belt, then the waist button before she slid down his zip. She was on him, and he felt her try to move them toward the king size bed.

Breaking off from the kiss momentarily, he panted, "Let's do it right here, against the window."

She looked at him with devilment in her eyes. She glanced back over her shoulder at the view and the bank of windows facing them. "I love the way you think, Gregory."

"It's not that dangerous," he gasped. "They'd need binoculars to see us."

CHAPTER FORTY FIVE

AFTER STAYING IN BED THE following morning for a lie in, Alec took a relaxing salty bath.

Chelsea had come very close to eclipsing his evenings at the farm. Almost, but it still left him with the thought that another man would be able to sample her like he had, and he didn't like that thought at all.

When he'd returned home last night, totally exhausted, he'd called his brother and had asked him to get a couple of steaks out of the freezer and to get some potatoes and a prepared salad, along with some breakfast food. He also asked him to put some Champagne in the fridge and to buy a couple of bottles of decent cabernet.

Feeling much better after the hot bath, Alec had his normal breakfast of avocado on toast with some coffee, then called Sinead to ask her out for lunch next week.

She sounded thrilled to hear from him. She'd probably thought that having two boys would have sent him running, but the fact that she was upfront about it put her in his good light. She was very excited to accept his invitation and asked him to call her when he got a reservation.

They also talked about their upcoming weekends. She had to go to one of the boy's football games, and they also wanted to go to the movies, so it was going to be busy for her. He told her that he had to deal with some clients over the weekend who were in town, so he, too, was going to be busy, although he didn't appreciate them taking his weekend away.

He guessed that the mood she was in after he called would make her weekend a lot more enjoyable for them all.

He lounged around for the rest of the day, watched the Friday sports, and took a nap after having some lunch.

After he finally got dressed, he renewed his overnight bag, took it to the car, and put it in the trunk. Ready, he drove down to Aisha's apartment.

He called her after he'd parked out front and watched the door as he waited for her, hoping no one else would be around when they departed. It was still quiet when he saw her through the door as she got out of the elevator. He bounded out of the driver's door to meet her and take her bag. Like him, she was in jeans and sweater, except hers were much tighter than his.

Her bag was stuffed, and she carried a wool jacket, which he took from her as he kissed her hello.

Her sweater was a pink turtleneck, and she wore a black belt over it that was fastened but loose, making her waist seem thinner, and she matched it with some toeless black heels. It looked like she'd had a pedicure, along with the manicure.

He held the passenger door open for her and got a good look at her rear as she climbed in and smelled her perfume as she brushed against him. He put her bag and coat in the already open trunk, closed the trunk, then got back into the driver's seat. He leaned over to kiss her again before he put on his seat belt.

"Did I tell you how delicious you look?" he asked her as he started the engine.

"Good enough to eat?" she teased.

"I'm already ravenous."

"If you're that hungry, Christos, we could go upstairs before we go. Really."

He looked at her, realizing she was serious, but he set off anyway. No one had seen them leave, and he didn't want to jinx it.

"We'll be there in less than an hour. I think I can wait that long, but not much longer than that. Put some music on if you like, it will help take my mind off you while I drive."

She fiddled around with the radio and searched for a station before settling on a hip hop setting.

"I like your car, is it new?"

"No, but almost. Whoever got it before me didn't like it for some reason, so I got a great deal."

"I like it," she replied as she played with her seat settings. "Are we going to be alone?"

"Yes. Is that a problem? Do you want me to invite some other people over?" he said lightly.

"Oh no, don't you dare. I wanted to be sure no one was going to arrive unexpectedly."

He looked across at her. She was reclined with her legs crossed, and her eyes were directly on his own.

"No one at all, just you and me."

He got a smile in reply as she sang softly along to the music, which thankfully she hadn't turned up to a headache inducing level.

As they cruised up the freeway, he took her left hand in his right. She sucked his fingers, and he felt her tongue licking them, very softly. He had to take his hand back on exiting and kept them on the steering wheel along the winding road to the farm. It was too dangerous to drive with one hand.

It was dark when they arrived, but George had left the porch light on for them. As he pulled up, Christos wasted no time in getting out of his door.

"Here we are," he declared. "I hope you like it."

"It looks wonderful," she replied, taking off her seat belt.

He opened her door for her and retrieved their luggage, then carried it all on one arm as he took her hand and led her to the front door. It was unlocked.

"Is someone home?" She sounded worried.

"No, they didn't go that long ago, so they said they'd leave the door open for us."

"Okay. But make sure you lock it behind us, I don't want them to come home early and surprise us."

She had a look of deviousness on her face that Christos really liked, and he led her inside and turned on the lights.

"Oh, this is really nice, Christos," she commented as she looked around the family room.

Christos put their luggage down, locked the door, then turned on the fire and some lamps before he picked up the luggage again and led her upstairs.

"I'll show you our room, then I'll get us a drink and make some dinner."

"We're sharing a room?" she said mischievously, putting her hand on his denim bottom.

"I hope you don't mind. I promise not to touch you."

"That's a promise I don't want you to keep," she whispered as she turned him around and put her lips to his, her hands exploring him.

He broke off their kiss and deposited the bags, telling her to make herself at home as he went to get them a drink.

He went downstairs and turned off the main light, leaving the lamps on. Now that the fire had burned for a few minutes, it was nice and warm. He went into the kitchen, turned on the light, and opened the fridge to retrieve a bottle of Champagne.

He opened it with a pop and found two glasses, then carried the bottle and the empty glasses as he headed back to the stairs. But before he made the first step, he saw that Aisha had preempted him.

Aisha was lying on the rug in front of the fireplace. Her face was down with her head propped up by her elbows. Although she faced the fire and not him, she was totally naked. And she had the most amazing body.

"Are you going to join me?" She asked. She turned her head around and watched as he put the glasses and Champagne down on the stairs and removed his clothes.

She liked how unabashed he was, as, naked, he picked up the champagne and glasses and walked toward her, so she turned herself around but remained on her elbows, exposing herself.

He knelt beside her and poured their drinks, handing her one.

"You are magnificent, Aisha."

"You are pretty good yourself, Christos."

They clinked glasses and took a drink, their eyes exploring each other in the flickering light of the fire and the subdued lamps. Aisha got to her knees to face him as they drank, and they looked and stroked one another with their free hands.

Christos was so happy he'd brought her here. This house was magic!

CHAPTER FORTY SIX

THE FOLLOWING DAY, GEORGE TOOK the unconscious Aisha away. Alec helped with the clean-up by stripping the bed of its soiled sheets and putting them, along with the smudged pillowcases and used towels, in the washing machine. Then he remade the bed.

He retrieved her cell phone and would check it out later, but there were no new messages on it, and she hadn't used it the previous night. George returned and took the rest of her things, so Alec took his bag back to his car and got out the new computer for George.

The salesman had shown him how to transfer everything to the Mac, so after talking to George he set it up and began the process. He liked how the laptop operated. His brother had said that he'd better keep the old computer for now, otherwise Jane would ask questions. As she had stuff on it, he couldn't very well transfer her files without telling her.

Alec understood, but he warned George that if they should leave, then if there was anything on the old computer that he didn't want anyone to see, then he should email them to a new address and delete everything. Alec also told him how to revert the computer back to an early date. Failing that, he urged George to just throw it in the incinerator.

George told Alec the location of his escape bag. Now the new computer was inside the escape bag, if George wanted to transfer anything else, then Alec would do it for him the next time he was here.

Alec's time with Aisha had been amazing, everything and more than he'd even dreamed of, and he was extremely happy when he drove away. He was already thinking of where he could meet more prospects.

Since laying his eyes on Aisha, George had been itching for his brother to leave so he could have his time with her. He'd spent the previous evening at Jane's house, but his mind had been here, wondering what beauty Alec had brought over.

Jane had thought him distant for the whole night, so she wasn't at all bothered when he'd left that morning for the farm. She said she'd call him the following day when, hopefully, he'd more responsive to her.

George was pleased to hear that. He didn't want to see her this evening, not when he had one of Alec's girls on his table. As Jane had slept, he'd showered and shaved. He wanted to be as clean as Aisha shortly would be when he washed her, when the fun began.

He cleaned up the house in record time in his haste to savor her, although he was still careful. Her scent seemed to be all over the house, so he opened windows and sprayed air freshener. It wasn't that he was trying to pretend that she hadn't been here, Jane already knew that Alec was staying and would no doubt have company. It was more that he didn't want Jane to duplicate her smell.

He could smell it when he browsed through her luggage, admiring her skimpy underwear and slender clothing that Jane would never be able to fit into.

Alec was almost home in the city by the time George returned to his table to wash her. He'd been thinking of where he could meet more prospects over the next few days, as he was again down to just one.

He didn't want to go to Berkeley. He might run into Kim there, and he doubted if she'd ignore him. She'd probably make a scene, which could be very embarrassing, but also would also ruin any hope of taking someone from there to the farm.

He was thinking more of going over to Oakland and perusing the bookstores and galleries there, maybe the Bookmark Bookstore or the Swarm Gallery.

Tomorrow, he'd leave a message on Aisha's phone, then dismantle and dispose of it, possibly go and walk on the Embarcadero, if the weather was agreeable.

Alec had thoroughly enjoyed his week. After he ordered another car wash for his almost spotless car and entered his home, he made himself a huge sandwich, poured a glass of Merlot to wash it all down with, and settled in to watch college football.

CHAPTER FORTY SEVEN

DETECTIVE

GARCIA DIDN'T THINK SHE was getting anywhere with the two blondes who were missing. She had nothing apart from an "extremely handsome guy." One of the uniforms had even sat through hours and hours of security tape from a bunch of restaurants and had come up with zilch.

The Walnut Creek hooker was going nowhere either, and her pimp was none too happy about losing his "best friend," as he called her. He was harassing the station over there practically non-stop, asking why she couldn't be found.

The pimp had no doubt that she'd been taken. She wasn't the type to run away, and he said that he always looked after his friends. As the police were always harassing him, it was now his turn to return the favor.

Now another beautiful woman was missing. This time she was black, but her actions were like the others. She'd met a very handsome guy. Her phone was disabled, and a message had been sent to her friend saying she was off sick and would be back at work in a week. The detective was going over to her apartment and meeting the friend.

She and the super were waiting, and as the super hadn't seen her leave or even set sight on her for a while, the detective let him go when he opened her door.

The detective went in alone to check things out. Apart from clutter, there was nothing, so she went to get the friend. The friend, Mandy, was a plump girl and would be far prettier if she lost a few pounds. But Mandy was very distraught about her BFF, as she called her.

It was Wednesday, and Mandy hadn't seen Aisha since work on Friday. She hadn't worried too much until she realized Aisha's phone was turned off. She hadn't replied to her messages or texts, so Mandy had reported her missing.

Apparently, Aisha had met this gorgeous guy. Unusually, in this day and age, he'd taken his time with her. He'd never tried to take advantage of her, just taken her out for lunches and dinner and hadn't even been in her apartment or taken her to his place. Aisha had thought he was very gentlemanly but suspected he might be married. But when he invited her away for the weekend, she'd jumped at it.

Then she'd sent the text on Sunday, which Mandy showed Detective Garcia. It read: "Hi, had a wonderful weekend but not feeling well, taking a few days off, don't worry, love A."

The detective asked Mandy to forward it to her and gave her the number, then they looked around the empty apartment.

Aisha wasn't the tidiest person, she had stuff everywhere. Dishes were in the sink, and her fridge was a mass of fresh and take out foods. Her bathroom was no better. It reminded Garcia to get her own house in order, as she'd hate for something to happen to herself and have someone rummaging through her mess.

She picked up the laptop that was open on the coffee table and, having found nothing else of note, started to make her way out. Mandy waited by the door, about to shed a bucket load of tears.

"Mandy, do you know what this guy is called?"

"His name is Christos, but I don't know his last name."

"Do you know where he lives, or what he does?"

"I know he lives in the city. I don't know where, but Aisha said he worked from home as a business advisor. And he was rich."

"So, good looking and rich, there's a losing combination," said the sarcastic detective.

"He's very good looking. Do you want to see?"

Detective Garcia could barely believe what she'd heard, but she kept the hope out of her voice. "You have a picture of him?"

"I was looking out the window the other day after lunch and saw them returning to the office, so I took a few snaps with my iPhone. Here, take a look."

She handed over her phone, and the detective went through her snaps. She'd taken some good photos of them.

"Do you mind if I forward these?"

"I just hope they help find him. Do you think she's okay?"

"I hope so, Mandy, I really do. I may want to ask you more questions later. Is that okay?"

"Whatever you need, I'll be glad to help. She's my best friend."

"Do her family know she's missing?"

"I don't know, I don't know who to call. She has family in Sacramento."

"We'll find them, Mandy. Maybe she's being taken care of up there. We'll keep in touch with you, and if there's anything else you can recall, here's my card. You can call me any time. Thank you, Mandy, you've been a huge help."

"Just find her, detective. Please."

Mandy was crying, and the detective gave her a hug. It helped a little but not entirely, and she was still crying when they left the apartment building and went their separate ways after the detective's offer of a ride was politely refused.

Garcia was sure this guy in the picture was behind the disappearance of the three women. She didn't think he'd resort to a hooker when he looked like he did, but she wanted to find out who he was, and quickly. This was the first break she'd had.

CHAPTER FORTY EIGHT

ALEC WENT TO OAKLAND ON

Monday but had no luck in the bookstore or the coffee shop. It wasn't that he hadn't been attracted to anyone, he had. But the ones who caught his interest had all been with friends or their partners.

He wasn't too despondent about it, even he struck out sometimes. And if he hadn't been particularly looking for someone alone, then he would probably have gotten somewhere.

He did start chatting with a woman who, like him, was traveling back to San Francisco on the Bart. He was already seated when she entered the train, and they exchanged friendly smiles as she took her seat immediately in front of him. Like him, she wore a raincoat, as there had been light showers throughout the day. Her white coat had the collar up, and it framed her boyish face and short black hair. Beneath her buttoned and belted coat, she had on light blue cropped pants and similar colored sandals that didn't have much of a heel. The skin that was on show had a nice tan.

She carried a large attaché case that looked heavy. After she took her seat, she opened it to retrieve something, and some of the papers fell to the floor, a few to the side of Alec. He hadn't planned on speaking to her, but when she lost the papers, he helped to gather them. She was very thankful, so much so she engaged in conversation.

She worked for the city and had been over to the Oakland office to liaise with them on a joint parks project they were doing. It very rarely happened, so rather than have endless telephone conversations with a voice with no face, she'd arranged to meet with her opposite in Oakland to speed things along. She thought it had been a great meeting, and they seemed to share the same thoughts and vision.

Alec thought her very pleasant. She wasn't great looking, but she had unusual light blue eyes that caught his attention and a nice, even smile. She was also easy to listen to. She was obviously used to speaking to strangers, so there was no nervousness in her voice.

Of course, she asked Alec what he did and why he was on the train, then she also inquired what his wife did and where his children went to school. To fend off suspicions that he might be gay, Alec told her he'd recently split up from his fiancée as she wanted to relocate and he didn't, preferring to stay in San

Francisco. As for children, no, he didn't have any. They had discussed it, but now the subject was kind of moot.

They eventually introduced themselves as Dana Ashton and Peter Zarros.

From what he could make out, Dana was in a long term relationship that didn't seem to be progressing much. Apparently her boyfriend was happy to still be living as a single and avoid the next step. She seemed to be in her late 20s or early 30s, but Dana was worried about time passing her by, how quickly the years were going. And she was tired of being single.

She seemed to like her job, and she got a great salary and benefits. Although she hated it when the elections were coming around, as everything was put on hold or was completely changed.

Most of her family lived in Stockton, but she didn't see them much these days, apart from at holidays. Her parents preferred to spend their time with the grandchildren that her sister and brother had provided, who were also in Stockton.

When Peter asked for her number just before his station, she thought for a few seconds before getting out a business card and writing another number on the back. Peter told her that he'd had the most delightful journey and really enjoyed her company. Then he told her that he'd just changed his number, so he wrote it on another of her cards. Peter also told her he'd really like to have lunch with her one day, that he'd call. He gave her his most disarming smile before he got off the train and gave her a wave.

Over the next couple of days Alec made several calls and not only arranged a lunch date with Dana for Friday, he also met again with Sinead. Made a date at the Redux Lounge with the woman Gina who'd passed him her number when he was with Jenny, and he got some good information from his various contacts.

He didn't take Sinead to lunch as he'd promised. Instead, he took her for afternoon tea at the Top of the Mark Lounge, inside the Mark Hopkins Intercontinental Hotel. Although he'd been to the hotel recently, he wasn't exactly a regular. After the time he'd had with Chelsea, it was now established as a wonderful place to go.

There wasn't much about the English Alec liked, but he did like their clothes, their accents, and their afternoon tea. He thought that was very civilized.

Despite living just down the street, Sinead had never been to the Intercontinental, She loved the view from the top of the hotel, not to mention the tea. He had the Earl Grey, and she had the Darjeeling, sharing the tiny delicate sandwiches, pastries, and the scones with thick Devonshire cream and jams. It was a meal in itself.

She came dressed for the part in a light brown autumn dress, short sleeved with a round neck, flaring out from her waist. He would have liked to have seen her twirl in it or to stand over a gust of air like Marilyn Monroe did one time. He didn't tell her that, he just complimented her leafy dress and how beautiful she looked.

She liked the attention he gave her, the slight touches on her hands and arms. Her gaze never wavered as they chatted, and he listened to her talk about her failed marriage and lack of a social life. Her ex had visitation rights, which always seemed a burden to him. She guessed that if he was able to stop the child support, he would also stop seeing them, as he seemed to relate one to the other. Sinead also said that he'd have them the following weekend after the boys came home from school on Friday.

Although the boys never complained, she thought they missed their father and doing things with him. She wanted Alan to meet them sometime soon, as she thought they would like each other, and that maybe he could come over for dinner one night.

Alan had no intention whatsoever of meeting them, but he went along with her, saying the right things. He made plans for them to have lunch on Monday.

Later, he called George to let him know that there was a possibility he'd be staying at the farm on Friday night but wouldn't know for sure until late that evening.

CHAPTER FORTY NINE

PETER MET DANA OUTSIDE

THE Zuni Café on Market Street before noon on Friday. It was quite mild that day, and Dana wore black jeans, a simple pink top, and a long black cardigan with pink flower embroidery. She apologized, saying it was casual Friday and she didn't want to dress up and cause suspicion with her co-workers.

Peter thought she looked very nice and told her so. She was quite shapely out of her raincoat, a little bigger than his usual dates but not overweight, and she hadn't overindulged with make up. No doubt worried about her colleagues' suspicions.

She'd been in Zuni's before, so once they were seated she recommended their roast chicken special for two that came with lava beans and a bread salad. They also ordered iced tea. The food was so good and filling, they didn't need dessert, although Peter had a coffee.

Dana felt guilty about having lunch with him. It was very unlike her, but she'd enjoyed meeting him and wanted to see him again. She also said that he looked yummy in his black cashmere jacket, white shirt, and blue jeans, but he was also way too handsome for her.

Peter thought she was funny. He attempted to be modest but thanked her for her praise, telling her she was too kind.

She didn't seem too thrilled about her upcoming weekend. She wasn't going out that evening, and her boyfriend had more or less invited himself over to her place for a dinner that she would have to cook and clean up afterward. They would probably watch some horror movie that he chose, he'd drink a twelve pack of beer, and then he'd wonder why she didn't seem to be having fun.

She asked Peter if he had a date for the evening, and he said he was going to see a friend in Berkeley, they'd have a nice dinner somewhere, and then he'd go home. His friend was female, a student, and it wasn't a sexual relationship. She was an old family friend who happened to be nearby.

When she asked Peter what his last date was like, he told her that he took her for a really nice dinner, then went dancing for a while before he took her home. They shared some champagne and he'd made breakfast.

Dana thought that sounded divine and bet that his date was very beautiful, probably a Victoria's Secret model. Peter denied this, saying models were too thin for his taste and that he preferred shapes like Dana's, which she thought was possibly true with the way he was looking at her. For the first time in a while, she felt desired and wished that her boyfriend looked at her like Peter was doing in the middle of the restaurant. She felt herself blush.

When she told him she was blushing, he told her that he loved looking at her and that he wanted to see her again. Just lunch, no pressure, similar to today.

She was afraid of that but also excited, and agreed instantly to his request, asking him to call her on Monday with the details. When they left the restaurant and she returned to work, she had to work hard to remove the smile from her face before she faced her workmates.

Alec rested when he got home. Napping in front of one of the televisions before having some soup and bread. Then refreshing himself with a wash, cleaning his teeth, adding more deodorant and cologne, and changing his shirt. He then left in his car for Walnut Creek and the nightclub.

He was already in the club and seated in a dark corner when he saw Gina arrive. It looked like she meant business. She was dressed very provocatively in a black mini skirt. Her long tanned legs were supported by black stilettos, and her ample breasts were barely contained in a very low-cut red top. The spaghetti straps were joined by her red bra supports. Her dark hair had been turned into a mass of waves and curls, her eyes were enveloped in black eyeliner, and her lips were a dark pink. She looked like a mixture of seductress, hooker and too-good-to-be-approached.

A number of men were at the bar. It wasn't full, but Alec watched them as she entered. Although they looked, none of them made a move. She probably scared them.

She was with a friend who looked almost as intimidating, and when they stopped, the friend kissed a guy at the bar. Alec stepped out of the shadow to wave at Gina, who saw him and kissed her friend, then made her way over, being eyed all the way by the other guys at the bar.

She was actually better looking than he thought, which was probably why she intimidated, and her smile was genuine when she joined him. She immediately kissed him on both cheeks before she sat down and crossed her legs for maximum effect.

Alec ordered drinks from the waitress, a glass of Merlot for himself, vodka and tonic with a twist for Gina.

She was actually more demure than her appearance or actions implied. She didn't like being manhandled or groped, but she did like to tease with her legs and breasts, putting them on show at every opportunity.

Although she didn't like to be touched much, she did like to use her long hands, Alec was explored by her fingertips from every angle, and when they danced she liked to demonstrate her prowess with her pelvis. After a couple of hours in the crowded club, she said they should go. She retrieved her coat and they left. Alec took her to his car, where she poured herself on to him once they got inside. Now he was allowed to touch.

When he suggested they go to his place, she told him to hurry there. They were barely inside the door when he had her peeled to her lace underwear, leaving a trail of both sets of clothing all the way to his bed. She may have been protective in the club, but in the bedroom she let it all go, much to Alec's complete satisfaction.

By the time he had cooked her breakfast and taken his photos, he was extremely happy he'd kept her number. She had exceeded all of his wants and needs as he bade her goodbye.

CHAPTER FIFTY

GINA WAS REPORTED MISSING

ON Monday morning at the Walnut Creek police station.

Detective Garcia heard about it a little while later, but she had no idea if it was associated with her missing women in San Fran- cisco. Gina had told her friend she was going to spend the night with a smoking hot guy, but her friend didn't have a description of him. She just saw him wave from a dark corner in a dark club. Even the waitress, who remembered getting drinks for Gina, could only come up with the simple description of "a dark-haired guy." The police there were going through the security tapes from the club.

The detective wasn't full-time on missing persons. She and her partner worked in the Robbery and Homicide Department, and they investigated the missing while continuing their other work.

Most of the missing wanted to be lost, or they had mental problems and wandered off, usually ending up as homeless on the streets. The detectives in the whole department shared the cases, and usually it only needed one of them to do the initial inquiry. But if anything developed, then they'd involve their partners.

It was just by chance that Detective Garcia got the first case. When one of the next ones seemed similar to the one she was working on, it was passed to her. And now the whole department was looking at them as being very suspicious.

Detective Lorena Garcia was in her early 30s, married for five years to her husband Jose, and despite pressure from their parents were childless but still happy. Jose was a very good mechanic with a Ford dealership and his job was safe, so they weren't stressing about having a family. They figured it would happen one day when the time was right.

Her partner was Detective Chad Stafford, a twice married, unfit, burly blonde who was rapidly losing his hair. Stafford was quite gruff, but they got along great and always had each other's back.

She'd had the photo of the guy with Aisha circulated to the whole department in hopes that someone would know who he was, and uniforms were going to ask around to see if they could find him. Aisha's family had heard nothing from her, and now they too, were extremely worried.

The detective, as well as her husband and partner, were sure the women were being killed, but as yet they didn't have a shred of evidence to go on. They really needed a body to show up somewhere.

Most of the cases they were assigned to were pretty simple. Generally, criminals are quite stupid and leave evidence everywhere, then react with complete amazement when they are caught. Some of the stories the department told were hilarious, tales of cell phones being left at the scene, criminals smiling into security cameras, home addresses on the back of demands to bank tellers, even using their own cars for getaways. This guy wasn't that stupid though.

They knew that all they could do was hope for another break, a mistake made somewhere, old-fashioned grunt work.

She also couldn't help wondering how many more women would have to go missing before he stumbled and let them in. After speaking with her partner, they thought their best chance of solving this was to find the guy and follow him.

It seemed he was taking the women on Fridays, so they probably wouldn't have to follow him too much, and it would be hard to justify overtime on what was basically a hunch.

They thought that he had to be going out of town or that he had come up with some ingenious way of making them disappear. Perhaps he had a mansion with underground cells where he kept them prisoner.

First things first, they had to find out who he was and take it from there. To that end, Detective Garcia took copies of the photo to the modeling agency to see if it jogged anyone's mind.

CHAPTER FIFTY ONE

ALEC HAD GONE ALONE TO the

Stanford game on Saturday, George had declined as he said he had too much to do, which Alec didn't ask about.

The Cardinals and the 49ers were having good seasons. Although the 49ers were on an off week, they'd beat the Lions the previous week in Detroit who'd previously been unbeaten, and the Cardinals kept winning emphatically. Last week had been 44 – 14, and this week they had won 65 – 21.

Before the game on Saturday, Alec had stuck to one of the very few habits he had and went to the bar before the game, even though he wasn't meeting his brother for once. It was routine. He'd sit at the bar unless there were no stools available, in which case he'd take a table and order a glass of draught light Coors, along with a shot of malt whisky with a drop of water. He'd also order a cheeseburger with fries. He'd usually have another order of drinks and then leave for the game.

Although he was never chatty with the staff who worked the weekends and midweek during the baseball season, he knew them by now, and they'd comment on the upcoming game or make small talk. He'd never propositioned any of the female bartenders or servers, and although one or two of them had come on to him, he'd never taken them up on their offers. So by now, they didn't bother him any more.

After he found a bar stool and ordered his usual, he was surprised when Julie, a very attractive brunette who liked to show off her figure to get maximum tips, asked him if everything was okay.

When he asked her why, she said a cop had been in barely an hour before showing his picture, asking if they knew him as they had some information that they needed to relay to him. On being assured that he wasn't wanted for anything, Julie told the uniformed cop that she'd ask around if he left the photo with her, and call him to let him know.

Julie showed Alec the photo, and he knew instantly where it had been taken.

Alec handed the photo back to her and told her he had no idea what information they had for him, but he told her to call the cop and tell him that he went into the bar on game days and would always be able to find him there.

He was very nonchalant about it, Julie thought, so much so that he obviously had done nothing wrong, and his smile and ordering another drink after his burger only enforced that opinion. When he left for the game and thanked her again, leaving her a good tip, she was still of the same opinion, but resolved to call the cop on Monday sometime.

With the amount of cell phones and security devices around, Alec knew that he'd appear in a picture at some stage, there were just so many cameras. One photo with Aisha outside her place of work was no big deal, but he knew he'd have to be extra careful now.

On Monday morning he called Dana, then he had lunch with Sinead at the Waterfront Restaurant. She looked most delightful in a light brown trouser suit with a matching turtleneck sweater. She seemed more radiant each time he saw her, the smile broader, more confidence in her whole demeanor.

For lunch she had a Louis salad with Dungeness crab, Alec had halibut with brown butter Hollandaise, and it was delicious.

All through lunch, Sinead had looked like she wanted to say something. She was attentive yet distracted, and it wasn't until they were having coffee that she finally got it out. She wanted him to go to her place for dinner on Friday, and maybe stay over.

Alec had been wondering about Sinead since he'd seen his photo. He really wanted to take her to the farm, but now he thought it foolhardy, so he gladly accepted her shy request. When he said yes, he saw her eyes widen and could imagine the cogs whirling as she thought of what she'd cook and wear. Although he hadn't picked her up at her home, she didn't realize that he knew where it was.

He walked her home, and when he left her with kisses on the cheeks, she told him to come over around 7:30 pm, well after the two boys had left with their father.

After a busy afternoon, on Tuesday morning he walked into the San Francisco Central Station on Vallejo Street and asked the desk sergeant why they were looking for him. The sergeant looked at him with total bemusement, so Alec told him that a cop had been taking his photo around town and asking if anyone knew him. He was told to sit down, someone would come to see him.

Detective Garcia was shocked when the sergeant called her, and she asked him to send him up. She'd just heard from a uniform only the day before that the guy in the picture frequented a bar on Market Street, and now he was here. She hadn't wanted him here, she just wanted to know who he was so she could observe him from the background.

A uniform brought him up to the squad room, and when they walked through the door, the whole room recognized him from the picture. A couple of the female detectives really looked at him. The detective could see why, he had the aura of a movie star but was taller and better looking than most of them. When he approached her desk, she could smell his scent and admire his expensive clothing.

She didn't stand to greet him, she wanted to appear aloof, like an authority figure, looking at him disdainfully over the top of her computer screen.

"Good morning, sir. Will you take a seat, please?" Was her greeting.

"Be glad to, and a good morning to you too," he replied. "Can you tell me, please, why you are looking for me? Have I done something wrong?"

He didn't appear to be at all worried to be in the squad room, in the detective's opinion. He sat quite calmly and didn't fidget, just looked around at the typical squad room scene. His voice was calm and controlled.

The detective's partner came over and sat at the side of the desk facing Alec, and Detective Garcia introduced herself and her partner.

"Thank you for coming in sir. Now that you know who we are, can you tell us who you are, please?"

"Alec Savvas." He gave them his address and handed over his driver's license when asked, watching as Detective Garcia did some typing and glanced at her screen, finally handing back his license, which he returned to his wallet.

"Thank you, sir. The reason why we have been looking for you is because you were seen with this young lady. Do you recall this photo being taken?" She handed over the photograph as she spoke.

Alec looked at it as if for the first time. "I certainly recall the young lady. She is called Aisha, but I don't remember the photo being taken. Is there something wrong?"

"I don't know if you are aware, sir, but she was reported missing. You were one of the last people to see her before her disappearance." The detective was going through her notes while her partner looked at him. "Can you tell us why she called you Christos?"

"It's my middle name, and I use them both. I quite like being called by my middle name sometimes, it's something my mother used to do. You said that Aisha is missing. You mean no one can find her?"

"Like I said, sir, she is officially missing. She told her friends she was going away with you on the weekend of the 14th, so can you tell us what happened?"

Alec was very calm and collected. He'd shown shock at the news of her disappearance, frowning and showing concern. "I did see her that weekend, but I didn't take her away. She came over to my apartment on Friday and left the following morning, I walked her down to her apartment. We had thought of going away. I thought of maybe driving up to Tahoe, but instead I took her to my home."

"Is there anyone who can verify that, sir?"

"I'm afraid not. I live alone."

"So no one saw you arrive or leave your apartment?"

"No, I don't think so."

"Are there any cameras in the foyer?"

"No. There's a doorman during the day, but the rest of the time we use a key for the front door or drive into the parking garage and open the gate with a remote. The residents have discussed the option of having security cameras in the foyer and garage, but it hasn't been approved yet or how it would be monitored."

"Is the remote for the garage electronic?"

"No, it's like a normal garage door opener. But once we get in, then we have to open a door to get to the elevator, and we use the same key as the entrance."

"So you spent the night with Aisha and then took her home the following morning?"

"Yes."

"Did you try to call her after she spent the evening with you?"

"Yes, I think I called her on Monday to ask her out again, but didn't get hold of her."

"You think?"

"It was either Sunday or Monday, I'm not sure which."

"Why didn't you get hold of her?"

"I don't know. The phone rang and didn't go to voicemail. I figured that maybe she didn't want to see me again."

"Really? Why not?"

"I have no idea. We had a great evening, but that happens sometimes.?

"Does that happen to you, sir?"

"Sure. Some things don't seem right or don't click, you just never know."

The two detectives exchanged glances.

"Do you know where she is, sir?" Continued Detective Garcia.

"No, I'm afraid not."

"Did she say anything when you took her home, any indication as to what her plans were for the rest of the weekend?"

"No. She asked me if she'd see me walking on the Embarcadero, but that was all."

"Did she seem pre-occupied with anything, was something worrying her?"

"No, not at all. She seemed fine. Do you think something's happened to her?"

"We don't know, sir," replied Detective Garcia, "that's what we're trying to determine."

"Well, if I can help in any way, you only have to ask."

"Actually, sir, now that you mention it, do you mind if we take a look around your apartment?"

"No, not at all. Feel free."

"Thank you, sir. We'll take you up on that." The detective rustled through more papers and handed some over to Alec. "Have you seen any of these other women, sir?"

Alec went through them, Rebecca, Jenny, Gina, and someone who looked like a hooker. He picked out the one of Jenny.

"This one looks slightly familiar, but I can't recall from where. It's like I met her somewhere or saw her, but I don't know her name."

The detective took back the photos. "Well thanks for looking. If you remember anything, then give us a call. Here is my card. Do you date a lot, sir?"

"I don't know whether it's a lot, but I do date frequently. I'm still reasonably young and single, so why not?"

"Quite. Well, that's about all we need to know right now. Thank you again for coming in. Will it be okay to ask you more questions, if need be?"

"Sure, anything to help you find her."

"Did you walk here, sir?"

"Yes, it isn't far from my home."

"If you don't mind, we'll give you a ride home and take a quick peep, if that's okay."

"Yes, no problem."

After a few minutes, they took Alec home. He took them into his apartment, letting them roam and snoop. Both detectives asked more questions as they went from room to room. He also took them into the garage and let them look in his car.

They didn't stay that long and after they shook his hand and thanked him for his assistance, he showed them out and escorted them down to their car, telling them he needed to go and pick up something for lunch.

Once he was back home, he called George from one of his "other" phones.

CHAPTER FIFTY TWO

AS THEY DROVE BACK TO the police station, Detective Garcia asked her partner what he thought now that they'd met their, so far, only suspect.

"Lorena, I think he's our guy. But we've got our work cut out trying to prove it, unless we can find one of these women and find some evidence. He's not going to admit to anything, I thought that when you showed him the pictures of the other women he'd react in some way, but he didn't flinch, not one little bit. He almost seemed to know that all we had on him was the photo with the black girl."

"I got the same impression, Chad. He was very cool and collected, didn't trip up anywhere and didn't give us a thing. I was almost speechless when they called from the front desk to say he was there and wanted to know why he was being looked for."

"Do you think he's behind all the disappearances with these women?"

"I certainly think he took our women. The ones on the East Bay don't seem to be as beautiful as those who are missing here, so I doubt if they're his. I can't see him picking up a hooker. Why would he need to?"

"How does a guy like that attract such gorgeous women?"

"Are you serious?" She looked at her partner incredulously.

"Okay, I see your look. To me, he seems gay. I know he's good- looking, I can see that. But the way he acts and dresses seems gay, doesn't it to you?"

"No, not at all. I can see where you're coming from, Chad, but just because a guy dresses well, smells great, and is very well groomed doesn't mean he's gay. Most women, despite what men think, don't like tufts of hair below the bottom lip. We don't like beards, we don't like looking at armpits or pot bellies, and we don't like seeing the crack of your ass when you bend over. We actually like men who dress well, are well groomed, who smell nice, talk politely and have manners. We don't like guys farting and belching, swearing at everything and everyone, smelling of beer and cigarettes, and wearing what they wore yesterday. This guy has all the attributes that women like, plus he's good looking and rich. And did I say he was good looking?"

"So you'd go for him as well? I saw the looks he was getting in the squad room, I don't think I've ever had a woman look at me the way they looked at him, and I've been married twice."

Lorena looked at her partner. He didn't get it, and she couldn't help but smile at him. "Sure, I'd go for him. Jeez, I'd sleep with him for his apartment. How does anyone afford an apartment like that? But I'm not his type. He obviously has a thing for these "model" kind of women. But if I was, then yes, I would. With all his attributes, good looks, and wealth, it would be hard not to. It would be like you turning down one of your movie star crushes."

"Okay okay, I get it. He still seems gay to me, though. So what next?"

"I think if you look into his phone and credit card details, I'll find out about his family and background. Did you notice that there wasn't one family photo in his apartment?"

"Yeah, weird. Even in my place I have to look at the wife's ugly relatives all the time."

Lorena laughed at her partner. "We're going to need evidence that sticks, Chad. This guy will walk with a jury of women. They won't buy into coincidences or circumstantial stuff."

"We can always get a jury of men. They'll convict on his looks alone," Chad joked.

"We might need some luck, Chad, but we need to keep tabs on him, especially over the weekends. Hopefully he'll lead us somewhere, and we can take him. He won't be able to stop now, so we need to be there. Don't you think?"

"Yes, I agree. This guy thinks he's clever, that he has all the answers. But we'll get him. He'll trip up somewhere, and we'll be there to see it. He's the guy, Lorena, so let's get after him. Okay?"

"Okay, Chad. Let's get to work."

CHAPTER FIFTY THREE

PETER MET DANA THE

FOLLOWING day at the Absinthe Brasserie and Bar on Market Street. She wasn't in Friday casual, she'd made more of an effort, but she was obviously still worried about her colleagues and their opinions. It was a damp day, so below her blue raincoat she wore a dark blue form fitting skirt to her knees, with a teal cardigan over an untucked pale yellow blouse. She'd had a manicure, her fingertips were evenly cut and were white, and her hair looked freshly cut.

He complimented her on her looks and how well she smelled, making her blush a little and bringing some extra redness to her cheeks.

Dana replied in kind, saying how nice he looked in his brown wool sport coat with darker brown pants and an ivory shirt below his stone-colored raincoat.

She let him kiss her when she arrived, on the mouth, and they were shown to their table in the romantic, richly red, and very French restaurant.

They both ordered the French onion soup, then Peter had the coq au vin while Dana had the pork prime dip. Both had water, but Alec took a shot of absinthe as well before having coffee. Both meals were very delicious and greatly enjoyed.

Peter had realized at their first lunch that Dana liked being listened to and looked at, the two things she was being denied by her boyfriend. Peter made up for it, listening to her and looking her over.

Her weekend hadn't gone particularly well. It had been the usual stuff of beer drinking and mainly boredom, watching bad movies, and eating junk.

Alec told her he'd had a delightful meal with his friend in Berkeley, some nice wine, and had even found a little jazz location before he took the last Bart train home. On Sunday he'd exercised on the Embarcadero, had some brunch alone in one of the cafes there, then had returned home and had later grilled a steak for himself with a nice salad and a baked potato. Nothing fancy, just a simple Sunday.

Dana looked very envious of the thought of a nice relaxing Sunday without her beer-swilling boyfriend and asked what the rest of his week looked like after their lunch.

"Oh, I don't know. I don't seem to be busy on Friday, so I was thinking that I might go to Ruby Skye tomorrow night, after a nice dinner somewhere nearby. Would you care to accompany me?"

It didn't seem like she'd envisioned being asked out. Her look was total astonishment that he'd asked her, so he added further to her dilemma.

"Maybe you could call in sick on Friday or just be late?"

She leaned in close to him and whispered, "What about my boyfriend? What would I tell him? I can't just go out and not say anything."

He knew he had her, he just had to close the deal. He took hold of her clammy hand in his own and kissed the back of it.

"You could tell him you were staying with a friend for the night. She's not well, and she lives alone, so you want to look after her, make her dinner or something. You could change at my place, we could have dinner, do a little dancing, have a nice evening. You'd see him the following day like nothing happened, and it doesn't need to. I have a spare room you're welcome to. We could have dinner at Scala's Bistro, they do good Italian food, plenty of carbs for dancing away. What do you think? Will you join me?"

Dana didn't need a lot of persuading. Her biggest concern was thinking about what she'd wear or if she needed to go shopping. It had been quite a while since she'd dressed for a night out, and she didn't want to look dated or out of place. She knew she could still look pretty good when she wanted to, even though she wasn't as thin as she'd like to be or as tall.

She was preoccupied for the rest of the afternoon at work, and when she got home she looked in her closet and underwear drawer for suitable clothing.

After her boyfriend came over and they had dinner, she left him to his beer and television while she put her things together in a bag. She'd pick it up after work and go along to Peter's apartment, and he'd meet her outside when she called. He'd told her where he lived, and she knew the area. She couldn't believe she was doing this, but after seeing her boyfriend open his second six pack, her reservations rapidly diminished. She was excited and could barely wait.

Alec had kept his eyes open when he left Dana for signs of someone following him. When he went to the police station, he'd looked at everyone around and thought he'd be able to recognize anyone who might follow him.

That was his biggest reason for going there. He felt sure that if he'd left it up to them to find him, then they wouldn't have spoken to him. He also wanted to know if they had other photos. He was positive they hadn't, they would have had to say something, as he'd then be more than one date for just one of the women.

He did feel like a suspect though, so now, instead of following his prospects, he looked around to see if someone was on his tail. He thought it was exciting, and he wondered if his prospects felt the same sensation.

He actually wasn't watched that day, or the next, but he was picked up on the Friday evening when he left his apartment to go to Sinead's.

He spotted the tail before he left, as he'd been waiting at one of his many windows. He was sure it was the detective he'd talked to in person, Garcia, as she was fairly short and squat. A baseball cap pulled down to her eyebrows failed to disguise her figure when she stepped out of the unmarked car opposite his building. It was where he would have parked if he was waiting to follow someone, as it was the only place someone could see both the garage and the front door at the same time.

It was also restricted parking there, so it was practically guaranteed someone would receive a ticket from one of the many officers who constantly patrolled in their tiny carts, but her car was ignored. There must have been something on the unmarked car to distinguish it from all the others, a secret sign known only to law enforcement.

As Alec made his way to Sinead's with a very nice bottle of Bordeaux, he recalled his previous evening with Dana, which made him smile as he walked.

She'd called him on her way over, and he'd met her outside. After taking her small bag, he'd led her to the elevator and his penthouse. She'd thought it was wonderful, and he showed her around before he opened a bottle of Chardonnay and shared a glass with her. He'd known she was nervous so didn't push, and he took her to the spare room to change and wash up.

She must have been in there for an hour when he knocked on the door to see if she was okay. When she told him to come in, he found her applying her make-up, seated in front of the dressing table.

She was wearing a burnt orange dress with black pinstripes, with sleeves to just below her elbows. Her stockinged knees were exposed as she sat on the stool and applied her eye liner. Her hair was still damp from the shower she'd had, the towel lying on the bed beside her neatly folded work clothes as he came up behind her with his refreshed glass in hand. He smelled her washed skin and perfume mingling in the air around her.

He wore a violet shirt above his black pants. The shirt was open at the collar, but the cuffs were closed with gold footballs.

The dress was v-necked, and he saw her cleavage as he stood above her and exchanged looks with her in the mirror.

"You look beautiful," he whispered into her right ear as he kissed her neck. "And your scent is delicious."

He nuzzled her neck some more, watching her breasts rise and fall with each breath. Then he caught her eyes in the mirror and noticed they were both smiling.

He moved around her so that his back was to the mirror, and his kisses went up her chin to her mouth, where she joined him, kissing him back with vigor. Still kissing, she got to her feet and pressed herself into him. He had to remain stooping, as she'd yet to put her heels on, and let his hands roam her figure. He stopped the kiss. As she sat down again, she said, "That was nice, just what I needed."

"I've been wanting to do that since I met you," he replied, taking a drink of his wine. "Now I can't wait to do it again."

She smiled some more as she put on her costume jewelry of gold bangles and a whale pendant. When she put on her heels, he got a glimpse of her suspenders.

"I'm so glad you came tonight," he continued, still looking at her.

"You know something?" She took a sip of her wine, "I am too."

They had a terrific evening. Peter kept his alcohol consumption to a comfortable level. He didn't like drinking a lot any way, and Dana appreciated him not doing so. He gave her all of his attention for the rest of the evening and well into the morning, and when she left late for work, she was radiant and alive again.

Alec had returned to his bed after she left. Her scent on the sheets welcomed him back to sleep. When he awoke again, he took a relaxing bath and got ready for the evening, putting on his black cashmere sport jacket over grey pants and a grey shirt. And once more he unbuttoned the collar.

When he got to Sinead's building, he glanced around when he pressed her apartment number. He spotted the detective as she dived into a doorway.

"Hi, it's Alan," he said when Sinead answered the call.

"I'm on the third floor. I'll be waiting at the elevator," she said before pushing the button to open the door.

He opened the door, found the elevator, and pressed the button. The door opened immediately, and he entered and pushed number three, watching the numbers on the floor indicator then feeling the elevator slow to stop on three.

As the door opened, he saw her standing and waiting, her arms behind her back, her long copper hair having a sheen to it as it framed her face that was smiling, her body enveloped in a little black dress. She was standing with her legs crossed at the ankles, and she stayed like that as he approached her, admiring her short, armless, but high-cut dress.

"You look wonderful, Sinead. Thank you for asking me over." He opened his arms to embrace her as he went to her.

"It's my pleasure, Alan. Thank you." She mirrored his movement by opening her arms, taking a look to the sides as she did so.

As he kissed her on both cheeks, she kissed him on the lips before he could move his head away, her tongue darting into his mouth.

"That was a very nice welcome," he said when the kiss stopped.

"I hope you didn't mind, Alan. It wasn't too personal, too soon?"

To answer her, he kissed her again, leaving her in no doubt as to how he was thinking.

"I think you'd better come in. Dinner is almost ready, and I don't want to put a show on for my neighbors. And you look great, by the way. Come on, let's go inside."

She took him by the hand and led him inside, closing the door and locking it.

"Now that I have you, I'm locking you in," she said, seeing his look.

"I'm not going anywhere," he replied, putting the bottle down on a table before he put both arms around her waist and pulled her to him to kiss again.

They had each other undressed very quickly, and Alec eventually found himself on her family room carpet watching Sinead as she got up and put on his shirt over her naked body. She tossed him his boxers and said, "Just put those on, I'm not quite finished with you yet. Would you like to open the wine while I get dinner?"

"You mean there's more to look forward to?" he replied, putting his arms around the back of his head.

She stepped over him with a foot on either side of his hips then knelt down to kiss him, whispering "A lot more, lover. I've been without sex for some time now, so I aim to make up for lost time. If you're up for it." She kissed him very tenderly as her hair covered their faces. When she got up, he already wanted her again.

She went to the kitchen, and he put on his boxers and took a look around, her boys in evidence everywhere with photos, clothing, toys, and school books. They each had their own rooms, but the apartment was small, no room was large. And the kitchen and family room were basically the same room with just a table in between.

There was nothing special about the apartment. It was more practical than aesthetic, with fitted carpets, inexpensive furniture, and family pictures rather than art. Both boys had their own laptops in their rooms, along with the usual posters of sport stars and female singers. Their beds were small and masculine.

Sinead's bedroom was a mass of colorful cushions. Although her pillows and bedspread were white, the cushions overpowered the whole room. The queen-size bed more or less took up the whole room, so Alec guessed that she had the cushions to watch her flat screen TV, as there was no space for a chair.

Her bathroom and closet weren't too small. She had a separate shower, but it was a mass of female paraphernalia. Like the rest of the apartment, it had pale blue walls, white fixtures, and standard beige carpets that had obviously been vacuumed that day.

He heard her calling his name, and he replied that he'd be right there. He took a peek into her nightstand and found her tampons, pads, and vibrator. There were no condoms and no men's deodorants or shaving kits, so she didn't have any male callers.

He made his way back to the living room and noticed for the first time that the table was set for two with linen napkins, silverware, a lit candle, and two empty glasses. He went to get the bottle he'd brought and took it into the kitchen, where Sinead was dishing up their meal.

Putting his arms beneath the shirt, he stroked her skin, his head to the back of her neck, smelling their aroma. "Do you have a bottle opener?"

Her hands covered his as he grasped her breasts. "Later, let's eat first," she spoke over her shoulder as she followed his hands with her own, debating whether to forget dinner altogether.

He took his hands away and went to open the bottle, filling their glasses when he did so and sitting down as she brought over their plates. He made a toast when she sat opposite him. "To a most enjoyable meal and to an even better evening!"

"I'll drink to that!" She concurred as they clinked their glasses. "I can't wait!"

She didn't have to wait very long. As soon as he finished his meal of roasted chicken with potatoes and asparagus, he helped her put everything in the dishwasher and was then all over her, but letting her do as she wished.

All the while he was there, which was all night, he thought of the detective waiting outside for him, probably retrieving her car to stay warm in, and it made him feel very special.

He went home the following day, but he returned later and spent another night. Sinead was thrilled about this, and they never left her apartment.

He took more wine back to her, and they ate snacks and pizza that were delivered early in the evening. He watched college football until she paraded around in some very sexy underwear. They showered together, fed each other, and played like two teenagers given free range on a first date.

He looked out the window on many occasions. He thought they changed shifts once or twice, and knowing they were around just fed his hunger.

Although Sinead wasn't complaining at his prowess, she thought she could get used to it.

When Alec left on Sunday morning, he told her he'd call on Monday and that he'd love to have another weekend like this. He said that she should have her boys spend more time with their father. She knew he wasn't serious, she knew what he meant and appreciated the thought, herself not wanting the weekend to end. She felt great.

Alec saw Detective Stafford crouching in his car when he departed, and he smiled all the way home.

CHAPTER FIFTY FOUR

GEORGE'S

WEEKEND HAD STARTED poorly, as Jane had come around and they'd had an argument. She wanted construction to start as soon as possible on their house, and George wanted to go over the plans again. He didn't want to rush.

Jane had thought the plans were final. They'd talked about them enough and had incorporated everything that George and she wanted, so she couldn't understand why he wanted to delay. She wanted the concrete poured and the frame up before winter came. Otherwise, they'd be waiting for spring to get it done and before they knew it, another year would have gone by.

Getting nowhere with his stubbornness, her annoyance grew, so she went home and said she'd be back on Sunday night, after he got back from the 49er game.

George knew he was being unreasonable. He was in a mood and couldn't shake it, taking it out on Jane only because she was there. He felt bad about it when she went home.

He stomped and banged his way around for at least a couple of hours but his mood remained unchanged, and he could lay no fault with Jane. He was just in a pissy mood.

He hadn't been drinking, so he eventually picked up his keys and went for a drive, heading toward Walnut Creek, not to anywhere in particular, just driving with the window down and getting some fresh air.

He very rarely went out at night, so when he was driving toward the DMV he was surprised to see a nightclub opposite. He'd never noticed it before, and he pulled into the DMV parking lot.

Other people were parking there as well, and he watched as they headed into the club, which was called Vice. The folks he saw were around his age group, and a mixture of caucasian, black, and Hispanic. He decided to go in.

He had no problem at the door. After they took his $10 cover charge, he went inside and sat at the bar, ordering a beer as his ears got used to the loud beat of the hip hop music blasting out of the many speakers.

Although he watched the dancers on the floor, he kept to himself, slowly drinking his beer as his mood calmed down and disappeared.

"You buy me a drink, Senor?"

George looked around to his right where the voice had come from and found a Hispanic woman sitting there. She wasn't bad, a tad overweight maybe, chubby some folk would say, and not dressed for a club, at least in George's opinion. Jeans and tee shirt didn't seem right to him. Her face was pretty, though, and she had brown eyes and black hair with bangs, straight and to her shoulders. She seemed to speak good English but with a heavy accent.

"Sure miss, what can I get you?"

"Margarita over ice. Top Shelf, please."

George ordered her drink and another beer for himself, amused at her audacity. The bartender asked if she was bothering him, and he looked at the woman with suspicion but George said she was okay, she was a friend. He wasn't thinking of anything, and when the drinks arrived he turned his attention back to the dance floor after she thanked him for her drink.

"You wanna take me home, Senor?"

George turned back to her, looking her in the face to see if she was serious. When he didn't reply she continued, "I'll be good to you Senor, you'll see. We'll have a good time."

She wasn't talking loud enough for others to hear, just loud enough for George to hear over the noise of the music.

"What do expect from me?" He asked her, wondering if he was being set up.

"Give me a hundred dollars," she leaned in to speak into his ear, "and you can have me all night, any way you want. Only a hundred dollars. I'm very sexy, Senor."

"Where at, miss?"

"You come with me, $100. If I go with you, it's $200. Any position you want, and you can slap me if you want. I'm worth it, Senor, you'll see."

"Okay, miss. You can come home with me. I'm parked across the street, and I'll flash my lights when you come out. I'm going now, and I won't wait. I'll pay you when you get in my truck. Okay?"

"Okay, Senor. It's your lucky night. I'm worth it, you'll see. I'm just going to the bathroom, and then I'll come outside, don't go and leave me," she replied, finishing her drink and kissing his cheek as she got up and headed upstairs to the bathroom.

George had just started the engine when he saw her emerge. She was alone, making her way through the crowd trying to get in. He flashed his lights.

He kept his eye on the door as she made her way over. It looked like no one followed her, so he handed her two crisp $100 notes out of his bulging wallet when she opened the passenger door and climbed in.

As he drove away, she offered him a blow job as he drove. He declined, as he didn't want to have an accident, but told her he'd accept her offer when he got her home.

As soon as he pulled up and put the truck in park, she was pulling down his zipper, and he let her get on with it, satisfying him within a few short minutes.

Telling her to wait for a couple of minutes while he got something from the rear seat, he quickly immobilized her before carrying her to his table and putting on the straps. He'd enjoyed her going down on him, but now his real fun began, as she was about to discover.

At first she thought he was just kinky, she'd heard about guys like this, but this was her first experience. Not that she was experienced in any way. She needed to earn some money for her family, and she'd resorted to this. She hadn't yet tried to pick up anyone on the streets, she just did bars and clubs and stayed in casual clothes so that she wouldn't be spotted. And so far it had worked out for her. Until now.

She had no idea how she'd gotten onto this table, but she was scared now, and her body wouldn't obey any of her commands. She could see and feel the pig doing things with her. This wasn't worth the $200 he'd paid, she should have charged him a thousand, and the bastard wasn't even putting a condom on. And why did he wash her? She wasn't dirty, the guy was a pervert, and she swore to get her revenge.

George kept her until early morning and put a few extra things in with her before setting the timer.

Truth was, he didn't have such a good time with her. She wasn't scared enough for his liking, but she'd served her purpose, and now she was gone.

He stayed busy for the rest of the day, helped his new farm manager Jose with a couple of things. As it was Jose's weekend to work, he arranged with him to take him to the Bart station tomorrow as he'd be going drinking with his brother and didn't want to be tempted into driving, so he would take a cab home.

After Jose left, George cleaned out the incinerator and washed it out as he'd done with the table and the cot.

As he was in a cleaning mood, he took the truck for a wash and dropped off a bag of trash on the way. He felt refreshed after all his cleaning, and when he returned home he cooked himself a nice steak with a couple of fried eggs and some fried potatoes. He also opened a good bottle of wine and watched some sports as he ate and drank, cheering on the Cardinals as they won again, 56 – 48.

He opened another bottle and watched a soft porn film on one of the cable channels he got with his sports subscriptions, then went to bed after a busy day.

The following morning he had a good breakfast of bacon and eggs. As Jane was coming over tonight, he got some lamb chops out of the freezer and left them to thaw under some plastic wrapping.

After Jose arrived, he got the bag he'd prepared and threw it in the back of the truck, and Jose drove him to the Bart station. He told Jose that the bag was for his brother, he'd left some things at the farm that he needed so he was taking them to him. George told Jose to just put the truck keys on the doorstep, he would pick them up later.

Jose told him to have a good time when he dropped him off, and George told him he would see him tomorrow morning, bright and early. George threw the bag over his shoulder and entered the station.

CHAPTER FIFTY FIVE

ALEC HADN'T SEEN HIS TAIL

since the night before outside Sinead's home. He'd stopped a couple of times to pick up a coffee and to tie his shoe laces, but no one had seemed out of place.

Sinead had exceeded all his expectations, and the suppressed passion she'd stored since her break-up was all poured onto him. She hadn't pushed or demanded, she'd let him nap when he needed to, but then with a look, or a touch, or some enticing clothing she re-aroused him.

As he walked home. he was exhausted but elated, still thinking of her and their love making, and the cop having to sit outside and freeze while he was naked and sweaty. He couldn't help but smile and giggle.

George was waiting for him in the lobby, and they went up to the penthouse. He dropped the bag just inside the front door.

Alec led the way into the kitchen and turned on the TV, checking the scores before asking George if everything was okay.

"Yeah, it's good. Jane's coming to the farm tonight for dinner. We had a bit of a fight on Friday, but it's all okay now. I was just in a bad mood," he replied as he sat on a kitchen stool.

"You want some coffee?"

"No I'm okay, I'll have a beer soon at the bar."

"I'll just have a quick one then. Otherwise, I'll go to sleep." He put a little container in the coffee machine and pressed a button as he put a mug under the machine.

"Did you have a long night, Alec?"

"I tell you, George, you need to date a divorced woman who hasn't been with a man for a long while. They get crazy wild."

"I'll take your word for it, Al. Are you going to get changed? We need to go soon."

Alec looked at the kitchen clock, picked up his mug of coffee, and headed toward his bedroom. "I'll be right back, George, ten minutes. I've got my clothes all ready."

George didn't reply. He was watching football and one of the teams was in the red zone, struggling to score after flying down the field with ease.

He was surprised when Alec reappeared within the ten minutes. His brother always took forever getting showered and changed. He was worse than a woman.

"That was quick, Al. You feeling okay?"

"Just fine, George. I don't want to be late for the game, it's looking like a good season for once."

"When you went for a shower, I don't know whether you saw it, but this team on the TV are like the 49ers. They easily get to the red zone and then they can't get a touchdown, have to settle for field goal."

"I saw some of it. I bet we have to put up with the same shit today but as long as we win, who cares?"

Alec was now dressed like his brother in the 49er gear and didn't seem to care that his hair was still wet, which to George was completely out of character for him.

"You going to go out with your hair wet?"

"Sure George, why not?"

"Wow, I'm impressed, You should date more divorcees."

"Sarcasm becomes you, George. Come on, let's go."

Alec didn't tell George he'd been tailed, he didn't want to freak him out, but he didn't see one on their way down to the Sutter Station Tavern. He relaxed a little, although he wasn't that tense to begin with.

The bar was hopping when they entered, and they just managed to squeeze themselves to the bar. Alec stood as George took the one stool.

Julie was working today. When she saw Alec come in, she made her way over and greeted him, despite serving one of the other customers. Her tee shirt was more revealing than normal. All the customers were getting a good eyeful of her cleavage and legs, and lots of hands were trying to gain her attention.

"What can I get you guys?" She yelled over the noise, pouring a glass of beer from a pump before them, beads of sweat on her forehead and chest, as she smiled and shook her hair back.

"Two Coors and two cheeseburgers, hold the pickles on one of them," Alec yelled back.

She nodded and was back within a couple of minutes, pouring their drinks directly in front of them.

"So, did you sort it out?" She asked as she poured.

"Yes, thanks. Seems it was someone I dated that they thought was missing, but she'd just gone home to L.A."

"Is that all? I was hoping it was more, you know, dangerous!"

Alec read her face and thought it would be a good idea to take her out, see how much danger she liked.

"It was nothing. She just didn't tell anyone she was going anywhere. But anyway, I still need to thank you. Would you join me for dinner one night?"

"Oh, I don't know," she replied lightly. "Would you behave like a gentleman?"

"Only in public. In private, I'd be all over you. Can I have your number, please?"

Julie didn't say anything as she put the drinks in front of them, and as other customers were calling her she turned her attention to them.

George had been watching all this, especially Julie and her outfit, amazed yet again at his brother's audacity.

"I reckon you struck out this time, Al. What does it feel like?"

Alec took a swig of his beer and looked at his brother, who was also drinking. "We'll see, George. She didn't say no."

Their burgers arrived about ten minutes later, and Julie brought them over, asking if they wanted ketchup, which they did, and who wanted the one without pickles, which was George.

She leaned in as she put Alec's basket in front of him, handed him a card and said, "I'm off on Tuesday and Wednesday. Call me tomorrow, and I hope you're as good as I think you are."

Alec leaned really close to her, and his nose almost touched hers, "I'm better than you think. Thanks for your number, I'll be calling."

She looked at him and her intuition told her she was in for a great night, so she winked and said, "Can't wait, darling," before she moved down the bar.

"You know something, Al? You make me sick!"

Alec looked over at his brother as he was making inroads into his burger. Laughing as he picked up his own, "Sometimes George, it's just too easy."

"Like I said, Al," breaking away from his burger, "you make me sick."

They had another beer before leaving, and Julie gave discreet little touches to Alec when she served them. Her fingertips touched his as she passed the beer over, and her meaning was very clear.

George watched and commented, "I can go to the game on my own, you know."

"It's okay, George. I'm going to the game. I wouldn't miss it for anything."

The 49ers beat the Browns 20 – 10, and Alec and George complained throughout the whole game about the 49ers failure to score touchdowns in the red zone. They won, but it was annoying to them. The score should have been more emphatic in their favor.

Like everyone else in the stadium, or at least the home fans, they stood and complained, cheered at the few scores, had more beers, and had a good time.

Even on their way home, they were still bitching and complaining, wondering how they'd actually won but thankful they had despite the lost opportunities.

They returned to Alec's apartment and had dinner at the Big 4 restaurant just a short walk away.

On returning to his penthouse, they left together in a cab very shortly after.

CHAPTER FIFTY SIX

DETECTIVES

GARCIA AND STAFFORD WEREN'T very happy on Monday morning. They'd sat on Alec both Friday and Saturday night, and he'd led them nowhere, apart from an apartment building on Taylor Street. Despite them both being convinced that he was responsible for the disappearances, he had caused them both to have cold nights on surveillance with little or no sleep.

"That felt like a waste of a weekend," Detective Garcia mentioned as they sat at their respective desks, opposite each other.

"Not for him it wasn't, Lorena. I think he had a great weekend."

"Did you find out who he was with, Chad?"

"Apparently," he replied, consulting his notes, "he was with a divorced woman on the third floor whose two kids were with the father. Seems they've been divorced for some time."

"And she hasn't gone missing?"

"No, she's still around."

"So, did anyone else go missing this weekend?"

"Nope, unless you want to look into some drug addict who walked away from a rehab program."

"I don't think so. So, when our guy dates divorced women, then nothing happens, We need to catch him with someone single, not many friends, young and beautiful."

"The divorcee is beautiful," replied Chad.

"You saw her?"

"No, but that's what they say."

"But the others were single, no kids. Maybe he has a conscience."

"I doubt it. Walnut Creek has another woman missing," Chad read from one of his notes.

Detective Garcia looked at him, confusion in her face, wondering what they'd missed or if they were looking at the wrong guy.

"What did you find with his credit cards and telephone, Chad?"

"Not much, Lorena," he replied, picking up the statements. "He only seems to use the cards on himself. He always buys gas in the city, and he makes a lot of cash withdrawals. The only dinner that was for two people was last night at the Big 4, which is practically next door to him. There are no hotel charges or anything unusual."

"The telephone is just as bland," he continued, switching papers. "A few overseas calls, and the only number he calls with any regularity is to George Savvas. There are no calls to any of our missing women."

Detective Stafford put his papers down with a certain amount of disgust.

"I understand your frustration Chad, he doesn't give us anything. George Savvas is his brother, and as far as I can tell," she paused, consulting her notes, "his only relative. He runs the family farm in Clayton, seems he farms sheep and they inherited the farm and a vast amount of money from their parents, especially the mother, who was a financial whiz.

"Apparently, both men are very intelligent, especially Alec. They both went to Stanford, where Alec especially was outstanding. Then their parents were killed in a car wreck, and that's about it apart from one interesting thing."

Chad waited for her to finish.

"Although he was never charged," she continued, "George was regarded as the main suspect in a string of rapes. Seems there was a lack of evidence, maybe some money changed hands. But neither he nor anyone else was ever charged. and he's been clean ever since."

"Do you think we've been looking at the wrong brother?"

"I don't know." She picked up some photocopies and handed them to her partner. "These are their driving licenses. Although they have certain similarities, as you can see George is nowhere near as handsome as his brother so you wouldn't think these gorgeous women would be attracted to him."

"True," added Chad, "but he's rich. You don't need looks when you're wealthy."

"These women don't seem like gold diggers, though. Aisha was seen with Alec, not George, I just can't see any of them with George."

"So what do you want to do?"

"Who is the new missing woman in Walnut Creek?"

Chad went through his papers again and handed one over to Lorena. "They were hoping to update the photo later. This was taken by one of her friends on her cell phone. As you can see, she's Latino and the cops there think she was hooking. She went to a club with her friend and left with some guy, and they're hoping to pick up some footage from the club."

Lorena looked at the photo. "Why do they think she was hooking?"

"No job, no visible income, and her friend was arrested once for soliciting."

"When did she go missing?"

"Friday night."

"Well it wasn't Alec, then. You think it was the brother?"

"Who knows?" Chad held up his hands. "But there's also this woman who disappeared from a bar, and they thought the husband was good for it," he continued, handing over another photo.

Lorena looked at the very attractive woman, and her gut was telling her this was another victim.

"The husband panned out?"

"It's actually the ex-husband. The friend who reported her missing said the ex was violent and very jealous, and as he didn't have much of an alibi they thought it was him. But someone has come forward and confirmed his alibi, so now he's out of the picture."

"Shit! I think we should have a road trip. Call the Walnut Creek station and see if we can drop by. We can also go to Clayton and see the brother, but we'll surprise him. This is getting worse by the day."

CHAPTER FIFTY SEVEN

ONCE THEY GOT OVER THE

Bay Bridge, the traffic to Walnut Creek was fairly light, and they reached the police station in about 40 minutes.

After checking in with the desk sergeant, they were escorted to the squad room and were introduced to Detective Helen Davis, who was in charge of the three missing women. The detective was fairly young. Her features were still fresh, with short curly brown hair, brown eyes, she was pleasant looking but unsmiling. They sat down facing her desk.

She had updated photos of the recent woman. One photo from the club showed her leaving just after a man, who was pictured on entering the club alone and he resembled George Savvas, which they mentioned to Detective Davis.

Seeing the look of consternation on Detective Davis's face, Lorena asked if there was something wrong.

"There's a George Savvas who was reported missing about an hour ago by his fiancée, a vet by the name of

Jane Lowell," she explained in her husky voice. "Is he the guy you want to question?"

"He is if he lives at Savvas Farm in Clayton," replied the worried Lorena.

Detective Davis looked at her notes and nodded.

"His fiancée said he never came home last night after the 49er game, although his truck is at the farm," she read from her notes. "She called him and his brother, but has been unable to reach either of them, nor have we. She said he never stays at his brother's place in San Francisco, he always comes home."

"Can you ask her to meet us at the farm?" asked the very dejected Lorena.

"Of course. Can I do anything else for you?"

"If you don't mind, that'll be great. Keep trying to get hold of them and call the provider to see if they can track the phones. I'll get someone from our end to check the airlines."

"We can do that if you want, it's no bother," replied the helpful Detective Davis.

"Okay, thank you. Call me if you learn anything, we're heading out to the farm."

The two detectives from the city left her their numbers, and they also got driving directions to the farm before they left the station. Neither was in a good mood any more.

They reached the farm in about 20 minutes, and as they drove up to the house, a woman was on the porch waiting for them, and she approached the car as they pulled up.

They introduced themselves, and Jane quickly asked, "Have you found him? Is he okay?" She was obviously beside herself with worry. "No ma'am, not yet. When was the last time you saw Mr. Savvas?" asked Lorena.

"Friday night. We had a bit of a fight, and I went home, but I said I'd be here for dinner last night."

"What was the fight about, ma'am?"

"Nothing much, we're having a house built and I thought he was stalling."

Lorena and Chad looked at the house behind her, wondering what was wrong with it. Seeing their look, she continued, "Oh, there's nothing wrong with this house, but it also belongs to his brother Alec, who comes and stays sometimes. We just want our own place."

"Don't you like your future brother in law staying with you?" asked Chad.

"It's not that. He's okay, but I want us to have our own place, not sharing."

"Is there anything missing inside the house?" Lorena asked.

"I don't know. I haven't really looked. I came over yesterday and cooked dinner, then when he didn't show I went home. I was worried still this morning because I couldn't get hold of either of them, so I came over. He wasn't here, and I noticed his truck out back. Jose, one of his farmhands, said he'd taken him to the station yesterday and that George told him he would get a cab home."

"Would you mind if we looked around? And we'll need to speak to Jose as well."

"Help yourself, the door's open. I'll go and get Jose."

The two detectives went inside the house while Jane went to fetch Jose, and they looked over the whole house, finding very little of interest.

They were in the kitchen when Jane returned, and Lorena asked, "Does Mr. Savvas have a computer?"

"Yes, it's in his office. Did you not see it?"

"We found the office, but no computer."

"Let me go and look." She returned within seconds, "That's odd. I wonder what he did with it?"

"You said earlier, ma'am, that you had a fight on Friday night. Do you recognize anyone in this photo?" Lorena asked, showing her the image on her phone.

"That's George. Where was it taken?"

"After you went home, he went to a night club in Walnut Creek. The picture is from a security camera. Do you know why he went there?"

"I have no idea. He never goes to clubs, he's always home," said the obviously shocked Jane.

"You don't know what's happened to his computer?"

"No, no idea. I use it sometimes, but he never said it was broke or anything."

"You said that his brother comes over sometimes. Do you know when?"

"Actually, I do. But what's that got to do with anything?"

"We don't know yet. But if his brother is missing as well, then it may be pertinent. Do you have that information?"

"Yes, but I don't see how it could be useful. I have it on my cell phone calendar, as I don't come over when he's here."

"Can you tell us why not?"

"No reason really, but his brother always brings over these gorgeous women. I kind of look very plain in their company."

"If you can give the information to Detective Stafford, I'll go and talk to Jose."

Lorena went back outside to meet Jose, and he took her to the truck, which was very clean. He also told her that George had an overnight bag with him which he said he was returning to his brother. Jose also confirmed that George said he was taking a cab home. She thanked him and let him go, just as her phone rang.

Detective Davis was on the line. They couldn't put a trace on the phones as they were turned off or disabled, but they had luck elsewhere. Last evening, the two brothers boarded a flight to Manila in the Philippines on a return ticket that would bring them back in two weeks' time.

Thanking her for the help and even more dejected, she made her way back to the porch where Jane and Detective Stafford were waiting. She asked Jane if they could take a look around. She said that was fine and that she'd wait at the house.

Lorena told Chad about the flight to Manila, and when he said the dates that Alec had been at the farm corresponded with the days that the women from San Francisco had gone missing, they were both mad.

"I wonder why the air tickets didn't show on the credit report?" commented Chad.

"They probably paid cash. But keep an eye on their credit card transactions. They might think we're stupid and come back on the flight they booked."

"Okay, so what are we looking for now?"

"I think Alec brought the women here, and they never left. There's a lot of land here, he could have buried them anywhere," she said, looking around.

"You think it was Alec, not George?"

"I think it was both of them, Alec couldn't have done it without his brother knowing about it, and Alec didn't do the hookers. But I think they're here as well somewhere."

"It very much seems like it, "replied Chad. "Let's see what's in here."

They had come to the barn.

On finding the recently scrubbed autopsy table and room, the walk-in freezer, and the hanging meat, they stepped outside and found the incinerator, clean and empty.

They didn't look any further.

CHAPTER FIFTY EIGHT

IF THERE WAS ONE THING that Detective Garcia hated, it was having to put a case on the cold file. Even more detested was having to inform the relatives and friends of the missing, or the deceased, that there was nothing more to be done.

The look on people's faces when they're told that their loved ones can't be found, or that there is no, or not enough evidence to convict someone of taking them, was just awful.

Detective Garcia waited for two weeks in the hope that one or both of the Savvas brothers would return from the Philippines and that she could grill them and get one of them to confess. She'd hoped, but neither had returned. They actually found some fragments of human bones but with no DNA on the farm, and that was about it. Knowing who the bones probably belonged to was purely circumstantial.

She didn't even know where the brothers were now. There'd been no credit card usage of what they had on file, no telephone calls, no nothing. The penthouse was being sold by an offshore company, the contents had been taken away along with the car, but for now the company was still keeping the farm and paying the two hands.

She felt helpless, angry, and pissed off that this could happen. Her colleagues kept telling her that it happened all the time with their cases. If the perpetrators didn't screw up or open their mouths, then there was a good chance they'd get away with it. The D.A. wouldn't take their cases to court unless they had proof. It was all a percentage game.

She couldn't even tell anyone who the suspects were, as they had never been charged with anything, and if she did she could be charged herself with defamation and would likely be convicted.

So she told everyone involved that the investigation had come to a halt. She'd keep the cases open for as long as she could in hopes that more evidence became available, and that she would always be available to talk with anyone at any time. It was all she could do, and it sucked.

CHAPTER FIFTY NINE

ALEC HAD DISPOSED OF HIS

and George's phones and credit cards before they left San Francisco and had given George some temporary new cards.

They went to Manila because one of Alec's contacts, who he gave business advice to, could get them authentic new identities. He was more than happy to do so as he'd made a vast amount of money with Alec's help.

Although they weren't going to completely give up their real identities, they traveled around the world at leisure with their new names, making up history as they went from continent to continent, spending more time with each other than they ever had.

Alec had George undergo several make overs, changing his hair style, doing some dental work, introducing him to skin care products, and giving him a better wardrobe. Although George was wary and not very cooperative at the beginning, once he discovered that he was noticed more in the new persona, he embraced it, and began to take better care of himself.

George also discovered bondage, which he greatly enjoyed. He found it took away a lot of his urges, although his brother couldn't see the attraction. Alec was now more attracted to divorced women. He had way more fun with them, and he no longer wanted to take a woman away every week. He found he could wait for months with no major problems.

They eventually settled in Argentina. Alec bought an apartment on the Avenida Del Mayo, the most prestigious address in Buenos Aires, and George bought an established 44-acre winery that came with a villa, a large deep lake, a huge basement, and the wine maker and staff.

He liked the change of scenery. The wine making process was interesting, and the wine was already established. It was only a couple of hours drive from Buenos Aires, and the brothers frequented each other's places.

Both properties only cost a million dollars for the pair, which after living in the Bay Area felt like a total steal. They also bought a property in the Italian Alps that they both went to during the humid summer of Argentina, which was January and February.

They didn't know if they would ever return to the family farm, but it remained in their thoughts. Jose sent regular updates to the company office.

George never contacted Jane again, but Jose sometimes mentioned her if he'd had to call her for one of the sheep. He never commented on her status or wellbeing.

The two brothers never discussed what happened with all the women.

Every day in America, thousands of people go missing. And while it is true that only a tiny percentage of those are young attractive women, almost 400 of them every year are never found. They fall off the face of the earth, and one can only imagine their fate.

The numbers get worse every year. Worldwide there are thousands of people who go missing each and every day, and no trace whatsoever is ever found of them. Nothing! The countries that don't make reports have even bigger problems, and whole communities can disappear into landfills or ditches, and even slavery.

Alec and George remained careful and alert in their new homes.

ABOUT THE AUTHOR

Peter was born and raised in the north west of England near Manchester, with two sisters and a brother.

Leaving school early, primarily because of family circumstances, he worked in many different fields but also spent many years doing seasonal work in hotels and restaurants.

He eventually trained as a Butler and worked for titled families in England, which he continued to do after moving to the USA after marrying his wife Debbie.

His first novel, Stonebridge Manor, was based on his working experiences in England as a Butler. It had always been on his mind, but he turned it into a murder mystery to make it far more interesting! He finished it late in 2011.

He currently lives in California, on the Delta in Rio Vista. His step children live in California, Florida, and in England.

A big soccer fan and golf enthusiast with a high handicap, he enjoys reading and movies, and networking with fellow Authors, Butlers and House Managers.

PREVIOUS PUBLICATIONS

Stonebridge Manor

UPCOMING PUBLICATIONS

CONSEQUENCES

Bullying is a huge problem, not only for children, but also for adults.

There is much said about it, but very little is done to actually stop this appalling behavior. Only four percent of teachers who witness bullying report it, over three million children are subjected to it every year, and over half of all adults in the workplace are affected by it.

James was bullied all through school and into his working years, and like most victims, he reaches his breaking point. He would prefer to get an apology from those who persecuted and mistreated him, but if they won't, then they have to face the Consequences of their actions.

THE INNOCENT CHILDREN

An indirect follow up to PROSPECTS, many of the missing children in the USA are taken by Human Traffickers. Thousands of children are illegally smuggled into the USA as slaves, working on farms, in homes, but mostly in the sex trade. Their ages range from 6 years old to 19. The average age is 12. The children are drugged and repeatedly raped, sold to the highest bidders, who can do what they wish to them.

The FBI do their utmost to stop this awful trade, and they have very many successes. The children they find often recover, with mental scars, but those who have been enslaved into adulthood, are generally lost.

The Innocent Children is a novel, but I hope it brings more awareness to this awful crime, and that people will keep their eyes open to what may well be going on behind their neighbors walls.

What people are saying about Peter C. Bradbury.

5.0 out of 5 stars
Eye Opener, September 15, 2012
By
Stan A. Grimes "saus" (saus) - See all my reviews
(REAL NAME)

This review is from: Prospects (Paperback)
Peter Bradbury's novel "Prospects" is a well written and solid novel that opened my eyes to statistics and truth about missing people in the U.S, especially missing women. You will pause and reflect while reading this novel. It was a mix of fiction and reality, which I happen to love. The late Gore Vidal was a masterful creator of this genre. Bradbury is not a Gore Vidal but his message is just as clear. I recommend this book to anyone interested in crime and suspense.

5.0 out of 5 stars
Terrifying to the bone- a real thriller!,
September 24, 2012
By
Bethany Michaels "B Mikes" (Outta this whirled) - See all my reviews

This review is from: Prospects (Kindle Edition) "Around 2,700 people go missing in the USA every day, and in California alone almost 15,000 women are lost each year." What a terrifying fact. In this spine chilling thriller, Bradbury tantalizes the readers senses, provoking goosebumps and the sudden need for your childhood blankie. The dialogue and descriptive detail paint vivid pictures of dark deceit and eerie realness. Alfred Hitchcock, known as the master of suspense, has easily been given a run for his money. Prospects is a gripping tale like Hitchcock's psychological thrillers with its disturbing and carefully crafted story-line. I would definitely recommend this book to anyone interested in real suspense.

A wonderful old fashioned murder mystery,
September 26, 2012
By
S. Appleyard "Sandy Appleyard" (Niagara Falls, ON Canada) - See all my reviews
(REAL NAME)

This review is from: **Stonebridge Manor (Paperback)**
This book was addicting from the first page. It was easy to follow, it kept the energy flowing and was very enjoyable. Peter gives a wonderful sketch of all the characters. He's especially good at this as there were many characters, which can sometimes be confusing, but he nailed it.
The behind the scenes action was most interesting. I loved the portrayal of Lady B; villain yet still loved by some. The story is told in such a manner that once the
trigger is pulled, everyone is a suspect. There is a nice balance of good and bad characters as well, and the reader gets to know each personally.

Very well told and I highly recommend it to anyone who likes a good old fashioned murder mystery.

Exciting read..., April 26, 2013
By
SC "SC" - See all my reviews

Amazon Verified Purchase(What's this?)
This review is from: Stonebridge Manor (Kindle Edition)
Well written storyline, wonderfully created characters, and some twists and turns make this a fun read! This book contains something for everyone. There's love, sex, romance, adventure, and especially a murder mystery! Follow along as detectives try to figure out who killed Lady Baldwin...was it her spin-off-be ex-husband, a spurned lover, or a disgruntled staff member? With a list of suspects, all who had ample motive and opportunity to commit the murder, and only circumstantial evidence the detectives and coroner have their work cut out for them for sure. This is definitely worth reading!!

61041090R00230

Made in the USA
Lexington, KY
26 February 2017